ARE
YOU
HERE
FOR
WHAT
I'M
HERE
FOR?

ARE YOU HERE FOR WHAT I'M HERE FOR?

Brian Booker

Bellevue Literary Press
NEW YORK

First published in the United States in 2016 by
Bellevue Literary Press, New York

For information, contact:
Bellevue Literary Press
NYU School of Medicine
550 First Avenue
OBV A612
New York, NY 10016

This is a work of fiction. Characters, organizations, events, and places
(even those that are actual) are either products of the author's imagination
or are used fictitiously.

Library of Congress Cataloging-in-Publication Data
is available from the publisher.

Bellevue Literary Press would like to thank all its generous
donors—individuals and foundations—for their support.

 The New York State Council on the Arts with
the support of Governor Andrew Cuomo and
NYSCA the New York State Legislature

  This project is supported in part
by an award from the National
Endowment for the Arts.

Book design and composition by Mulberry Tree Press, Inc.

Manufactured in the United States of America.
First Edition

1   3   5   7   9   8   6   4   2

paperback ISBN: 978-1-942658-12-2
ebook ISBN: 978-1-942658-13-9

For Mom and Dad

"Fear is only a dream . . ."

—from *The Night of the Hunter*

Contents

ARE
YOU
HERE
FOR
WHAT
I'M
HERE
FOR?

Brace for Impact

THE NIGHT D. CALLED ME out of the blue, wanting me to come out, I was home alone in the basement watching *The Silence of the Lambs*. It was late winter of senior year, and my parents and sister were skiing up in Pennsylvania. I was supposed to be recovering from mono. I'd been looking forward to holing up for the weekend with my movies. Normally I preferred horror over thrillers. In a thriller the madman was finally captured or killed, but horror could end in madness, because the bad thing might turn out to be inside you—*where it had been all along*. In a good horror story, you lost track of what was in your head and what was really out there in the world. The phone lines were cut. You were on your own.

I'd once read a story about a boy who developed a kind of cyst on the palm of his hand that, even as he tried to conceal it, evolved into a rudimentary eye. The boy tried to bargain with God to take away the eye. That story was on my mind because over the past few weeks I'd begun to develop strange growths on my hands. The first one was a hard little nodule in the dead center of my right palm. I thought it was a callus. I worried it with my fingertips, savoring the feel of its dry, grainy cap, until one day in the back of the art classroom I pared it down with an X-Acto knife until blood seeped out. It grew back and several more appeared on my fingers. I instinctively covered them with band-aids, as if they were something singular and shameful—seeds or pips rooted in the flesh, the fruits of an old story that had somehow infected me. Of course they weren't eyes; they were just warts.

D.'S VOICE GAVE ME A SHOCK. "May I please speak to Eric?" There was something touching about his politeness or caution, as if he shouldn't presume it was me he had on the line.

He asked what I was doing. I explained about the basement, the movie; I said, "*It rubs the lotion on its skin or else it gets the hose again.* . . ."

D. chuckled nervously. He didn't get the movie reference. We didn't have much in common anymore—but we had, sort of, in ninth grade. We'd gone to see *Total Recall* at White Flint. Another time we saw *Lord of the Flies*. D.'s father drove us. D.'s parents were cordial and smug. One or the other worked for the CIA. Both were tall and blond; they owned a split-level in the shadow of the high school, and hanging out at D.'s you felt the school peeking over your shoulder. Games were encouraged, displays of learning tacitly frowned upon. Their style of family authority was soft, insidious, secular. They kept innocent D. under their thumb. I could tell they didn't like me. After *Lord of the Flies* we were dropped off at my house, and D. slept over in my basement rec room. After midnight I took bourbon from the cupboard and we went in the jacuzzi out back. It was dark, windy, and cold. D. had never been drunk before, and the whiskey and steaming foam went straight to his head. He was beside himself and I had to keep shushing him. I felt like an older brother, initiating him or corrupting him in a way that would bond us. Afterward his face and limbs had been flushed; his soggy briefs hung from his hips like Balthazar Getty's loincloth in that movie. His legs dripped on the basement carpeting, and I could smell the clean chemical warmth coming off his skin.

"Hey, Eric," he said. "How about I come pick you up?"

I wondered if this could be some kind of an appeal to our old friendship, as if, now that we were a little older, those earlier times might be revived. I wanted to say, Yes, I'm alone here, come over. But instead I said it was late, that I was sick. I thought of D.'s sophomore-year girlfriend, Debbie Moffit, a fireplug, with her cigarette smoke and perfume, her flat freckled face, her astringent laugh of an older woman. She called D. "basketball star," as in *Hey there, basketball star.* (D. was already playing for varsity that year.) She was still in eighth grade. The guys called her Moffit. They hung out at her house on Monongahela Street. Her mother was rarely home, and when she was, she seemed to enjoy the company of the boys. They drank beer and watched TV while Moffit and D. were sequestered for hours up in the attic bedroom.

That had been two years ago. As far as I knew, there had been no subsequent girlfriends. Maybe it had something to do with the spook parents. Or maybe it had something to do with D.

I had spent recent weeks guiltily avoiding Bridgit Sparrow. She was fourteen, like Debbie Moffit had been. But we were seniors now, and several of the guys I still thought of as my friends were dating freshmen. Seeing me in the halls with Sparrow at my side, the guys gave me smirks of approval, and the senior girls looked at me askance, as though what I was doing was slightly sick, which also indicated approval, or at least registered a kind of normalcy. I wanted them to believe I was doing the things with Bridgit that they thought I was doing. Under their gazes I could think of myself as a guy who wanted, in theory, to do those things.

The mono diagnosis gave me temporary cover. *No exchanging bodily fluids,* my doctor had said. It afflicted the vital organs. It had, vaguely, the aura of an STD. It gave me permission to keep to myself, and to hide. It was like a vacation in a cocoon of moderate sympathy.

"How about I'll just swing by," said D. "Twenty minutes?" He wanted me to scrounge up some weed. I found a little bag of shake and a stubby metal bowl in my closet.

I WATCHED THROUGH THE FRONT WINDOW as the headlights of the Volvo wagon nosed into the driveway. I remembered the thrill, from earlier childhood, when the new friend comes over to your house for the first time, and crossing that mysterious boundary into your world, seems different, a little bit under your powers. Outside in the drizzling, breezy night, I thought I could feel a tenderness in my spleen. I felt conscious of not having showered.

The inside of the car smelled like leather and air freshener. It was his parents' smell, complacent and mind-controlling. His hand on the shift was clunky, unpracticed. I saw bemused hesitation in his big clear eyes. And behind that, something I didn't associate with D., something calculating. He swung the wagon out of the driveway, popped in a Counting Crows tape, and drove out MacArthur Boulevard. When he turned off the road into a park and pulled into a space behind the tennis courts, I got a flash of vertigo, a little wave of sickness, not knowing what he was going to do.

"Hot box?" he said.

"Your parents will kill you," I said.

"Let's crack the windows."

"They'll still smell it."

"Maybe I could stay over at your place," he said. "Give it time to air out."

The lung-scorching shag had been drying in the baggie since Christmas. I took deep draws and coughed wretchedly. The metal bowl conducted heat from the lighter, burning your fingers and lips. I knew D. could see the band-aids on my fingers, but he didn't remark on them. Nobody did.

"Where are we going?" I said. "Or are we just going to hang out here."

"Twin Falls," said D.

"Huh?" I was conscious of his big knobby knees on either side of the wheel, the buzz of hair on the back of his skull, the laundered smell of his sweatshirt. His body filled up the driver's seat with the muscle weight he'd put on.

"That's where we're going," he said. "Twin Falls."

"Oh." The pot had vacuumed me up into my head. My body felt distantly attached, as if by marionette strings. "Why?"

"You know Heather, right?"

"Heather . . ."

"Snoozy." He glanced at me sidewise and touched his lips to the pipe, sipping at the smoke. My hand trembled as I relit the bowl for him.

I hadn't realized D. was into Heather Snoozy. She was a freshman, tomboyish, with an impudent blue gaze and a prominent nose. She had a vaguely regional accent, a Chesapeake vowel.

"Hey," I said, "isn't Heather the girl who—"

D. nodded, grinning.

"—with the mother?"

He gave me a puzzled look. "The mother?"

"Yeah," I said. "The mother. A plane crash, or something?"

D.'s look of utter bafflement made me gag, and that set him off choking with laughter, heaving and hacking, jostling the car on its wheels. Tears welled up, spilled down my cheeks.

"It's not funny," I gasped. I was trying to explain that I thought Heather Snoozy's mother had been in a plane crash, but D. had no idea what I was talking about, and I thought it must be wrong, that I had the wrong idea, the wrong person. "Forget it," I said.

D. got back on MacArthur Boulevard and drove north. It was a twisty two-lane road, with the woods on our left, the canal and towpath, the warning signs telling you how many people had drowned in the Potomac that year. The Volvo seemed to hover like a helicopter while the road spooled under us.

"Are you okay to drive?" I asked.

D. appeared not to hear me. He drove stiff-backed. The

stereo had gone silent. We passed the naval research lab, a shed the size of a town. When I was little, my dad had told me how they simulated storms in a swimming pool, testing the strength of ships. An artificial ocean, manufactured waves crashing into walls of steel.

We followed the road past sleepy old homes in the woods by the river, and out into newer subdivisions, huge houses set on wide-open lots with small, freshly transplanted trees. He turned off on a street I didn't recognize. It was more like a dark country lane. We pulled up in front of a gated entry. Beyond the gate was a hulking Colonial house. Footlights in the shrubbery cast lurid shadows on the white brick facade. There was a long row of dormer windows, all of them dark. Bare branches tangled above the two chimneys. Who knew how many bedrooms were in there.

The gate's wings, cast-iron and spiked, stood open, and the car pulled through into a circular pebbled drive.

"Jesus," I said.

"What?"

"This place," I said.

"Heather's?"

"That's her house?" I couldn't square that mansion with my idea of Heather Snoozy.

"Where did you think we were going?"

"I don't know," I said. I had smoked too much. Maybe I hadn't been listening. D. hopped out of the car. I followed him up the pebbled path. A holiday wreath encircled the knocker on the glossy red door. D. went straight for the handle.

"This isn't a good idea," I said.

The latch clicked and the heavy door hushed inward. His face held an expression of hilarity, as though he couldn't believe his good fortune.

"Eric," he said. "Know who else is here?"

My stomach dropped. I knew what he was going to say.

"Bridgit Sparrow. Double date, man."

"Bridgit's in there?" I whispered.

"She's always here. They're friends. She knows you're coming. She's been asking about you."

D. strode across the foyer while I tiptoed behind, catching my reflection in a twilit mirror above a rosewood chest. You could smell the cool impersonality of marble, of polish. We went down a hallway, our footfalls muffled on the plush runner. Passing an entryway on the right, I heard a TV on low volume: a gunshot, a sense of laughter and applause. I stole a glance in there—a TV room or den—and caught the end of a sofa, picture frames on a side table, a wash of blue light on fine drapery. The light and sound and the look of the furnishings—glimpsed for but half a moment—gave me a weird impression of permanence or stasis, as if something had been going on in that room for a long time.

I could see a kitchen at the end of the hall—sheen of brushed nickel and glint of quartz—but before we reached it, D. went for a door on the left. I knew it would open on a staircase that went down and down and down.

THE GIRLS WERE CURLED UP TOGETHER on a sectional sofa before a huge TV. Heather, lips pursed, dressed in baggy soccer shorts, ran around the sofa and leapt onto D. like a monkey, wrapping her legs around his butt. "You reek," she laughed.

Bridgit approached me warily. She poked me on the breastbone and said, "Where have *you* been?" I took her hand, which felt small and cold. She wore a stretchy pinkish top baring her flat white stomach. I knew almost nothing about her, except that she lived with her mother in one of the high-rise apartment buildings across the road from Talbert's.

"Hibernating, I guess," I said. I bent down and she planted a quick kiss on my cheek. I could hear the glutinous smacks of Snoozy and D.'s long smooch.

The girls wanted to watch the end of their movie, so the four of us were arrayed on the sofa, Heather sprawled against D. with one leg propped on Bridgit's knees. Brad Pitt stood in a stream, whipping around his fishing line in the bright western sun. *I'd say the Lord has blessed us all today. . . . It's just that He's been particularly good to me.* The dialogue was hitting me with an intolerable, dumbfounding vividness. I got up and looked around the rec room, which had an unstocked bar, a pinball machine, a pool table. It all had an air of newness and neglect. I stalked around the pool table, lining up shots, trying to steady my hands. Sometimes my cue spastically grazed the ball and sometimes I shot it dead in the corner pocket. I kept peering over at the sofa. The girls were misty-eyed. It seemed to me that D.'s long arms were enfolding both girls. I racked up the pinball machine, which, oddly, had a duck-hunting theme. No one seemed bothered by the jangle and clatter.

I hoped things might carry on like this until it was time to go. But the movie credits were rolling, and Heather and Bridgit were in whispery consultation in the shadows of a little hallway leading into some further extension of the basement. I heard a giggle, a cackle and shush; they kept glancing back at D. It occurred to me that D. might bed both girls in tandem, or rather both girls might bed D., each pulling one leg of his jeans, each pulling off one tube sock. But Heather took D. by the hand and led him back into the hallway, and Bridgit appeared at my side.

"I've missed you," she said.

"Me too," I said, slapping at the machine's buttons. "Is there anything to drink?"

Bridgit bit her lip. "I think the booze is upstairs."

I realized I had always disliked pinball. The game was finally about nothing but gravity. The ball always won, rolling inexorably between the outstretched tips of the vainly flailing flippers. Game over.

"Come sit down here," said Bridgit, moving to the sofa. I obeyed her.

"Can I ask you something, Eric?" she said.

I suddenly felt terrified. I didn't want to know what the question was. As if to preclude it, I leaned in and kissed her. When she slipped in her tongue I backed off. "I'll make you sick," I whispered.

"I don't care," she said. "You can give it to me. I probably already have it."

"Really?"

"I don't know," she laughed, stroking my thigh. "If you're afraid to kiss me, there are other things we could do." She clambered onto my lap. She blew in my ear. It sent a chill down my spine. She shifted her hips: I knew she could feel me underneath her, and that my body wouldn't respond the way it was supposed to. As if part of me were dead. Or something was abnormal in my wiring. I thought of how, when the ball landed in D.'s hands, some gland started squirting and his brain sped up. He didn't have to think: it all happened without effort.

I was kissing her again, and when I opened my eyes her eyes were wide open. She looked beautiful and frail: the hollows of her cheekbones, those enormous eyes which, in my memory, would gaze back at me like the eyes of a religious icon or a Keane picture. "What's wrong?" she asked.

"The mono," I said.

"It's okay," she said. "We both have it now."

"I don't feel well. I think I need water or something."

I turned away from her confusion, her disappointment. She must have felt something was wrong with her, something other than mono. I would never know any of this, what she really thought.

"I'll be back in a minute," I lied. "I promise."

Climbing the stairs I heard Bridgit's voice drift from the sofa: "You shouldn't go up there, you know." When I turned back to look, she'd enveloped herself in a blanket.

THE HOUSE TREMBLED AND THE BLOOD THROBBED in my head. Beyond that leaden pulse I could hear TV music drifting from the den: a woman singing. I tiptoed to the fridge and cracked the door. It was bright and loud and crammed with food. My eyes feasted on the things I might have: bagels and cream cheese, sliced turkey, hummus. Red peppers like tongues nestled in a jar of liquid. I picked up the jar and turned it in the light, watching the translucent seeds lift off the bottom, twirl and subside as in a snow globe.

It slipped from my fingers and smashed on the tile. I froze, listening, watching the liquid pool around my feet.

The damage was appalling. A pungent smell expanded in the room like a fart. The song from the den sounded closer now. It was an old melody, like a lullaby.

"Amparo?" called a woman's voice. "Amparo, is that you?"

I stood still, and could feel time passing. I heard a soft metallic whir—and a motorized wheelchair, bearing a female, rolled into the kitchen.

Her ghoulish girl's face emerged from the dimness: eyes set in grayish hollows, a wide pale forehead tapering down to a thin mouth and sharp chin. Her lap was covered with a plaid blanket in the manner of an invalid. The drink in her right hand was balanced on the chair arm; she worked the control with her left.

She maneuvered closer and stared up at me. I saw the hardness of her fine-boned face, the dull pallor of her skin. She was a woman in her forties. I realized this was Heather's mother. Mrs. Snoozy. I had thought of her as someone who was dead. But she was a living person, in a wheelchair, in this improbable mansion, which must have come from an insurance settlement. It made sense. All of this was about that plane crash.

When she leaned forward to peer down at the broken mess, I saw the white scalp line in her hair.

"Ah," she said stoically, as if she'd expected this. "Amparo!" she called. Then, turning to me: "What do you need?"

"I'm so sorry," I said.

"You're going to be sorry, boy-o."

Her eyes ran down then up my body. She wore a low-cut shirt of netlike material embroidered with black flowers. Below the hem of the lap blanket her shins were sheathed in tights, and her feet, strapped into shoes of red patent leather, rested on the footpad.

"Amparo! Here, I'll do it myself," she said, reversing the chair and turning.

Just then a stout woman in a green blouse bustled into the kitchen, muttering and softly chiding the woman in the wheelchair, and began to address the broken jar. I stepped clear and watched from the other side of the kitchen island as Amparo swept the mess into a dustpan.

"You're hungry," the woman in the wheelchair told me. "How's a sandwich? I'll get you a sandwich—"

Amparo intervened: "What you like. Turkey, PB and J . . ."

"No thank you," I said, "I'm okay."

"He don't want it," said Amparo.

"He wants it," said the woman. "PB and J. He wants something sweet."

When Amparo had prepared the sandwich, the woman in the wheelchair took the plate from her and balanced it in her lap. She motored around the kitchen island and handed me the plate.

"See. That wasn't so hard. It's just a sandwich."

She regarded me curiously. I wondered if she could read my mind, or whether, from the fact of my presence, she could infer what was going on in the basement. Silver bracelets jangled on her wrist when she brought her glass to her lips. She pointed to the table: "Sit and eat." Amparo had vanished. It seemed like the kind of house where people could disappear if they wanted.

"Are you Todd?"

I chewed and swallowed with difficulty, the gooey clumps catching in my throat.

"Eric," I said gruffly.

"Molly's friend Eric?"

I didn't know who Molly was, but I nodded.

"You have a lovely voice, Eric."

"Thanks," I said, polishing off the last of the sandwich.

"Your eyes are a little red. What are those band-aids on your fingers?"

I stiffened. No one except my little sister had had the audacity to ask me about them. "Cuts," I said. "Scrapes."

"Scrapes on just parts of your fingers? How do you scrape them like *that*?" She smiled: big teeth fanned out from her gums.

I felt my cheeks flush.

"Is this bothering you, Eric?"

"No," I lied.

"Then what's with the band-aids?"

"I don't know. Warts, I think." The ugly word was sluggish in my mouth, a bloated syllable. "It's warts."

Her eyes widened. When she closed her lips and her expression turned solemn, I saw again the hardness of the bones in her face. She set her drink down and motored around the island to the fridge. She was rummaging in a crisper, then removing things from a silverware drawer. When she came back she had several items in her lap. She rolled up next to my seat and placed on the table a paring knife, a potato, and a wooden cheese board. I could smell her perfume.

"Give me your hand."

"Why?"

"Eric," she said impatiently—and was opening her mouth to speak when I gave her my right hand. She turned it this way and that. "Such a smooth hand," she said, tracing along the middle knuckle. "Are they always this cold?" She picked with her bloodred nails at the edge of the band-aid on my ring finger. "Is there a little wart under there?"

"Wait," I said as she took up the paring knife.

"Shh, Christ, I'm not going to cut you."

She slipped the knife tip under the rim of the band-aid, scoring it. Then with her nails she pried away the gummed-up bandage, revealing a pruned band of grub white skin where a wedding ring would go, or a class ring—and in the center where a stone would be set, a plump pinkish nubbin the width of a pencil eraser.

She took a long breath. "It *is*," she purred, impressed. She set the potato on the cheese board and sliced it in half. She cut the potato in quarters, eighths. "Let me give you a word of advice, Eric—"

I waited for her to continue—somehow hypnotized by the careful, deliberate movements of her hands—when I became aware she'd stopped cutting. I looked up; she was glaring at me fiercely.

"You know what?" she said. "You are very—." She let the knife drop on the cheese board. "You are very, very rude."

"Huh?" I said.

"You know, forget it," she said, lifting her glass. "Amparo!"

A balloon of fear expanded in my chest. We both listened to the house, for the stirring of Amparo, for footsteps.

"I'm sorry," I said. "What did I do?" My head felt shimmery. The only sound was distant music from the TV in the den. The woman seemed to be listening still, or paused in thought, her head cocked to the side, eyes closed, her lids delicately veined and subtly twitching. With a finger she absently flipped back the side of her hair. I caught a glimpse of her right ear: a fused lobe of bright pink flesh. The burned skin extended down the back of her jaw, onto her neck.

"It's the eye rolling, Eric. The sighing." Her eyes fluttered open. "Am I wasting your time? Am I in your kitchen, rooting around in your fridge, breaking things?"

"No no—please."

"Forget it," she said again, and took a breath (to call out for Amparo, I thought).

"Wait!" I said. "I really didn't know I was doing any of that. The sighing . . . and what else?"

She lowered her eyes. I could feel her deciding to lay off, to accept my plea for mercy. To my relief, she resumed cutting up the potato. I wondered if her hair was a wig.

"It's not your fault," she said. "I have a headache that never goes away. It will never go away."

She glanced toward Amparo, who, I now saw, had been watching us from the edge of the kitchen.

"It's nothing, honey," the woman said to Amparo. "I forgot what I wanted." Amparo glanced at me with unveiled suspicion, then ducked out.

She took one of the cubes and began to lightly press the moist potato flesh onto the wart on my ring finger, swabbing it. The wart was inert: it felt like nothing.

"It's the anniversary this month," she said. "Molly told you about it? The accident?"

I blinked at her, then shook my head.

"She wouldn't have told you about it. Are you an older child?"

I nodded.

"Heather's the younger child. She knows every detail. That's because she always wanted me to tell her the story. But Molly never wanted to hear about it."

Her voice had changed; she spoke ponderously, almost as if she were falling asleep, or slipping into a kind of trance. She took the knife and scored the other two band-aids on my right hand and peeled them away. She talked about a birthday party in a place called Cremona, New Jersey, and a ride in a commuter plane, and her concern for her mother, who'd been acting spacey, losing her keys, forgetting things. "That's how it all started with *her* father," she said. "Of course if you bring any of this up she gets terribly upset and defensive. Anyway, *that's* what I was thinking about, when suddenly there was a tremendous *boom* and the whole cabin shook. I thought another plane had crashed into our plane. That was my thought—that's just what it felt like. People were screaming. It's hard to hear that. You know when you're on a plane and the turbulence gets *really* bad, you say to yourself, It feels like something's wrong here. But everyone's quiet—some people don't even seem to notice. You say, If something were *really* wrong, people would be screaming. Well, now they were screaming. The captain came on and said we'd only lost one engine. He sounded calm and in control. We only had the one engine, but the captain would land the plane. People stopped screaming. For a while everything almost went back to normal."

When she'd finished with my right hand, she went after the two band-aids on my left, repeating her careful procedure. Something like a trance had fallen over me too, a kind of veil interposed between myself and the sensation of moist gentle handling, the smells of perfume and bourbon, the tinkling of bracelets, the melody drifting from the TV in the den.

She said the plane had begun *rolling* from side to side, and she heard a man behind her say, *The pilot is flying this plane in a very strange way*. When the captain came back on he said he was losing control of the plane. She remembered how the captain said, *We have to prepare for the worst*, wondering what it meant to prepare. She could hear people crying and a woman repeating the Hail Mary. "It felt like I had woken up from a dream into a different dream. But it was real. And I thought, *Well, this is me here. This is my life.* I didn't wish or pray to be anywhere else. I retied the laces on my tennis shoes. I always wear tennis shoes when I fly."

She swabbed the cube around and around on my pinkie-wart. When she finished she dropped it onto the little group of infected potato pieces lying on the cheese board.

Then, she said, she was lying on the ground in the cold. She felt like she had been conscious the whole time, but later they told her she hadn't. From where she was lying she could see a sign for a laundry-mat, a yellow sign with blue and white soap bubbles. She could hear traffic somewhere. She could see a chain-link fence, and some pieces of garbage, shiny hamburger wrappers stuck in the bushes. "When I was in the hospital, I saw us on TV. I heard a woman tell the news reporter, 'This was my first plane crash.'"

She smiled strangely, baring those buckteeth, and emitted a dry cluck of laughter. She licked two of her fingers, then wiped her hands on the blanket on her lap.

"Let me tell you something, Eric. I am more alive in my body than I ever was before the accident. Do you believe that?"

I WASN'T SURE IF I BELIEVED in *her*, or that house, or in what was going on in the basement. Had I really been there, with the strange woman undressing my fingers, hearing her story which seemed so doubtful? *I didn't wish to be anywhere else.* She could have been insane; she could have told all manner of story to any captive audience. And she had no more reason to believe in me, or to remember me, a ghostly stranger in her house. Boys would come and go, creeping up and down those basement stairs.

But in years afterward, whenever the bad turbulence hit, miles above Wyoming, or off the coast of Newfoundland, I'd feel the floor drop, hear bolts wrenched, the ripping of metal, a calamity of noise and wind, and think, now it gets real: and if you could surrender to that, how terribly fear, infinitely precious fear, would fall away: and that's what it would be like to be seen by God.

"LET THAT AIR-DRY," SHE SAID, having finished with my hands. "It's a cure. It doesn't matter whether you believe in it or not."

I asked her if she had some band-aids to replace the ones she'd removed.

"No point," she said, shaking her head. "Everyone can tell." She sipped from her drink and, pushing the lever with her other hand, began to reverse the motorized chair away from the table. "Trust me," she said. "Everyone can tell."

Just then the timid squeak of door hinges summoned up the basement rec room in all its chambered mystery. Heather appeared, wearing an oversized fleece and those baggy soccer shorts. She pushed her hair out of her face and blinked sleepily at the scene before her. She came blithely forth, barefoot, and plucked her mother's drink from out of her hand. She peered into its dregs of ice melt, shook it a little, and downed it. Then she slid her teenage bulk onto her mom's blanketed lap and, placing an arm around her neck, turned to regard me—they both did, amused, unsmiling—and I saw then how much more alike they looked than I'd realized.

D. DROVE US HOME IN THE MIDDLE OF THE NIGHT. He looked sober and thoughtful, steering his parents' Volvo down the snaking road. He might have been eager to talk, but I was in a fugue state, watching the dark woods and vague houses drift past. Not till we'd reached Glen Echo did he tell me what he'd done with Heather Snoozy. I was shocked when he admitted it had been his first time. I had assumed he'd been doing it since sophomore year, since Debbie Moffit and the attic bedroom of the house on Monongahela.

So D. has now fucked, I thought. D. has fucked. It was so conclusive. It determined everything. I knew I should have said something encouraging, given him by heartiest attaboy, but my heart felt so heavy.

"How did it happen?" I said.

"I don't know," he said. "I just put it in."

The idea was crushing. He just put it in. I tried to picture it. I asked him if he had used a condom. That was the second shock: he said no. This changed my picture again; it gave me a gnawing thrill, made me even more envious.

"That's bad, D.," I said. "That's really bad."

I said, "You know how to put it on, right?"

He grinned sheepishly and mumbled something I didn't catch or remember. Then he asked if he could still sleep over. I had thought he would want to go home. Maybe it was only because of the pot smoke in the Volvo. Still, it was a gift: I wanted badly for him to sleep over.

Ten years later I saw him at the wedding of a mutual friend in Miami. D. had been divorced and single for some time. We didn't exchange more than a few words. By then I'd long since mastered the subtleties of evasiveness. (Arts of survival or deathly arts . . . exhausting, whatever you call them. I told myself, *After this wedding, no more.*) Some of the guys who hadn't been invited to the rehearsal dinner went bowling. I remember seeing D. standing by himself on the sidewalk outside the bowling alley, waiting for a cab back to his hotel. He wore pleated khakis and a yellow golfing-style shirt—he looked very grown-up.

Once I caught a post by Heather Kristopoulos, née Snoozy, on a social media website. *I can't believe it's really been fifteen years since the accident. Not a day goes by when I don't remember that day.* . . . The post made it seem as though Heather had been in that plane crash with her mother. I had never realized this. But in the archives of a local paper I found an article that confirmed it. American Eagle flight 147 had crash-landed in the parking lot of a shopping center in a place called Sewell, New Jersey. Six of the twenty-eight passengers plus the copilot had died. The article mentioned the mother, whose name was Lydia Vogel, and her children: Molly Snoozy, eleven, and Heather Snoozy, nine.

I thought of Lydia Vogel, nodding off in the den of that silent mansion, watching an old movie, while somewhere else, in reaches of the house she couldn't access, her very young daughter was having sex with an older boy in a spare bedroom.

IT WAS THREE OR FOUR A.M. BY THE TIME I TURNED THE KEY in the lock of my front door. The house, emptied of family life, seemed paused in an attitude of expectant stillness. We passed by the door to the basement and went upstairs. I showed D. to the guest room. My mother had decked out the bed in white pillowcases with fancy embroidered trim, a white duvet on the goose-down comforter. Everything looked immaculate. D. closed the door partway. I heard him taking off his shoes.

In my own bed I tossed and turned. Eventually I got up and went into the hall. Through the ajar door, in the faint dawn light coming through the curtain, I saw D.'s sleeping face in profile, his bare shoulder, his arm hugging a pillow to his chest.

I slipped into the bathroom and examined my hands. In the vanity light the warts looked obscene. I fished out the last two band-aids from the box and affixed them around the two fingers with the ugliest warts. The tightness of the clean band-aids felt good.

I went down to the basement and stretched out on the couch with a blanket. I played *The Silence of the Lambs* from where I'd left off. I would follow for a few minutes before it fused with the scenes my dreaming mind was playing, and would never cease playing. *Don't you feel eyes moving over your body, Clarice? And don't your eyes seek out the things* you *want?* The thriller, barreling toward its climax, was like a prologue to sleep.

A Drowning Accident

A TIDAL WAVE EMERGED from between two hills, reared up, and fell down on top of our town. It happened at night, and many people drowned in their sleep. The lake on top of the mountain above the town had never been much in people's minds. They had been warned about trouble up there; but they'd been warned so many times that perhaps they'd grown tired of waiting for a disaster that never happened—until it rained so much the earthen dam broke and the lake came pouring down the valley. Growing up, I sometimes felt I was living among watery ghosts. I sought reassurance from my mother that the flood was in the past, long before I was born, and could never happen again.

My mother had three miscarriages before me. When I was a little boy, she and my father took me on a picnic up the mountain to the place where the lake had been. There was nothing but a wide depression in the ground. A solitary house, with a front porch and steps that led down to a field of grass, stood on the hill facing the depression. My father, a happy man who liked jokes and stories, said, "That was a lakefront house. And there were sailboats on that lake. Sailboats on the mountain! Imagine such a thing. It seems impossible."

The house was empty. A man called Colonel Unger

had lived there during the flood. When he saw there was nothing he could do to save the dam from breaking apart, he sent a message to the town saying *Notify the people to prepare for the worst.* Then he took to his bed, as though he were ill. He never recovered. Meanwhile, the workmen who had been waiting for the colonel's next orders climbed down to where the lake had drained away, and saw the fish twitching and gasping in the muck, and not knowing what else to do began scooping them up with their hands.

In my dreams I saw the ghostly sails, gliding pale against the dark forest, across a glassy lake with sky and clouds in it. My father had told me what a flood survivor had written, many years later: "It just seemed like a mountain coming." The thought of a mountain falling down a mountain, a mountain tumbling over itself, gave me a queasy feeling, like the aftertaste of a fever. I imagined the people paralyzed before their fate, unable or unwilling to move. *It's coming*, they would have thought; *this time it is real*. Why didn't they climb, get up high to safety? Because it still seemed impossible. Unger had sent the message, and a mountain was coming.

WE LIVED IN A HIGH NARROW GRAY HOUSE up on Strayer Avenue, a street cut into the hillside on the north end of town. From our front porch you could see across the rooftops of the houses in the street below us, out into the misty blue basin of the town, cupped by a ring of steep hills. From our back door it was a short walk up through the woods to the ridgeline; from there the town looked even deeper, shrouded in mists or dissolving in its watery depths, the church spires sticking up narrow and brittle like points of deep-sea coral.

When I was eight, my father was hit by an automobile on the highway behind the mattress factory. He lived for a couple of days—sleeping, I was told—before he died. My mother grew silent; she began to consult doctors, complaining of noises in her head.

I was a shy, friendly, nervous, good-humored, independent boy. I spent idle days, in the summer after my father died, exploring half-forbidden parts of the city with Wilkerson, a boy with whom I had developed a kind of friendship. We would ride the funicular railway (the steepest of its kind in the world) up the mountainside to the platform where you could look through a telescope into every crevice and corner of the city; or throw stones in the culvert behind the I. X. M. Creamery; or walk on the train tracks behind the factories on the west side of town. Sometimes we went to a place called the Penn Hotel. It was a narrow four-story building at the end of a block in the far corner of town, past the YMCA swimming pool and the Coney Island Hot Dog cafeteria, across the train tracks from the Iron Works. It was a sad, quiet, empty block, and I liked it there because it was lonely and strange, and a queer feeling came over me as I lingered there with Wilkerson in the afternoons before the time when I would have to go home for supper. The Penn Hotel had a saloon on the ground floor, with a broken clock over the door. A legend in the brickwork between the third and fourth stories read *1890*, which meant it was built in the year after the Flood, so that the building itself had no memory of that catastrophe.

The Penn wasn't really a commercial hotel, but more of

an irregular boarding-house. Looking from the street you could see men sitting in chairs or staring out of the upper windows with blank expressions on their faces. These tired, solitary men came and went on vague business. Other men who lingered around the Penn were drifters. They arrived with the railroad on their way west, knocking at people's back doors for something to eat. The ones who couldn't afford a room for the night slept, I think, in the woods above the train tracks. Now and then alarming stories appeared in the *Tribune*:

TRIED TO FORCE BABE TO DRINK WHISKEY, CHARGE

Elijah Jenkins and Charles Wilson were sentenced by Mayor Franke today to pay a fine of $100 and costs or spend 20 days in jail. They were unable to pay their fines and were locked up. The men are alleged to have attempted to force a small child to drink whiskey.

The child was sitting on a door step on Franklin Street, near Washington Street, when the men came by, it is said. One of them held the child while the other attempted to pour the liquor down its throat. The child's screams attracted pedestrians. One of the men had a large razor.

My mother showed me this article, buried in the back of the newspaper among other stories: a child in Cresson who was dead of spinal meningitis, a miner who had lost his eyes in a dynamite explosion. I was meant to understand it as a caution.

As the summer wore on into hazy August days, I became aware that I preferred to go to the Penn Hotel without the company of Wilkerson. I began to make excuses so that I could have my adventures alone. Because it was remote, and because it was forbidden, I went there as if in a dream; or as if by straying from the bounds of the life that was meant to contain me, I became someone else, a ghostlike personage, invisible and oddly free. In the saloon I was permitted to buy a fruit drink from the bar. There was a man there who noticed my presence; he invited me to sit with him while I finished my fruit drink. He said that his name was foreign but that I should call him Jack. I didn't know whether he rented a room in the hotel, but he was usually in the saloon, sitting by himself at a table, drinking a glass of beer and idly stirring the sawdust with the heel of his boot.

I knew that I should not be spending time with Jack. I could see from his clothing, which was tidy but not clean, and from his face, which was cheerful and inquisitive but also not clean, that Jack was what people might have called a tramp; but his manner of speech and oddly elegant comportment suggested a man who aspired to a certain measure of respectability. He asked unusual questions, and alluded to movies and theatrical performances he'd seen or heard about, and recounted stories about trains and mining accidents and places he had visited in states in the West. He had a book that he carried with him at all times. He called it a "dream book." I was given to understand that Jack's dream book was filled with mysterious and extraordinary information. The book was more like a thick pamphlet. It was filled with messages and codes, legends and numbers; its full title was *The Original Lucky Three Wise Men Dream Book: The Science of Numbers Revealed.* I understood that Jack used the book for gambling.

"Do you remember your first dream?" he asked me.

I said, "Oh, I don't know. Once I dreamed it was Christmas."

"Christmas, Christmas . . ." He looked up the dream in his book. "If you dream of Christmas, then your lucky numbers are 15, 25, and 35."

"What's lucky about those numbers?"

Jack shrugged. "It all depends on you." He consulted the book. "If you dream of seeing a ghost, for instance, then your numbers are 14, 56, and 65."

"What other dreams are in there?"

"All of them."

"Like what?"

Jack smiled. "If you dream that your left eye jumps, your luck comes with 6, 16, and 18. If you dream about stealing, then you want 10, 16, and 45."

"And a train wreck?"

"5, 14, and 41."

"And a volcano?"

"21, 69, and 70."

I wanted more. Jack indulged my curiosity, wetting a finger on his tongue with a grin and flipping through the worn newsprint pages of his book. He told me that making whoopee was 7, 11, and 44, while a funeral procession was 9, 17, and 36. A bell ringing in your ears was 2, 43, and 66, and a drunk woman was 3, 13, 18, and 20. A strange city was 10, 20, and 22; a colored baby was 13, 32, and 50; and a dog howling in the night was 5, 14, and 24.

"A hunch of death," he said, "will be signified by 24—37—and 42."

This information seemed thrilling and urgent; I wandered the streets in a reverie, thinking about the hidden significance of my dreams. But when school began in September, the world of the Penn Hotel and the tramp Jack grew distant in my mind. My mother seemed to know that I'd been going to places where I wasn't supposed to go, and in the house she looked at me askance. She'd been spending time with a new friend, a cigar salesman named Mr. Schrock, who came to our house two or three times a week for supper. Mr. Schrock also looked at me askance. And I found that I saw very little of Wilkerson. My absence during the latter part of the summer must have hurt his feelings; I noticed he had drifted away from me, involving himself with a new group of friends.

It became clear that it was going to be an unusual school year. At the end of September, Mayor Franke ordered the theaters, saloons, dance halls, and moving-picture houses closed. There were rumors that some people in nearby towns had fallen sick. No one I knew at home or at school seemed ill. Mr. Schrock declared firmly, "That doesn't have anything to do with us," and my mother agreed with him. But a few days later, the ice-cream parlors were closed, and then the churches. Public funerals were banned. Stories in the newspaper used the word *quarantine*. Others referred to an "epidemic wave."

There was a cartoon in the newspaper called "Petey Dink," and in one strip Petey was reading the newspaper in his overstuffed chair, smoking a cigar, and saying, "Oh, well—best thing to do is not to be afraid of it—I'm not afraid of anything like that."

School remained open. The mayor proclaimed that *children in well-ventilated schoolrooms are reasonably safe, certainly much safer than in moving picture halls and other places badly ventilated.* I tried to imagine why the moving-picture halls were so dangerous. I thought of rows of silent people closing their eyes and quietly dying in their seats while the light from the screen flickered on their faces and the waves of music rose and fell in the dark theater. I told my mother that I wanted to stay home from school, but she pointed to the newspaper and said that it was safe. She said that I had to go. *I'm not afraid of anything like that*, said Petey Dink in his chair.

I was daydreaming at my desk with my red geography spread open before me. I was thinking of a hotel at the edge of a continent, looking out from an upper window at a sailboat tiny in the distance, and the tiny people in the boat peering over the edge, wondering how deep it was. Then I sneezed. Mrs. Miller looked up from her desk. Other children had turned to look at me. When I sneezed again, the teacher called me to her desk. She had a strange expression on her face. I stood with my back to the class; I felt eyes on the back of my head, eyes from the corners of the room. She said, "William, you are dismissed. Go right home to your momma." A boy giggled from the back of the room. In the silence I took my cap and left. When I shut the door behind me, I could hear the muffled voice of Mrs. Miller speaking to the class, and I wondered what she was saying. My footsteps echoed in the empty hallway. When I opened the door into the blinding sunshine, it felt strange to be walking freely forth into the outside world in the middle of the morning, in the middle of the school day which had suddenly come to an end for me. I thought of the hours that lay ahead, when all the other children would still be confined to the classroom, moving through the prescribed motions of the day without even thinking about it—but I would not be there. I would be somewhere else. I felt like a thief, a secretive person stepping into danger.

I walked north across town, past the cigar shop where Mr. Schrock was bent over his counter working. I saw him through the window, but he didn't look up. I passed the YMCA; the side door was open and I could see elderly men in bathing costumes groping their way feebly along the watery lanes like blind people or sleepwalkers. I bought a hot dog at the Coney Island Hot Dog cafeteria and ate it at the counter. I felt fine. But I also thought of how I'd been sent home by Mrs. Miller, and wondered why this was so. Perhaps I had done something bad that I couldn't remember, or hadn't even noticed. Perhaps the whole thing was a mistake.

My mother had remarked on a story in the *Tribune* about saloon keepers getting in trouble for remaining open and serving liquor to men despite the mayor's ban. I wondered if the Penn Hotel would be closed. When I got there, I looked up at the top floor. In the window directly above the *1890* legend was a man in a blue work shirt, with a white surgical mask over his mouth. He stared at me; then he disappeared into the room.

The saloon was open. Through the grimy window I saw men sitting at the tables. But Jack wasn't there. I ordered a fruit drink from the bar. The saloon keeper eyed me suspiciously, as though he didn't recognize me from before, but served me without a word. I sat at a table, and after I'd finished my drink I began to feel tired. The afternoon wore on. I must have sat at the table for a long time, feeling sleepy and comfortable as murmuring men shuffled past amid clouds of cigar smoke and the sour smell of beer spilled on the floor.

When the late-afternoon shadows were gathering in the street outside, Jack the tramp appeared before me.

"Hello, friend." He smiled; his teeth were stained from tobacco, and his eyes looked reddish and dreamy.

"I got to leave school today," I said.

"You must be a lucky boy," said the tramp.

I said I supposed I was. "They closed the school," I lied. "Because some boy in the class got sick."

Jack said nothing. I asked him if he had his dream book. He nodded, dipping his hand into a hidden pocket in his coat.

"Getting sick, getting sick," he spoke, licking his thumb and paging through the pamphlet. "If you dream of getting sick, you would be wise to choose 10, 20, and 30."

I nodded.

"This boy who took ill," said Jack. "He is your friend?"

I said that I didn't know the boy; he was just a boy from class.

"Do you have a good friend?" Jack asked. "When I was your age I had a friend."

I told him I did, and gave the name Wilkerson, though as soon as I did I wished I hadn't.

"If you dream about your friend," he said, peering into the book, "you can tell him to keep an eye on 5, 45, and 54."

As the tramp continued to read to me from his book, I felt I had fallen back into an old rhythm. The time since school began seemed to dry up and blow away, and I was back inside the dream of a humid summer afternoon. He spoke in a measured, soothing tone, which caused me to fall into a kind of empty, unfocused gaze, forgetting about the supper that would be waiting for me at home, forgetting about the strange day and what had happened at school. He told me the numbers for dreams about needles and onions, freckles and candy and measles. He told me the numbers for a black pussy cat, and a hunch of bad news, and a knife, and muddy water, and a pretty girl. He told me all the lucky numbers for grave diggers, gravy and gold teeth; a glass eye, good luck, and a giant; a gift, a guest, and a gallows.

A distant bell tolling from the Methodist church roused me. The saloon keeper, wiping out a glass, glanced over at us. I thought maybe he assumed we were father and son.

"If you dream of the sea, you get 17, 34, and 42. But if you dream of drowning in the sea, then 8, 32, and 60 are your numbers."

Jack must have sensed my distraction. He looked worried—concerned, perhaps, that I was growing bored with our game.

"You know this was all underwater." He leaned forward, close to my face; his breath smelled faintly rotten. "The very place we are sitting."

Of course I'd known that; everyone knew about the

flood. But I didn't like him saying it; for some reason the way he said it annoyed me.

Still he tried to hold my attention. "If you dream of a boy," he said, flashing his ugly yellow teeth, "your very best luck comes with 1, 12, and 40."

"I have to go."

I rose unsteadily from the table (my right leg must have fallen asleep), mumbled a thanks and a good-bye to Jack and left the saloon. When I had crossed the street I stopped and looked back at the Penn Hotel. In an instant every detail of the building seemed to leap forth in the twilight and imprint itself on my mind—the broken clock over the door, the white window shade half-closed on the third floor, the *1890* legend carved in its lozenge of pale mortar, the chipping green-painted cornice—and it occurred to me that everything seems most real at the moment it is about to, indeed has already begun to, dissolve.

My mother was furious. She asked me was it true that my school had been ordered closed for fumigation that very morning, because a case had been discovered there. She asked, if it was true, where I had gone all day instead of coming home. After a bout of questioning, to which I could give only vague, halfhearted replies, she sent me to bed without supper. I had no appetite anyway. I tossed in the sheets in my hot room, imagining a coal furnace glowing and smoldering under my bed. I was plunged into dreams that swamped me like waves, rolling over and under themselves in endless repetitions, churning me downward, their force black and mindless and insupportably heavy. Then clear vistas opened before me: I saw a funeral procession marching into the sea, and Christmas bells howling in the night, and a girl with freckles dangling limp from a gallows, and a black cat with glass eyes scratching away in a grave. I dreamt of a giant shoving an avalanche down onto a train, and a boy with a gold tooth and measles lying faceup in a pool of muddy water, whispering *Good-luck, good-luck, good-luck,* the words bubbling up through the filth. And all the while strings of numbers reeking of mustard chugged on like angry machines, like a train of infinite length and energy spinning its wheels on a track that could lead nowhere. *Good-luck, good-luck, good-luck, good-luck, good-luck* . . .

Someone pressed a cool wet cloth to my forehead. I could hear my mother breathing loudly through her nostrils. When I opened my eyes, three faces with ghostly surgical masks hovered there: my mother, and Mr. Schrock, and a man I didn't recognize. "You can see the one pupil is larger than the other," said this man. "It is a symptom of the ailment I was explaining to you." Mr. Schrock said, "Don't go back to sleep, William. You can stay awake now, can't you?"

But I couldn't stay awake. I felt myself sinking through the deeps until I came to rest at bottom. My body was as dead as a stone, but my mind was strangely lucid—and this sensation was vaguely familiar, as though I had met it before in a dream. I felt as though I had returned to a home I had once known but forgotten.

Against my will I was called back to the world. Tears streamed down my mother's face. There was something, I saw, that she needed to tell me but couldn't. I watched her face impassively; she wore an expression of beseeching, but I didn't know what it was she wanted from me.

She seemed to be saying there was *some bad news*. My friend had been in an accident. But who was my friend? Wilkerson, or Jack? I tried to ask what was wrong but couldn't understand her reply. I was slipping back into sleep, and in my dreams the notion got mixed up, so that it seemed to me it was I, and not my friend, who had been in the accident. The whole town was talking about it. I felt thousands of eyes from the hundreds of homes in the valley, and the homes nestled in the hills that ringed the town, all turned in my direction, waiting to hear the news. I saw families watching through their curtains and shutters as the floodwaters came down the street and rose to their doorsteps, and kept rising, until the water was level with their parlor windows. They looked out into the underwater world, and asked, *What is going to happen to that boy, the boy who had the accident? What is going to happen?*

I slept through the fall while the quarantine was lifted and the town came back to life. The sourwoods blazed red against the pines, men and boys went hunting in the mountains, and deer meat hung in the butcher shops. Winter was coming, when people would take sleigh rides to Gallitzin, and join in tobogganing parties, and ice-skate at Von Lunen Pond, where the silhouettes of skaters would glide against a pink sunset, their blades describing slow arabesques on the powdered sheet of ice.

On Halloween my fever was gone. From my bed I looked out the window at the children parading through the street below. They all wore white gauze surgical masks no matter what their costume, laughing and shouting and setting off firecrackers in the street. I watched until the parade was past, then lay back on my pillow in the lamplight.

In the middle of November I returned to school. Mrs. Miller said how wonderful it was to have me back. She asked me how did I feel. I said I didn't know how I felt. My reply seemed to perplex her. I felt like a ghost in the presence of the other children. I limped toward my old desk, thinking of how it had been empty during the many weeks, and how perhaps the children had avoided that desk, as though the residue of a frightful sickness lingered on it. Seated again with my red geography open, I remembered the day I had sneezed. I tried to think of the time that had passed between then and now, and a wave of dizziness washed over me. I tried to concentrate on my lessons, but the words jittered on the page and the numbers looked bent as though refracted through liquid. I squinted, and felt the others watching me strain over the page. Before recess I asked the teacher why Wilkerson wasn't there. She said that he had the flu but would be back soon. On the playground I heard a girl say, *He looks funny*, and her friend say, *He's cock-eyed, isn't he?*; and I understood they were talking about me. A boy named Franco asked what had happened to me; I lied and said I had been run over by an automobile.

But more than anything I no longer understood why I was there in the school. I remembered how I'd felt the day I was sent home, when I'd walked down the silent hallway and opened the door into the bright sunshine— how strange it was that I could be anywhere at all. I sensed that this displaced feeling, this anxious shiver of a vague, indeterminate thrill had grown inside me, had made some irrevocable claim on my being. And so, in my first week back, I began to wander out the doors of the school, in the middle of the day, during recess or after I had asked permission to go to the bathroom. I walked through the park in the town square, past the gazebo and the stone monument to the Great Flood, where in the warm months a Venetian fountain sent jets of water pluming into the air, creating a mist under the oak trees, which gave the place a dreamy, underwater feeling. I faced the monument and thought of the sailboats on the mountain lake, expecting the terrible falling sensation I used to get whenever I imagined the tidal wave appearing from between the two hills, the impossible feeling of a mountain tumbling over itself. But instead I felt nothing. It was all in the past; everything was in the past; the wave had come and covered everything, and everything had already drowned before I was born.

What remained was only this: new snowflakes flurrying through the bare branches—the first snow of autumn. People in the park looked at me, noticing my limp and my squinty eye, but they didn't know who I was.

The theaters and ice-cream parlors and saloons and moving-picture houses had reopened by decree of Mayor Franke. I went to the Penn Hotel, where the saloon's front window was fogged up from the heat inside. The saloon was crowded with men drinking and talking. I looked around at the faces of the men; Jack wasn't among them. A man I hadn't seen before was tending the bar. I described to him Jack's appearance, to see if he knew where the tramp was, if he still lived at the Penn Hotel. The man gave me a dark look; he asked me how I knew this person, what my relation was. I lied and said he was a friend of my uncle's. Then he brought up a week-old newspaper and pointed to an article. I told the man I couldn't read because my head had been injured at birth; I asked him if he would read to me what it said in the paper. He sighed and read it.

DESTROYED SELF WITH BELT, COAT HOOK, AND A BED

Mr. Jacnin's body was found this morning by fellow boarders in his room in the Penn Hotel. Circumstances attendant upon the supposed suicide are so suspicious in the minds of police authorities that a rigid inquiry is being conducted.

I interrupted him: "Jack's name was *Jacnin*?" A giggle erupted from my mouth. The bartender looked horrified; then he became angry. I tried to explain that I hadn't meant to laugh, that I hadn't meant anything—but he told me to get out.

I seldom went to school. I walked past the Penn Hotel but never went inside. I threw my schoolbooks down a grating in Washington Street. Sometimes I wandered up into the hills above the train tracks to see the tramps who lived there, but it was winter now and they were all gone. One time I saw a woman standing in the water in Stony Creek, holding up her dress around her knees. She said the hospital had tried to keep her there against the law but that she had escaped. She said she knew Mayor Franke personally, and warned me not to tell anyone about this, and if I did, something awful would happen to me that she knew about but couldn't say.

At home I had spells. Something came alive inside of me, and I would shout or kick or slap at my mother, but never at Mr. Schrock. I couldn't sleep at night. Lying in my bed I would whistle or sing to myself; Mr. Schrock said he had never heard of such behavior in a child. "He's different from the first day out of bed," I heard him say. My mother said, "I fear the illness may have touched him."

Once I was crying in the night and my mother came into the room. She asked me what was wrong, and I complained of a pain about my heart. She asked me when had it started; I said after someone had thrown a frozen snowball at my head.

Then she, too, began to cry. "I thought it was all over," she whispered. "I thought you were going to be better now." I said that I felt fine and that nothing was wrong with me, except that I couldn't see right because I had been hit in the head by a westbound train. I said all the fast trains had accidents and only the slow trains were safe. I said the people on the train were escaping from the hospital because they knew a flood was coming and nobody else believed them. I said the mayor was driving the train, and he had hit me on purpose because I was cockeyed. I said that each person on board had dreamt of their lucky number, but everyone kept it a secret.

My mother asked me why I was lying, why I told so many lies; I said that I didn't know.

When the doctor was summoned to our house, I watched through the keyhole. They whispered in the kitchen. It was difficult to hear—there was a rushing, crackling noise in my ears, like water flowing under the surface of a frozen creek.

"... you would hardly expect a child to think of ..."

"... that certain—*moral*—defects have been noted in cases where ..."

"... ate a piece of candy he found in the gutter ..."

"... masklike condition, a 'smoothing' effect ..."

"... insomnia and ..."

"... colony for the feebleminded in Ebensburg, where formerly incurables ..."

I went to my room and began to hiccup. I couldn't stop hiccupping, and my stomach began to hurt, but still I couldn't stop, even when my mother came into the room with the doctor and Mr. Schrock and told me they had decided it would be best if I took a trip to the sea-shore, to a place on the East Coast that Mr. Schrock's aunt knew about, a rest home where people and children suffering from nervousness could benefit from the fresh sea air and the hot baths. I was told that I would take a train there. Mr. Schrock would accompany me on the journey, while my mother would remain at home. A trunk would be packed tonight.

MR. SCHROCK SAT STIFFLY IN THE TRAIN COMPARTMENT, wearing his white gauze mask. He wore it even though the ice-cream shops had reopened. His wearing it made me feel ashamed, but he gestured vaguely out the window and said, "We just don't know what's going on out there." Mr. Schrock and I had the compartment to ourselves, except for a man in shabby brown suit and a brown hat who slouched on the bench opposite. This man looked like a traveling salesman, with his leather-bound sample cases loaded on the rack. His hat shaded his face as he slept. From time to time he opened an eye and seemed to regard me and my older masked companion.

My mother had packed a hamper with pieces of chicken wrapped in tea towels. Once the train was flying across the valley where the smooth barren hills rolled softly, brown and gold and white, Mr. Schrock lowered his mask and we helped ourselves to the chicken, gazing out at the fields and licking the grease from our fingers. Then I fell asleep. Once I heard Mr. Schrock say the word *nervous*—he might have been speaking to the traveling salesman, or to himself. When I woke up it was dark. The compartment door was open and I heard people dragging luggage in the passageway. I heard a woman's voice: "My older brother is retarded . . . What? . . . An institution in Delaware." A second woman, with a European accent, said something I couldn't understand; the first woman replied, "Meningitis. He never . . ." A bell clanged. Mr. Schrock whispered in my ear: "Newport. We're not there yet." I heard his breathing through the mask. I fell back asleep. The train's monotonous rhythm lulled me; its vibrations enclosed me like a womb. I dreamt of the world's smallest train striving up a steep mountainside, grinding and struggling on the narrow-gauge switchbacks, to deliver vaccine to the people in a town at the top.

When Mr. Schrock shook me awake the sky outside was pink. The man in the brown suit was gone. As we unloaded my trunk onto the station platform, a salty, putrid odor in the cold air tingled my nostrils. There was snow on the platform. My trunk and I were loaded onto a boat waiting at a dock next to the depot—a ferry, said

Mr. Schrock, to take me across the bay to the rest home. Someone, he said, would meet me there. The ferryman stood silent; gulls cried in the air; and the few other passengers looked like statues against the fiery dawn light, which rippled in bands on the glassy dark water. The boat was untied, and slipped away from the dock toward a flat horizon with fire burning below it; and the last thing I saw was Mr. Schrock, waving from land, his face unreadable behind the white gauze mask.

THE BOAT PULLED IN AT THE PIER. Men were pushing broad shovels across the boardwalk, heaping up snow and shoving it off the edge onto the beach. I was approached by a gaunt elderly man in a long wool apron, pushing before him a white wicker chair on wheels. He had large moist eyes and a melancholy smile and a worried brow; he introduced himself as Mr. McCord, and coaxed me into the chair. He pushed me in silence, as the sun's disk broke the horizon, up the boardwalk toward our destination.

Set back from the boardwalk on a sandy lawn was a white three-story house with a gabled roof and steps leading up to a broad front porch which girded the house. A middle-aged woman in a black dress and tinted spectacles came out and stood with her hands folded. Her gray hair was pulled severely back in a bun, and she smiled warmly. She introduced herself as Mrs. Gritman, and took me inside while Mr. McCord hauled my trunk up the steps. She asked me how my journey was; I said I couldn't remember. She asked me if I knew why I was here.

Because of a flood, I meant to say. Because the train's gone. Because everything was underwater.

I said that I was very sleepy; that sometimes I couldn't go to sleep at all.

"But I think you will be able to sleep here," she said. She took me up the stairs to my room at the end of the hallway. I asked how long I would have to stay at this house. She shrugged, smiling. "It could be a few weeks," she said. "Or a few months, or a few years. It all depends on you."

A few years, I thought, stepping across the threshold. The meaning of the phrase, so far away and opaque, was bound up with the sensation of being in this new room. I tried to stretch myself out over that span of time, to see what it looked like on the other side, but I couldn't think that far. *A few years*. It was impossible. I would be someone else by then; it would be someone else in this room.

I thought of the solitary man in the window on the third floor of the Penn Hotel, the man with the mask who watched me, then disappeared. If I dreamed of getting sick, my lucky numbers were 11, and 25, and 40. But if I dreamed about a strange city, they were 20, and 33, and 47. Anything could happen to anybody—the secrets were all printed in a little book. And maybe it wasn't good to know them. Maybe knowing them could somehow make them come true.

"I'll leave you for a short time," said Mrs. Gritman, shutting the door.

I stood at the window looking out at the ocean. I hadn't realized, during the short boat ride, how truly enormous it was. How boundless and immovable, how unlike the floods I had dreamed, bursting their dams and tumbling forth with a thunderous smashing down into the valley. The ocean rippled and frothed in countless little white peaks, and the waves crumbled softly on shore, smoothed themselves out, withdrew, and curled up into new waves. This ocean gave me a peaceful feeling deep in my bones; it seemed the place that was the end of all floods.

TWICE DAILY, AS PART OF MY REST CURE, I got bundled up in blankets and mufflers and Mr. McCord pushed me up and down the boardwalk in the rolling chair. Gaily painted placards along the storefronts lured passersby to amusements that wouldn't be open till summer: Kipple & McCann's Sea Baths, the Alhambra Dancing Rooms, the Gigantic Sea Elephant, the Haunted Swing, the Whirlpool. At the very end of the pier was the Deep-Sea Net Haul, where, Mr. McCord told me, twice daily in summer the net was raised from "The Living Gulfs of Doom," and whatever cold-blooded monstrosities chanced to have been trapped in that abysmal region were dumped on the planks in the light of day, displayed for all to see.

Although the shore was mostly deserted, we occasionally passed winter visitors strolling on the boardwalk. Some of them still wore the white gauze masks. They must have looked at the elderly man pushing the bundled child in the rolling chair, and wondered who we were. Once we passed a dressed-up young man and lady in a bicycle rickshaw, a JUST MARRIED—'HONEYMOON CLUB' sign attached to the back of their seat. Their eyes looked happy; both of them wore masks.

Mr. McCord walked behind me. He liked to speak; his

voice was disembodied, monotonous, soothing. I couldn't see his face, and often I imagined my father floating behind me, his ghostly arms propelling my chair into the windy afternoon. He told me things I couldn't have imagined. He said the epidemic swept over the whole country, into every city and town, every village and valley. A lot of people didn't want to know about it, he said. They tried to pretend that nothing was happening.

Sometimes we stopped at a bench and I sat next to Mr. McCord while he read me headlines from the newspaper, picking out the most gruesome ones, which he knew were my favorites. "DEATH SHIP: ENTIRE CREW FELL ILL: No survivors in Labrador village where sick mail boat docked. . . ." "THE MYSTERY MALADY: ALARMING SPREAD OF SLEEPY SICKNESS. Children among the victims . . ." The news was scary and thrilling, but I wasn't afraid because I huddled close to Mr. McCord.

"You ought to consider yourself one of the lucky ones," he said.

One night I awoke suddenly; Mr. McCord stood over me with a candle. With a finger at his lips he signaled quiet. He had come to take me for the special treat he had promised. My heart raced with excitement as I got out from the blankets and he assisted me in getting dressed. He bundled me up in mufflers. Out on the sanitarium porch, the wind blew fierce off the ocean. I told Mr. McCord I could walk, but he insisted I get in the rolling chair.

From the boardwalk we slipped underneath an archway, through a door, down a narrow hall glowing with gaslight, and into a large dim room. It was a moving-picture hall, where a midnight clam supper was taking place. Men and women sat at long bench tables eating plates of steamers and drinking mugs of beer, while the pictures flickered onscreen and the organ music rose and fell. The film was about a group of picnickers in bathing costumes, who were so amused with themselves they didn't see a tidal wave was coming. They kept rebuffing an exasperated lifeguard who was trying to warn them, waving his semaphore flags and pointing at the sea and comically running up and down. Even when the wall of water was towering above them, like it could wipe out the whole city, the picnickers still couldn't be bothered about it. But when the wave reached the shore and the lifeguard had given up and run for cover, cowering under an umbrella, it turned out to be no more than a little spout, and splashed over the picnickers, who jumped about indignantly as if their picnic had been spoiled. The people in the hall roared with laughter as the picnickers shook their fists and chased after the poor lifeguard, who clambered up the lifeguard chair to safety.

I started to laugh. It came out of me like a convulsion, I shook and sobbed with laughter—the people at their suppers turned to look—and Mr. McCord rolled me down the corridor and out the door onto the boardwalk. The wind was wild; Mr. McCord was laughing too, gulping and hacking. We raced to the end of the pier where the Deep-Sea Net Haul was drawn. The wind ripped the clouds apart, revealing the moon, a ceiling of stars above the black ocean.

"I'll be in the newspaper," I cried, catching my breath. "How about 'A DROWNING ACCIDENT THIS DAY. One boy, attempting to bathe in sea during winter season, unfortunately drowned. . . .'"

Mr. McCord, invoking a lofty, sober tone, suggested "'INVALID CHILD IN ROLLING CHAIR PUSHED OFF END OF OCEAN PIER. Suspects questioned . . .'"

"'SEASIDE MOURNS. Body unclaimed . . .'"

"'MYSTERIOUS ROLLING CHAIR FOUND WASHED ASHORE NEAR LEWES. Nearby sanitarium astir . . .'"

"'INLAND BOY FLEES FLOOD. Came to land's end and plunged himself headlong into Atlantic Ocean. . . .'"

We went on like this, trading headlines and choking back laughter and tears until it was too cold to stay. We fell silent as Mr. McCord pushed me back to the house. Warm in my bed again, I thought of other headlines, other news. BOY BRAVES ILLNESS. CHILD'S MIRACULOUS RECOVERY: ESCAPE FROM THE JAWS OF DEATH . . . MAYOR'S PROCLAMATION: NEVER BEFORE HAS SUCH COURAGE BEEN SEEN IN A BOY.

NEWS DID COME THE FOLLOWING WEEK. In the evening, Mrs. Gritman brought the letter to my room. I asked her to open it for me.

> *Perhaps I shouldn't be writing to you about this but I thought you must know. The epidemic has returned in a second wave. No one can believe it. We all thought it was over for good. Mr. Schrock is gravely ill. He has been taken to a hospital they have set up in the town hall and of course I am forbidden to visit him. It is much worse this time. Everyone*

is very much frightened. You cannot go into any-
one's home, or speak to anyone since we are under
full quarantine. Children are forbidden to go in the
streets. No one can board a train without a special
certificate. Even if you came home, William, I fear
you wouldn't be allowed off the train. Although it is
sad, I am glad that you are so far away from here. I
am glad you are far away where it is safe.

Even if you came home ... The strangeness of those
words haunted me into sleep.

I dreamt of a train carrying me by night away from
the shore, back into the mountains. Nothing moved in the
hillsides; even the forests were silent. Nobody was in the
streets; crepe hung on every door, black and white and
gray; and I wondered if I was even in the same place. But
then I saw: they were all watching from behind windows.
In the windows of every house and hotel and shop I saw
the faces looking out, wearing the white masks over their
mouths.

"I am returned!" I cried. My voice echoed and died
in the street. "I am strong again!" But the people just
watched. They had been weakened by the illness; their
fear had diminished them to ghosts.

And then night fell; the rains came; I was in the little house up on the mountain by the lake, where Colonel
Unger lived. He lay in the bed, unable to move, conceptions
of horror stirring in his mind. His face was my father's
face. "There is nothing I can do," he said. "The dam will
go; the wave will fall." He wanted me to a deliver a message—*Notify the people to prepare for the worst*—though he

knew it was too late. He had tried to tell them. He had tried, and it had not been enough. The colonel turned his face to the wall and closed his eyes. In the last light he saw the future crushing in, monstrous and blind.

"You are far away, where it is safe," I told him. "It can never happen again."

Are You Here For
What I'm Here For?

THEIR HOTEL RESEMBLED a pink many-layered cake encrusted onto the side of the hill. As they drove up under the portico, Gina heard music and saw a man shouting through a bullhorn and gesticulating. The man resembled Moammar Qaddafi and wore wraparound sunglasses, salmon trousers, and a Liberace shirt unbuttoned to mid-chest. "Welcome, ladies, ladies and gentlemen, welcome to paradise!" he implored through the bullhorn in an indeterminate European accent, helping Gina and Harry and the other passengers down from the shuttle. A festive merengue song blared tinnily. Staff members appeared bearing yellow daiquiris. Gina accepted one, her throat parched, as bellhops made off with the luggage. The Qaddafi figure exhorted the travel-weary guests to form a conga line and, in this way, pass into the lobby dancing.

"Sun Club! St. Ri-ta! Sun Club! St. Ri-ta!" the impresario chanted through the bullhorn, pumping his fist to the beat.

"This isn't very relaxing," Gina whispered to Harry, but he couldn't hear her. She kept a big midwestern smile plastered on her face, glancing embarrassedly at the hotel guests who paused to observe the new arrivals shaking their rumps and shuffling along in their rumpled airplane clothes.

Their room was on the fourth floor. They stepped onto the balcony and took in the view: the moon-shaped cove with its crescent of white beach, coral reefs like cloud shadows lurking under clear water. At the far end of the cove, a ruined fort atop rocky cliffs. Windsurfers languished on the unruffled sea. Scattered white umbrellas pocked the beach. Directly below their balcony, multiple terraces staggered down the hill, flights of limestone steps overhung with bougainvillea and hibiscus, ornamental gardens of volcanic rock and flowering cactus.

All of it shimmered in the sun; it wasn't quite real. A shriek issued up from the pool deck, the sound a crystalline miniature. Gina's head felt glasslike.

"Not too shabby, eh?" said Harry, wrapping his arms around her from behind, nuzzling her neck.

IT WAS 1985 AND THERE WERE TWO POSSIBILITIES: Gina Maisley was dying, or Gina Maisley was not dying. The very ground she walked on felt ungroundlike. Her days were a tightrope over the winking, beckoning void. Really this was nothing new: dying had always been with her, a secret Idea. Recently, after a string of low-grade fevers and lingering odd infections, she'd gone to Andy Cerbone, family friend and physician, the way a young girl goes to the priest: to unburden herself, to feel concerned for, to go home corrected and reprieved.

She was fifty-two years old and this had always been

her ritual. Her illness—whichever it might be from one year to the next, a grim succession of -omas, each born out of some novel twinge or swelling—was an Idea. You had to *believe* somehow in your Idea in order for it not to be true, just as you shouldn't quite believe in the best things: your looks and good fortune, your husband's fidelity, your children's health and talents, all so precariously real.

It was a kind of spiritual camouflage: you disguised yourself in a cloak of misfortune to trick fate into passing you over. It was a kind of dark magic performed in the corner of your heart. It was vaguely shameful, and Gina knew better. But you stuck with what seemed to work.

She'd gone to Cerbone with her Idea, and instead of brushing it off, Cerbone had ordered bloodwork. When the bloodwork came back he grew sober, alarmingly thoughtful. His lower lip protruded and his moist black eyes, behind large glasses, looked involved in esoteric calculations. He spoke of *the emergence of a pattern we can no longer afford to ignore*. He invoked the Disease That Dare Not Speak Its Name. It left his lips like a profanity. It squatted between them like a toad.

She suddenly felt like she'd asked for it. Like a child who whines and begs for a prize, then abruptly gets it. *But I don't want* this *prize.*

"I shouldn't have gone there in the first place," she told her friend Gwynn on the phone. "I should have stayed out of doctors' offices." Of course they couldn't know for sure without a biopsy, the kind with the big needle.

"It won't be the bad thing, honey," said Gwynn. It was probably something murkier, something nebulously auto-immune. The kind of thing to keep an eye on, maybe for years; a shadow passenger, along for the rest of the ride. Hadn't Cerbone conceded as much?

"It's just this *house*," she told Gwynn. "I can't *stand* it here." She loved her house. It was as if the phone might ring and the news break in like a troop of gibbering weirdos, tracking mud or dog shit through each of her rooms.

And poor Harry. The day she'd come back from her appointment and tried to explain what Cerbone had said, Harry broke out in hives. He'd been planning, she thought, to make some gentle joke about yet another of Gina's false alarms. That night she woke up and he wasn't in bed. She found him at the kitchen table, hunched over the medical encyclopedia, with his broken reading glasses and his book light, his tongue in the corner of his mouth, his finger moving slowly down the page. She'd surprised him, and he gasped and cast her a guilty look.

"Don't overthink it, sweetie," said Gwynn. "It's *compli*cated, with these autoimmune things. What you need to do is focus on your *healing*. Get out of here! Go to St. Rita. Forget your troubles. Fall under a spell."

"Go to who?" said Gina.

"It's en*chant*ed."

"Is that a hospital?"

"It's an island. One of those Sun Club resorts. They have Sun Club Bee."

Gina misheard this as Sun Club B, as in a second-tier version of Sun Club A. An alternative for travelers willing to accept a slightly shabbier accommodation, or a second-best view of the cove. What Gwynn meant was Sun Club *Be**. As explained in the back of the brochure, Sun Club

*BE** offered "An experience for our guests whose journey includes a health challenge."

Was it experimental treatments? Health tourism? Gina pictured herself in a high-rise hotel that was actually a hospital, attended by nuns in starched habits, a Caribbean breeze blowing in at the window.

"The funny thing is," Gina said to Gwynn, "I don't *feel* like I'm dying."

She wanted her friend to say, *That's because you're not.*

What Gwynn said was: "That's the right *attitude*, Gina. Go to St. Rita and work on those healing thoughts."

Harry took vacation time—they would fly out of O'Hare on a Monday. Cerbone had assured them the results would be in no later than Friday. On Friday they would come home.

Harry had wanted them to call the kids, to tell Christopher and Becca what was going on. Gina forbade it. "It'll make them *sick* with worry. Let them live their lives. What would we tell them? We don't *know* anything yet."

So she agreed to a deal: by the time they came back it would all be settled, and they would tell the kids whatever there was to tell.

On the plane she thought of her little sister Frances, somewhere down there in the panhandle of Florida, by herself in the mobile home, or maybe with her friends at church. She had meant to confide in Francie before they left.

THEY WERE WAITING FOR THE ELEVATOR to take them down to dinner when a yellow-haired woman in a skirted bathing costume came sauntering past, bearing an exquisite piece of red coral like a brilliant calciferous bouquet.

"Oh. Do they sell those in the gift shop?" Gina asked.

The woman halted. "My coral?" she said.

"Yes—where did you get it?"

The woman brightened. "In the sea!" she said, gesturing at the door behind her, as if the sea were in that room.

"But how . . ."

"Go snorkeling," whispered the lady.

Remarkable, thought Gina. She wondered if it was legal. She felt she had to have a piece.

In the elevator she said to Harry: "I really think she must have bought it in the gift shop."

The gift shop was closed.

In the dining room, she noted with pleasure the Prussian blue carpeting, the white tablecloths with pots of orchids. Most of the guests were dressed nicely, even if some wore brightly colored loungewear and a few of the men wore shorts. (They always said sick people let themselves go, but she wondered if the opposite was true: you wanted to wear your nice outfits while you still had the chance, those blouses you really liked but for some reason had neglected.) The dining room was buffet-style. Gina and Harry loved buffets. She filled her plate with small portions of many things: snapper fillet, gratin potatoes, blackened shrimp, asparagus. The Qaddafi host made his rounds among the tables like the father of the bride. She heard him chatting with a couple in French; the three of them burst into laughter.

"Who is he?" Gina whispered, because Qaddafi was coming their way, still in the wraparound sunglasses.

"Russell," said Harry. "Russell or Raoul." Harry had eaten too fast again. He was muttering about a bad conch fritter, the heavy dough. Gina remembered how uptight she used to get when Harry drank and acted silly. He no longer drank. She didn't miss that, but sometimes she missed the silliness.

Russell/Raoul came up and said: "Cloudya!"

"Who?" said Gina. "No, I'm Gina Maisley."

"But of course Gina, how could I forget you, lovely Gina. You are here with your father, yes? Heh-heh. The show may not proceed without Gina. But of course you will be my date to the show?"

She held her face in a rictus of mirth, tugging her hand free of his grip. She couldn't shake the notion that behind the sunglasses Russell/Raoul had a milky white eye or a ghastly scar. "Then we shall see you in the theater," he declared.

Harry looked confused; his brow was beaded with moisture. On their way out of the dining room he made a move for the elevator, but Gina was anxiously torn. She didn't have high hopes for the show, but she feared future run-ins with a jilted Russell/Raoul. "I promised him I would go."

"Who?"

"Russell. The guy with the glasses."

"That jackass?" Harry said. He didn't look well, but she was reluctant to go alone. From the entrance to the Calabash Room came an upwelling of music and a garbled voice booming from the speakers. Gina coaxed him toward it, whispering assurances.

The theater was dark and laser lights played over the

seats, many of which were empty. She led Harry to a pair
of seats in the middle. Onstage, dancers in Day-Glo outfits
lip-synced to a pop song. She understood that the volume
and lights and razzle-dazzle were meant to distract you
from observing that the show was sparsely attended and
the content was poor. Russell/Raoul served as emcee, lingering at the edge of the stage with his microphone, firing
off quips at the performers and encouraging the audience
into weak hails of applause.

After the lip-sync dancers, a comedian was introduced. He told jokes about the foibles of resort life, marital
gags with sexual innuendos, potty humor.

"This is very tasteless," Gina hissed in Harry's ear. It
was her way of apologizing, of letting him know he was
right in not wanting to be there.

When the comedian took his bows, the emcee introduced a hypnotist.

"He is the superb Dr. Cline," proclaimed Russell/
Raoul. "But I know him as 'Sly,' or, as we say, the *régulière*.
So let us give it up for Sly!"

"Who is it?" said Harry, but Gina just shook her head:
she was focused on the hypnotist—a bald white man in
a black shirt, silver tie, and black pants—who, she saw to
her horror, was stalking up the aisle, selecting participants
from the audience. When the man made eye contact with
her—he was close enough that she could see a vein on his
forehead—she sent him a telepathic message: *Don't you
dare; I am a sick woman.*

His eyes slid off her and landed on a handsome young
man across the aisle to Gina's right.

She felt an ice-water trickle in her chest. The young

man rose hesitantly, grinning, against the silent objections of a middle-aged woman (his mother?) with whom he was sitting. Something in the carriage of his shoulders, the way he held his head, even the swells of his tanned calves as he stepped into the aisle to follow Dr. Cline, struck some intimate chord in Gina's heart. Who did he remind her of?

"Enough," rumbled Harry, hoisting himself up.

Gina gripped his arm and held him down: "Wait a minute. Please. I want to see something."

"What I am doing, ladies and gentlemen," said the hypnotist, "is putting these good people into a deep trance." The participants, about eight men and women, were seated onstage in a row of folding chairs. The hypnotist strode back and forth, touching the heads of the men, saying *sleep*. "When they awaken, they will believe they are contestants in a beauty pageant." The men, feigning grogginess, rose and began to mince around the stage, preening and striking poses. The handsome young man went gamely along, cocking his hips, flipping back his pretend hair.

Gina was riveted, seized with embarrassment for him. It was all a fake, of course. And it gave the hypnotist a cruel advantage. He barked out instructions and the men had to play along. The hypnotist held them hostage, not with mesmerism, but with emotional blackmail: *You wouldn't dare expose my act, would you?*

But even behaving in this demeaning way, the young man looked stylish and becoming, while the other, older men looked like maundering fools.

Dr. Cline put the men back to "sleep" and turned his attention to the women. When he counted to five, he said, they would feel sexy, ten times more sexy than they'd ever felt with their husbands.

"Okay," said Gina, "I can't stand this. Let's go."

That night she couldn't sleep, aware of bass thumping up through the floor.

HARRY WAS ILL IN THE MORNING. Then Gina revealed that she, too, was feverish. Harry emerged from beneath a mound of covers, tumbled and smelly, crooning sweet things. Gina rebuffed him, but he was mawkish and grave, fumbling at her, blubbering. He wanted to call Dr. Cerbone. He wanted to summon the hotel doctor. "Stop it!" Gina screamed. "No one can do *any*thing!" She watched herself lash out at her husband as though he were Sickness itself. She was a passive spectator, chiding herself to stop it. They sank into silence, went back to bed. Later she called for yogurt and ate half of it on the balcony. It was a brilliant sunny day. Guests milled about on the terraces. In the big pool a volleyball game was under way. Out on the water, the tiny prostrate bodies of the snorkelers. She closed her eyes, warming her face in the sun. When she opened them a lizard was poised on the railing. It was so still she thought it must be fake. Then she saw the crepe sac of its throat puffing in and out. Its eye was fixed on her, granular and unblinking, as though waiting for her to make a move.

Gina took her temperature, tried to read, returned to the balcony. Down below, a Jeep taxi was parked near the entrance. She saw the young man from the theater and the older woman standing next to the Jeep.

So that's *who he is*, she thought. The young man was
the spitting image of Eddie Marinowski, the lifeguard in
Waukesha. She'd obsessed about him all summer when
she was fourteen, willing him to notice her, pretty Gina,
hidden behind cat glasses and buck-teeth and adolescent
gangle. She made a deal with herself that she'd talk to
him by Labor Day if it killed her. Labor Day came; all
afternoon she waited for her moment, sending him mental messages, ignoring her little sister Frances, her charge.
The sky clouded over; a wind kicked up. Most people
had already left. Frances was impatient to go home. Gina
watched Eddie's well-muscled body in profile, talking to
another boy, fondling the whistle that hung on a cord
against his stomach. Frances whined, teeth chattering.
The moment didn't come; Gina was crestfallen. She felt
ugly. They left. Then the bus didn't come and Frances
caught a chill. Then she got sick, lost use of her legs; they
burned her toys in the backyard. She ended up in that
school for damaged children, sweet Francie among the
mongoloids and midgets, the floozies and delinquents.
Not long after that, they moved away. Gina's mother had
never let her forget that day at the pool.

A staff member was loading luggage into the back of
the Jeep. So the young man and the woman were leaving.
She went inside and tried to nap. Instead she cried quietly,
bitterly. Harry was snoring. She held vigil on the balcony
as the sea turned dark. Bats swooped in the dusk.

"I want to go home tomorrow," she said to Harry when
he woke up from his nap. "I want to change our flight."
Normally he wouldn't have believed her. He would have

urged her to wait and see. It alarmed her that now he just looked defeated.

That night she took two sleeping pills. As the drug drew her into its orbit, she saw the pale hands of the hypnotist, the blood-red coral, the face of the young man. She plunged to the deeps.

When she came up in the morning, a lightness lapped over her. She waited, doubting it, but realized she felt superb. There was no explanation. She took her temperature: perfectly normal.

Harry felt worse. He asked her if she still intended for them to go home. Gina said she hadn't made up her mind. She showered, did her hair, chose an outfit of white clam diggers and a silk print blouse over her bathing suit top, and drifted down to the dining room, where she assembled for Harry a plate of pastries and fresh fruit. She found herself meeting the untroubled gazes of the women she passed and wondering, *Are you here for what I'm here for?* To all appearances, it looked like a normal resort, a pretty classy one. She hadn't seen a thing about the SUN CLUB BE*. If there was some wing where the ill sought refuge, Gina wasn't aware of it. Maybe it had nothing to do with her. Maybe she was fine, and was just here to enjoy herself. She peeked into the gift shop but didn't see any of that exquisite red coral.

After she'd persuaded Harry to drink some juice and eat a little cheese Danish, she read the whiteboard easel in the lobby. There were pool aerobics, intermediate windsurfing, the botanical gardens (shuttle provided), a calypso luncheon, a sunset booze cruise . . . she saw nothing that might be related to SUN CLUB BE*.

At the concierge desk she asked about the snorkeling. The clerk was a pretty, freckled, heavily permed girl. She shook her head: "The class has already gone out."

"Oh shoot," Gina said. "Well." She thought of Gwynn. Leaning toward the girl and lowering her voice, she said: "I'm not sure how to put this. I was wondering about the *bee*. You know, the SUN CLUB *BE**."

The girl regarded her blankly. She pointed to the activity chart on the easel.

"I've already seen that. I can't find what I'm looking for."

A second staffer, seeming to overhear, came up and took over. This woman was beautiful, with warm brown skin and welcoming eyes. She said discreetly, in a mellow West Indian accent: "They'll just be starting the workshop, dear. Down that hall to your left, in the Manchineel Room. They recommend you wear a loose, comfortable clothing."

Gina was no good at walking into rooms full of strangers, but who was? She peered through the ajar door: the Manchineel Room was cube-shaped, with mirrored walls. A dozen people—mostly her age, a few elderly—were seated or lying on tumbling mats. The young man from the theater was not among them. Because none of them had caught her looking, she was able to slip away.

She struck up a chat with a friendly younger couple in the elevator, who assured her that you didn't need a class in order to snorkel, there was nothing to it. Their easy confidence emboldened her. She didn't get off at her floor, but rode the elevator back down. She made her way to the dive shack on the beach. The pro set her up with a mask and fins. He didn't even charge her. Minutes later she was floating on the Caribbean Sea.

Taking breaths underwater felt unnatural. It defied the body's logic, sucking air through a plastic tube while chilly seawater pressed against your face and throat, touched into your armpits and groin, sloshed across your back. At first she kept standing up to pop out the snorkel. The man from the dive shack had told her to float face-down so the snorkel pointed up, to simply breathe and look. Gradually the chill faded; the calm water became a neutral medium, buoying her. She quit thrashing her fins. Her breathing grew less panicked. The mask formed an airtight seal around her eyes. If she raised her face so that her mask was half-submerged, the world split in two: bright air above, blue shadows below.

The sun warmed her back. She drifted into deeper water. From a distance the reef looked like heaps of rubble. But up close, you saw the rubble was clothed in an infinitely variegated patchwork of substance, repulsive and alluring. Everything seemed to resemble something else: chalk and cheese, velvet and slime, needles and sponge and coarse nubbling. Her eyes grazed over jeweled deformities, stealthy lumps that quivered into motion. At the sense of her approach, tiny vermilion feathers waving atop barnacles sucked themselves down in their holes.

And the fish! A zebra-striped saucer with a big wary eye on each side. An oblong lurker, half violet half canary, darting out from a crevice. Peacock spots on transparent skin, dorsal spines tipped with gold. She watched a smiling, blunt-snouted fellow rooting like a pig in the coral, its eye tiny, its flank tessellated in emerald. A cloud of silverfoil butterflies parted around her, flashing spangles of light as they turned.

Life down here was so clear and nameless, resounding with an inhuman song. She yearned to keep some piece of it, an artifact of this dream. She touched the edge of a purple fan and recoiled at its slime. It looked rooted to the rock. She wondered how the woman in the hotel had come back with her treasure, so fragile and intact. Gina perused the sea floor and found a smaller, grayer fan lying on its side in a sandy shallow area. It wasn't exquisite, but it was something. She snatched it up—it weighed almost nothing.

She stood, feeling the weight return to her knees and hips. Liquid glugged out of her ears and the metallic lilt of reggae music drifted from nearby. The sky was clouding over; a breeze cooled her back and arms, and she wondered how long she'd been out in the water. She glanced around, disoriented, and realized the current had carried her to the far side of the cove. The cliff loomed over this end of the beach; she could see the ruined fort at its peak.

She waddled out of the listless surf in her clown shoes. She stopped to pry a flipper off her foot. Balancing on one leg, she tripped and fell on her butt. Sitting in the wet sand, she removed the other flipper. When she glanced up, her young man was grinning over her, shirtless. She'd dropped her piece of coral; the young man nudged it with his toe.

"Oooh," he said reprovingly. "Did you touch that one?"

Gina began to speak and realized she was still breathing through her snorkel. She spat out the mouthpiece and peeled the mask off her face. Her lips were shriveled from the salt water, her mouth chalk-dry. "Yeah," she said. Her teeth hurt. "I found it."

"They call it 'weeping-eye,'" said the young man. "It's a sea nettle."

"Oh!" said Gina.

"It blinded a girl. A young girl . . ."

Gina gaped at the young man in horror.

"No no!" he said. "It was only for a few minutes."

"The blinding?"

He nodded. "She's fine now. In fact, she is the daughter of a professional tennis star. They're in Luxembourg." His voice was deep and soft, like an actor's, with a trace, she thought, of the genteel South. Sun had honeyed his hair; the treasure trail of darker hair below his navel disappeared in the waistband of his trunks.

Gina looked past him to the cluster of chaise longues and white umbrellas. The older woman was nowhere to be seen. But on one of the chaises was a black man with long dreadlocks. He wore a white linen suit with a black tie, and chewed on a stub of cigar. At his side was a boom box playing the *chunka*-tink *chunka*-tink of a reggae song.

"Thanks," she said as the young man helped her up. He introduced himself as Steffens.

"But I thought you guys had left," said Gina.

"When?"

Gina wished she'd kept her mouth shut; she didn't want to seem like a snooper. "That Jeep taxi," she murmured.

"Oh!" said Steffens. "Just a visit to the botanic garden. For Chloris's sake."

Gina nodded. "You did a nice job of playing along last night. Or was it two nights ago? I'm sorry—I haven't been well. In the show, I mean."

Steffens looked puzzled. "Playing along?"

"Oh come on." Gina blushed. "I felt embarrassed for you. It didn't seem fair."

The young man raised his eyebrow: "What did I do? He put me in a trance. I have no memory at all."

"Oh, you're kidding me," said Gina. "Well, what about the lady you were with . . ."

"Chloris?"

"Didn't she tell you what happened?"

The young man shook his head.

"You pretended to be"—she could barely say the words—"a beauty queen. You had to—I don't know—prance around."

"I pranced?" he said, delighted at the word. He turned and began to bunny-hop away from her. "Like this? Is this a prance? Is this embarrassing?"

Laughter erupted from her mouth and butterflies swarmed in her stomach.

The Rastafarian man on the chaise longue bellowed in laughter that might or might not have been kind.

Steffens stopped hopping and shrugged. "I don't know how else to explain it to you. Dr. Cline's suggestions are powerful."

"They didn't seem powerful to me. He was making fools out of people—I don't mean you. He made a fool of himself. I felt like a fool, watching."

"But you weren't up there on the stage," he said. "With the lights on you. And all those eyes on you. Gina."

"How do you know my name?"

Steffens shrugged again. The Rastafarian man roared with laughter. Gina cringed. She wondered where the older woman, Chloris, was. A raindrop touched her cheek.

"Good-bye, then," Gina said. Traipsing back along the beach, raindrops prickling her shoulders, she wanted to stop and turn around. When she'd reached the dive shack, she looked back across the emptying beach. She'd left her fan of coral on the sand.

HARRY WANTED TO KNOW WHETHER GINA had been to a treatment center, had received some type of treatment.

"You mean the SUN CLUB BE^*?" said Gina. "Or what are you talking about?"

"I was under the impression that this resort had some kind of a treatment center. Like a spa or something." He was camped under the covers, spooning sherbet into his mouth, watching a grainy broadcast of a rugby match. "Isn't that why we came here? To St. Rita?"

She felt her chin quivering. Sometimes she got so exasperated with Harry's thickheadedness that she didn't feel like explaining. "You don't know what you're talking about."

She might have wanted to regale him with descriptions of her snorkeling adventure, but now found she felt disinclined to share it with him, that strange, separate world she'd discovered. Nor did she feel like telling him about her encounter on the beach. Nor the "workshop," which she hadn't joined because she was scared, or lonely. She didn't understand what SUN CLUB BE^* was, nor what it could supposedly do for her. She felt angry at Gwynn. They had only come here for distraction, to run out the clock.

"I can't figure out the rules of this game," noted Harry.

"But these sons of bitches are tough. Look at those legs. And look—no helmets."

She dressed up in her best outfit and went alone to dinner.

ON THURSDAY MORNING, GINA PRESENTED HERSELF at the Manchineel Room. She knew it would be her last chance.

The workshop leader, a perfectly bald man in his forties, caught sight of her lingering in the doorway and rose from his mat. He was barefoot, in a loose T-shirt and Spandex pants. It struck her that he resembled Dr. Cline, the guy from the stage show. She even noted the vein on his scalp. But he clasped her limp hand in both of his and introduced himself as Joel.

Joel's hands were moist and warm. He had a slightly lazy eye. (Had the hypnotist also had a lazy eye?) Pasted over Joel's left breast was a stick-on name tag that said

HELLO, MY NAME IS

—and below this, printed in black magic marker:

It is safe to be a man.

"I don't think I'm in the right place," said Gina, stepping back.

Joel laughed appeasingly; touching the nametag he leaned in and whispered: "Some of us find it helpful to wear our affirmation. It's up to you, of course." Gina saw that everyone else was wearing the name tags.

Joel installed her on a mat close to him, at the front of the group, but in the course of the stretching and movement—they breathed while circling their hips, shook stiffness from their hands, hissed like snakes at Joel's bidding—Gina managed to recede back into the thicket of bodies.

For the next exercise Gina found herself paired with a lanky middle-aged fellow with a mane of wavy hair, wildly flared nostrils, and sensuous lips. Gina tried to mirror him, bending deeply to the left, then to the right, but the man was extremely flexible and she couldn't reproduce his contortions. He stood on one leg and raised his hands in a V, grinning, fixing her with his gaze: the dilated nostrils gave to his blue eyes an appearance of crazed intensity.

She tripped, or her leg gave out—her butt hit the mat hard. She sucked in her breath. "Oh," she said. The nostril man began to help her up. "Wait a sec," she said as her vision dimmed and blurred. Through the glitter of her head rush (she hoped it was just a head rush) she saw Steffens in the mirror, threading his way blithely through the group, dressed in madras shorts and a seashell pink polo, against which his thin arms looked smooth and well browned. She hadn't expected him to be here, but she saw (with chagrin and excitement) how keenly she'd anticipated it. His presence in the room gave her a shimmery sense of wish fulfillment, of a magical thought realized.

There was a brief, whispered conferral between Joel and Steffens before the latter assumed his place on a mat.

Joel was jouncing on his bare feet, clapping, gathering himself to address the class. "I feel a lot of surrendering going on in this room. I've said it before, folks: I can't beat my illness unless *I am willing to surrender.*" The others chorused in on this last phrase. "And I can't surrender until I know that my body is a safe place for me to be."

Gina heard murmurs of assent.

"I can feel in this room a yearning for wholeness. You've paid your hard-earned money to come to St. Rita, the most beautiful place on earth. For a vacation. For re-creation."

The murmurs grew more enthusiastic.

"But what are we re-creating? Every man, woman, and child in this hotel—has anyone see a child in this hotel?"—there were titters here; in fact Gina hadn't seen one—"every *person* in this hotel is yearning for wholeness. But every person in this *room*"—Joel finger-scanned the guests, pausing on Gina—"has found the courage to ask themselves, Am I *willing* to heal? Am I willing to make the *choice* to take control of my healing process? I'm seeing some nods. I'd like for us to reaffirm that choice this morning. We have some new friends and some old friends with us. What I'd like for us to do is share with a partner something about the journey that brought you *here to this room today.*"

The group began to mingle and pair off. Gina looked for Steffens, but someone grabbed her hand—it was Joel: "Will you partner with me, Jean?"

"I'm Gina. Gina Maisley."

Joel shut his eyes, inhaling deeply. They sat cross-legged, knee-to-knee, uncomfortably close. Joel raised his hands and invited her to press her palms to his.

"This all must seem very new to you," Joel began.

Gina blushed. "I guess I thought it would be a little more like a spa," she admitted.

Joel nodded, seeming to reflect on this. "Are you well today, Gina?"

"I guess so," she said uncertainly. "Maybe not? The problem is it's all so *comp*licated—"

"Is it really, Gina?" Joel smiled. "Let me tell you a little bit about my journey. Years ago I learned to ask myself, What story is my body trying to tell me? Have you ever listened closely to your body's story?"

"Oh I have, I have," said Gina. She was having trouble deciding which of Joel's eyes to focus on. "But it's a little murky right now . . ."

"It isn't murky at all."

"No?"

Joel shook his head. "It couldn't be more clear. Gina, let me ask you a question. What happens when you hold on to resentment? When you hoard it inside and don't let it go?"

"Gee. It eats away at you."

Joel clasped his hands and raised his eyes to the ceiling as if in praise: "I couldn't have said it better myself."

Gina blushed again. It felt good to get the answer right, even for someone like Joel. She glanced in the mirror and locked eyes with Steffens—his half smirk, his wink. His partner was a heavy-jowled woman with a severe gray bowl cut and enormous culottes.

"I chose," Joel continued, "to hold my anger inside. The things in here"—he tapped his head, right on the vein—"became the things in here": he smoothed his palm down his chest and belly, over his pelvis and groin.

"I won't deny, Gina, that all of the work I've done—and I've been doing this work for years and it *has* saved my life—all of this work doesn't make it any less hard for me to share with you that I am a cancer survivor."

"Oh," Gina said.

"In the testicles," said Joel.

"Oh my Lord," murmured Gina. Did he mean both of them?

"What are the testicles?" Joel said. Gina opened her mouth to venture a guess, when Joel answered himself: "They are the principle of manhood. In my journey, I have had to teach myself that it's safe for me, personally, to be a man. And that I don't have to keep my fear of my father, and my resentments of my father, snarled up in here."

"Wait—are you saying you think that—"

"I'm saying I don't believe that I'm sterile, Gina. Why? Because for a long time I resisted the process of life, and the process of needing to go through the parenting experience. Whereas now I trust in the process of life. I am always in the right place, doing the right things, at the right time. I welcome my children. I know that when they are ready, if I am holding open the door for them, they will come into the world. I welcome them."

Gina was appalled, but the tears welled up in her eyes. When he asked her if she thought she could find the courage to name the place where she'd been wounded, she found herself nodding weepily. By the time she walked out of the Manchineel Room, she was wearing a sticker that said

Hello My Name Is:

I am safe and loved and totally supported.

She stood in the lobby in a daze as people dispersed around her. The air was thick with the smells of lunch. A woman seated in a wing-back chair was smoking and glaring at her with watery bug eyes. It was the young man's companion, Chloris. She had the air of a ruined southern belle, Gina thought, resigned and defiant in her red lipstick, floral-print frock, and white mules. She stubbed out her cigarette and rose from the chair just as Steffens brushed past Gina. Before he and Chloris walked off together, Gina noted the nametag on his polo shirt: *I am part of the Universal design.*

"Lunch*time*!" cried Russell/Raoul, clapping his hands. "Chop-chop! Gina! Lunch! We got to feed you pretty girls . . ." He swept past her toward the front entrance, where the same festive merengue song was playing. Another new group of arrivals, climbing down from the Jeep, getting coaxed into the conga line.

IT WAS A BRIGHT, WINDY DAY WITH SCUDDING CLOUDS and the agitated rustling of palms. From the balcony, she had seen how the cove was flecked with whitecaps—they'd looked motionless, as in a painting. The man in the dive shack had warned her: "I'd wait till tomorrow." But she couldn't tomorrow. It was her last chance to have this experience. Plus she was thinking about that coral.

So the water churned and heaved, jostling Gina's body

like an impatient mob. Waves broke over her, flooding her snorkel; she came up gagging, spitting salt water, sucking air. Underwater, the landscape was turbid, murky. She tried to float close enough to the reef to see it but found she had to kick her fins fiercely just trying to stay in one place. The swells shoved her forward—her face right up to the coral, a dazzle of color—then yanked her back, stealing the picture away.

It thrust her over a shallow part of the reef, so she had to suck in her stomach to keep it from grazing the coral; then it surged her over the reef edge, into the clear, and she found herself in a deeper place with only sand below, like the floor of an empty room.

As she floated over this desolation, she stewed. Joel had said she was sabotaging herself. But why would someone do that? Did she *want* to die? It was a scary thought, and shameful—she loved her children madly. Why should she want to die, when she wanted so badly to live? Yet how easy it would be to suck a breath of water. It would fill her lungs like cold lead; she'd subside into numbness. But she wouldn't subside. She'd choke and cough it out, her body would struggle viciously toward the air.

Out of the dim blue background a form emerged, a humungous drifting thing. *Shark*, she thought, releasing her bladder, the slight genital sting, then the warmth pooling against her belly and thighs. It was bigger than she was, and seemed to move with prehistoric slowness. She brayed into her mouthpiece, her voice vibrating in her ears. It turned, coming at an angle, like a stone statue, alert, impassive. Its body, she saw, was mud-colored and speckled, as large as a cow's. Gill fins bigger than dinner plates waggled blackly. The fish—for it was definitely a fish—frowned at her, its lips thick as bicycle tires, its eyes small nacreous beads. She felt an abyss opening beneath her and around her, the closeness of something immense and indifferent. She thrashed her feet and growled into her snorkel. In a blink the fish turned and sailed off into the shadows.

When she slogged out of the surf, shivering, she could hear the reggae music. Water had gotten in her mask, and when she pulled it off her eyes stung. Up ahead, the dreadlocked man in the white suit was sitting on his chaise under an umbrella. He saw Gina and beckoned. Steffens was nowhere to be seen.

The Rastafarian appeared to be in a heated discussion with a man she hadn't seen before—he looked like Woody Allen, but older and grayer, in an unkempt white undershirt. He seemed not to notice Gina, but was gesturing and pacing back and forth beside the dreadlocked man. "Oh yeah, oh yeah," he was saying, "that's just great, Thomas, just great. *All the little flowers in the garden*, right? Isn't that your trip? What a little *fasc*ist."

Who were these people? Gina wondered. Were they guests at the resort?

The dreadlocked man just laughed, seeming to goad his associate. "Yeah, I said it," the older man exclaimed in a whiny tone. "You know who you are. Go ahead and laugh, fascist."

The Rastafarian man, ignoring him, grinned and waved to Gina. "You a look fi yuh likkle fren?"

She smiled and shrugged; she didn't understand. The Woody Allen figure had stopped ranting; he studied her coolly.

"You cyah see seh 'im no want yuh?" continued the Rastafarian. "'Im a battyman—mi nah tell lie! 'Im head mess up. You tink 'im look good? You no waan fi touch dat. A dem tings ah di wages ah sin."

He threw back his head and laughed. Gina blushed, not knowing if it was a joke or an insult. The Woody Allen figure seemed to be leering at her. Then he, too, began to laugh, a wheezy chuckle and snort that joined the rich bellowing of the other. The edges of the white umbrellas shook and snapped in the wind. Gina grabbed her gear and fled, mortified. At the dive shack she found she had only one flipper to return.

HARRY WAS PROSTRATE IN A SUN CLUB BATHROBE, reading glasses perched on his nose, peering at her with alarm over the top of his Robert Ludlum novel.

"There's something wrong with my eye," Gina said.

She'd noticed the jagged sensation while climbing the steps from the dive shack. Sure enough, she'd peeled out her contact lens and seen that it was torn. But even after she was free of the damaged lens she could still feel an irritant, like a loose eyelash—what her optometrist would have called a foreign-body sensation.

Harry came alive with concern, as if her discomfort had infected him. With his thumbs he pried her lids apart, looking for the offending particle, a grave expression on his face. He wanted to take her to the hotel infirmary.

"Leave it be," she said. "It'll go away on its own."

"Maybe we should call Cerbone," Harry said. "It couldn't hurt."

This enraged her. "Don't you think he'll be calling us soon enough? Don't you think I have bigger things to worry about?"

She had a cry in the bathroom and took a long hot shower. When she came out in her bathrobe, she found a bunch of newly purchased products arranged on the desktop: two kinds of Visine, a tube of sty ointment, an eye-wash cup with sodium solution, and a ghoulishly white eye patch in plastic wrapping.

It flooded her with anguish. "Where did you get this stuff?" she cried, but Harry was out on the balcony, hunched in a chair, his back to her.

He was so single-minded and stubborn, like a big dumb compassionate beast. When all she wanted was a little sympathy, he took it as a call to set about trying to fix the problem. Harry guessed at the recondite transactions of her inner life; he dwelled on the periphery with tenderness and caution but couldn't really fathom it, could never enter.

He showered and got dressed up for their last dinner. He smelled nice but he looked like a wreck—she could see that he knew it—so she made him undress, and called up room service, and they ate their meal together in the bed.

THE WIND CALMED, THE PALM FRONDS SETTLED, stars filled the tropical sky. Tiki torches lit up the main pool deck, where a limbo contest was under way. Russell/Raoul kept up a continuous, suggestive commentary through his megaphone; each time a contestant fell or tipped the bar, he announced, in a matter-of-fact tone: *Sorry, but you lost!* It was the catchphrase of the night, and with each repetition it drew more hilarity from the guests. Gina watched from her balcony. She could also see, on one of the smaller terraces—above the pool deck but below her—Steffens and Chloris, seated at a small table beside a potted mimosa. She watched, filing her nails, until she saw them get up from their chairs. *Good-bye*, she thought; *good-bye for the second time*. But after the pair exchanged a few words, she saw Chloris exit the balcony and Steffens sit back down.

Harry was sleeping. Gina applied her makeup and slipped out to the elevator. She got off at the second floor, thinking this was how you got to the terrace, but it turned out to be wrong. She had to backtrack twice, and was sure she would lose her chance. But when she emerged onto the terrace, the young man was still there. When he noticed her, he smiled as if he'd been expecting her.

"Is it on account of that stinging nettle?" he said.

She frowned, touched her eyelid. "Is it still red? I tore a contact. Something like that isn't funny—an injury to the eye."

"No, it isn't," he said. "That little girl I was mentioning before—well, it wasn't from a nettle. But she really did go blind. And she isn't in Luxembourg. The last I heard she was in Storm Lake, Minnesota, on her grandmother's farm."

"Awful," murmured Gina. Steffens had risen and extended his hand. When she gave him hers, he leaned over and kissed it. "You have old-fashioned manners." She glanced up at the hotel facade, as if Harry might be watching from the balcony.

The young man shrugged. "You're looking at the last scion of the DuBrays." He chuckled weakly. "Steffens is just a family name." His upper lip curled winsomely, half-mockingly.

"It's a nice name," she said.

He took a sip from his liqueur. The blue liquid looked medicinal. He asked Gina if she wanted one, and when she said she did ("But what *is* it?") he disappeared for a minute and returned with a waiter bearing two curaçaos. The drink looked fruity, but when Gina tasted hers it was bitter.

"I saw your friend on the beach," said Gina.

"Chloris?"

"No no," said Gina, "the black man in the suit. With the music."

"That's Thomas," Steffens said.

"I had just come out of the ocean. I went snorkeling by myself and saw an enormous fish. I've never been so terrified in my life! I thought it was a shark. When I made a loud noise, it swam away."

Steffens asked her to describe it. "Goliath grouper," he said. "They call it a jewfish. Hulking old girls. But harmless."

"It was really scary," said Gina.

The sounds of calypso, the murmurous laughter and applause drifted up to them from the pool deck. In the faint light of the terrace—the fluorescent bug zapper; the glowing red glass of the votive candle between them—the young man's face didn't look so much like Eddie Marinowski's. Though it was a handsome face. His eyelids had a slight fold, which gave them an Asiatic tinge, and the eyelashes were lush and black in contrast with his honey-colored locks. It was a pretty, slightly strange face. He had a long jaw and a dimpled chin.

"Was it scary being in the workshop?" he asked. "It must all seem very new to you."

Gina cringed at the thought. "A little," she conceded. "I didn't know what to expect."

Steffens grinned. "I go practically every day."

"That name tag he gave you," said Gina. "Something about the universal something?"

"My affirmation."

"I'm sorry, this is none of my business," said Gina. "But I'm not sure I understand. Why you were there, I mean. You don't seem . . ."

"Ill?"

Gina lowered her eyes. "I'm sorry."

"Don't be," Steffens said. "You see, Gina, I'm . . . I'm what they call a sex deviate."

His words were like a slap to the face. Steffens held her gaze, his lips pursed, cheeks dimpled, black eyes glistering. "Does that offend you?" he said. "Or disappoint you?"

Gina shook her head, although it did both. She gulped down the rest of her curaçao. Steffens signaled to the waiter for more.

The DuBrays, he explained, were the last of the old Catholic families in their county. His father and mother were dead. He'd been brought up in a decaying manor house called Rountree. It was himself, Chloris, and a cook named Deedee. After the cook died when Steffens was thirteen, they'd survived on pizza and Chinese delivery. Chloris suffered from crippling hypochondria, and let him out of the house only for Mass. His boyhood was suffused with the funereal reek of lilies and the acrid breath of his home tutor, a dissolute cadaver named Spales. He'd been a lonely, silent boy—a "romantic virgin," as he put it—dreaming of Shelley in a walled garden overgrown with clematis. At seventeen he fell in love with a pizza delivery boy named Carter Holkins, who initiated him in the dark arts of male love. He endured a moonless August night of torment and bliss on a moldering picnic table in the walled garden. It was, he said, as though an angel had descended—but a saving angel, or an angel of destruction? Were they one and the same? The delivery boy wanted Steffens to come away with him; he said they would go to New Orleans and rent a room. But Steffens was afraid. He let Carter Holkins go. His heart was broken. Chloris never knew a thing. Then, last Christmas, he'd started getting fevers, night sweats. . . .

Gina gazed on the boy with mortification and pity. Gwynn had a nephew who was this way. Was that what he meant? She'd seen them on the news looking skeletal and horribly exposed in their paper gowns. She looked at Steffens' hands, his lips, and the hollows of his cheekbones in the candlelight, as though he were a kind of saintly creature—magical, dangerous, suffering.

"You must feel so unlucky," she said, fumbling in her purse for a tissue. "So betrayed."

A wince passed over Steffens' face. "On the contrary," he said. "I feel grateful. I feel forgiveness."

"Toward the pizza boy?"

"Toward myself."

"But why would you need to forgive yourself?" she asked (though she had an answer in mind: *For your mistake*).

"Because feeling guilty is what got me into this mess in the first place."

"I don't understand," said Gina, shaking her head.

"I'm talking about thoughts," he said, tapping his temple. "Subconscious patterns in the mind."

"Are you saying you made yourself sick? From thinking?"

"That would be blaming myself," said Steffens.

"But you *are* sick," said Gina. "Very, very sick."

Steffens grinned implacably. "If I say, I *am* sick, what I'm really saying is, I *believe* I am sick. But why would I *believe* such a thing, unless I wanted it to be true?"

"That sounds so sad," said Gina. "So terrible and sad."

"It shouldn't be," said Steffens. "It should be joyful. No matter how long you've been doing it—the thought patterns, I mean—you can change it today, this very minute."

"And how do you do that?" said Gina coolly.

"I say I am powerful and capable. I say I love and appreciate myself. I say"—the young man coughed—"I say that I was loved as a baby."

He turned aside and coughed repeatedly into his hand. When he recovered, he said: "I say that I am part of the Universal design." He smiled wanly. She thought he might be wearing a bit of rouge.

"You need treatment—real treatment," said Gina. "At a hospital. Not some place like this. It could mean your life."

"This *is* my life, isn't it?" said Steffens.

Gina was thinking of Joel, directing a beam of hatred at the image of his bald head. He *was* the hypnotist, she thought. It was a bunch of hocus-pocus. Of course the most desperate people were the most gullible. SUN CLUB BE*. Joel and his cancerous testicles. What had he said? Resentments. You stored them up and they ate away at you, and that was the cancer. Wherever Joel had gotten that malarkey from, it wasn't *his* —she knew because she'd heard it before. It was an old idea, that cancer was shameful, a sign of bad character.

But it *had* always made her wonder. If feelings could accumulate deep in her bones, worm their way into the very code that made the marrow new.

She thought of Frances in her nightie, draped over her crutches, a woman the size of a girl, gazing at the portrait of Jesus above the sofa. And she pictured a tiny flame of anger burning underneath the nightie.

It was Jesus who reached out and touched that flame; it burned His finger, and that was what turned it into love.

She shook her head. The eyes of Joel appeared in her mind, his eyes when they'd pressed hands; now she could see the wound there, and the hope when he welcomed his children.

She shivered. The blue drinks had made her head feel muzzy.

"I haven't been such a great person," she said. "Not all the time."

"But you have a good heart," said Steffens.

Gina nodded. "I think I might have made myself sick."

"You have to tell yourself," he said, "that you don't deserve to be."

"It's not a matter of deserving. I'm going to get some news tomorrow. Some very, very bad news."

"Hey, hey now." Steffens reached out and took her hand. "The only thing that matters is what's in your mind. You can change it now. This moment."

Gina cast a leery eye on him, then let her gaze fall. "I'm so ashamed," she said. "Not at being sick. I'm ashamed at being so afraid to die. It's the clinging. The regret."

"What? No," he said gently, taking both her hands and raising her up from her seat. The head rush rained sparks across her vision. He guided her to the edge of the terrace.

"Look!" he said. "What fun." Below them, the tiki torches blazed. The Qaddafi man incanted through his bullhorn. A heavy woman in a knee-length T-shirt took a running leap and cannonballed into the pool. "What life!"

Gina wept. "That's it," urged Steffens, "it's the fear. Just don't be ashamed." She looked into his Asiatic eyes. She wanted that angel of bliss or destruction, whatever he'd called it. It was crazy, an impossible thing. He bent to put a kiss on her cheek, but she turned so that his lips brushed hers—*there*—and his hand poked her breast. Had Steffens ever been with a woman? Maybe he was a creep and a liar, prowling the resort for desperate women. Maybe she wanted him to be that, instead of a sick, confused boy. "Don't be ashamed, Gina," he repeated.

"I can't believe I've said all this to a stranger."

"Am I a stranger?" said the young man, smiling.

THE CALL CAME BEFORE NINE A.M. First Harry spoke to Dr. Cerbone, then Gina. The results, he said, were ambiguous. Which, considering the options, was the best news they could have hoped for. Better than the best. (Gwynn, it turned out, could have been onto something with her idea about an autoimmune factor. Who knew?) They would have to monitor it, of course—he'd like to see her back in his office in six months' time. The upshot, he said, was that Gina was a healthy woman. Something was a bit odd about those numbers, of course, but . . . sometimes numbers were odd. Everybody, he conceded, was different. For the time being, it was important not to worry. They should be vigilant, yes, but not worry. She should relax. Enjoy her summer. Were they going on vacation? Oh of course, they were already *on* vacation. Well then. Nice timing.

Harry and Gina had a good cry and then, borne along on the flood of release, made love for the first time in months. In her passion, Gina thought of the young man's kiss, its small, unsavory thrill, faint as on the other side of a dream. They breakfasted in their room, scarfing rolls with mango butter, and then made love again, then showered and packed.

Harry was at the front desk, checking them out, when Gina turned and noticed Chloris watching her from the corner of the lobby. The woman stubbed out her cigarette in a potted palmetto and approached with a haggard look on her face. Gina quickly assembled a pleasant expression. It wasn't hard: she felt ebullient.

"Annabelle Duggan," said the woman in a smoky southern voice, shaking Gina's hand stiffly.

"No—no, my name is Gina Maisley."

The woman smirked. "I don't know who *you* are, lady. I am Annabelle Duggan."

"I thought you were Chloris," said Gina.

"I don't know *what* you thought, or what that boy *told*

you," said Annabelle, lowering her voice. "He's a sick boy. But not in the way you think. Like I said, I don't know *what* he told you. But you listen here—"

"My friends!" cried Russell/Raoul. "Gina and Annabelle! The sexy girls!" He put a hand on each of their backs, grinning from face to face. Annabelle gave Gina a hard look.

It gave Gina pause. *He's a sick boy.* She thought the kiss could not be contagious. It couldn't, could it? The question, that tickle in her chest, brought back the feeling of the deeper, colder place, like the floor of an empty room, where a shadow drifted toward her slowly, at an angle. She imagined Dr. Cerbone calling back with a careful apology—he had told them wrong; there was something else, which had gotten overlooked—but as quickly as the fish had darted away, the dread feeling left her.

"Gina," crooned their host. "I weep, Gina. I weep for the loss of you. Why do you leave us like this. You will come soon back to us, no?"

Gina giggled and aw-shucks'd him, casting her eye toward Harry, who had finished his business and was beckoning her toward the Jeep.

WHEN THEY LANDED IN CHICAGO, Harry broached the topic of their deal. They were to call the children, to tell them what they knew.

"Tell them what?" said Gina. What would happen, she said, was that in trying to explain the good news, they would only make the kids worry. "And it's all so *compli-cated,* anyway." Harry agreed that that was true. Francie, though, she would call. She would say as much as she could. As soon as she got settled back in. The cleaning lady had come during the week: the foyer smelled like polish and the carpeting bore the fanned traces of the vacuum. The rooms of their home felt ordered and replenished.

She met her old friend on a gorgeous spring Tuesday, at the place that had their favorite onion soup. They were to lunch outside on the patio, under the cherry blossoms, with the fresh breeze off the lake. Gwynn was already seated; when she saw Gina coming, she rose and stretched out her arms. As they embraced, Gina was taken aback by the sharpness of Gwynn's shoulder blades, and in the spring sunlight the smaller woman's face, though smiling, looked a bit pinched or wan. Gina wondered if her friend could be ill.

"So how *was* it?" said Gwynn.

It was paradise, Gina admitted. The entertainment was on the tacky side. But the *view*. And the *coral* . . .

(She had never gotten her coral. It had all gone by so fast, like a whirlwind.) "I must have been under a spell," Gina said.

But was it *healing*? Gwynn wanted to know.

She *felt* better, Gina observed. "We had good reason to worry, of course. But a lot of it, it turned out, was just in my head."

The Sleeping Sickness

THE HOLIDAY HAS BEEN SPOILED. From where I am lying on a straw pallet frozen hard as a bed of rocks, I can see, through a chink in the logs, snowflakes twirling downward in the moonlight. Somewhere here—on the floor/ground, I suppose—is a mess of scattered papers: my research, which had seemed so promising. Although I believe I have lost most of my senses, including smell and feeling, a phantom trace of vinegar, or rotten wine, haunts my numbed olfactory bulb.

It seems there's been an accident. Someone, I've heard, was hit in the head by a train. Although I am not sure who (or what such a person can have done to put himself in the way of such harm), I am confident that my personal conduct has been blameless.

Yes, there was the sniveling weirdo whose *least* crime was the interruption of my snack, the conductor of dubious innocence who may or may not have illegally tried to confine me, and the wholly unmerited hostility of some or all of the other passengers. But if there was a single moment when I should have been able to see the awful direction things were taking—the escalating series of misguided assumptions and malicious suggestions that seems to have conspired to land me here—I must have somehow missed it.

Or perhaps I merely caught the wrong train.

IT WAS THE END OF MY SABBATICAL in the picturesque hill town of Munktohnville, and I was on my way home for Thanksgiving. My wife and son, who often joined me on the weekends, had gone on ahead while I stayed behind to tie up a few loose ends in my research. I was completing a monograph on the history of the Munktohnville "Barn," an unassuming stone and mortar structure that now housed a small tourist office as well as Ted's Bait 'n' Bite. Yet according to records I had unearthed in the Munktohnville Library, the Barn had served as a plague hospital during the epidemic of "sleeping sickness," that most shadowy and ruinous of contagious neurological syndromes, which is now understood to have ravaged all of the larger cities (except Portsmouth) during the early years of the American republic.

What had happened was this: Infected city dwellers who would not or could not be kept shut up safely indoors were obliged to accept free transportation via "ambulance" (a crude wooden cart over unpaved highways) to the newly established "hospital" (an outbuilding on the property of a wealthy absentee flax planter) in the outlying hamlet of Munktohnville. This hospital—the aforementioned Barn—merely warehoused these patients, there being, then as now, no treatment for their affliction. Some victims must have unwittingly consented to be taken there. Others would have been more or less plucked off the curb and hoisted into the cart like bizarrely missculpted statues, all gnarled fingers and rolled-up eyeballs.

My hypothesis had evolved from painstaking archival work, in which I had to do what any serious historian does: conjure from the skeletons of newspaper articles and pamphlets the living tissues of a secret, truer, history. It is too intricate and exhaustive to reassemble here, but to put it in layman's terms: It is well established that in certain cases, and for reasons that are unknown, a victim of the sleeping sickness will "unfreeze" from his cataleptic stupor for a period of minutes or hours, and go about his business as if nothing has happened, before just as suddenly relapsing into that corpselike state that my colleague Otto Searl has referred to as a "psychic tomb, a paradox and a dead end."

According to my evidence, certain of the captured sufferers "unfroze" in precisely this manner, long enough to escape from the ambulance cart as it approached Munktohnville, and fled into the hamlet at large. We know that town officials and vigilante groups went to great effort to recapture these so-called walking cases before they could vanish, as it were, into the uninfected citizenry. There are even accounts of seemingly healthy Munktohnville residents who, caught napping on a streetside bench, were mistakenly identified as quarantine dodgers and expatriated straight to the Barn.

Just how many "walking cases" there were is a matter of conjecture and, no doubt, future controversy. I welcome it, just as I welcome the feigned indifference of certain of my colleagues. Professional jealousies will come and go. Sound scholarship is permanent. I will mention here that I was the recipient of a coveted grant from the Krupp-Nudenheim Foundation.

Most of my work, as I have said, was accomplished in the library. I only glimpsed the inside of the Barn on those occasions when I'd stop to chat with Tonya in the tourist office, or take my son Kenneth to shop for a few provisions. Ted's Bite 'n' Bait was nothing much. Yet even amid the meager shelves of Yuban and Swiss Miss, toenail clippers and motor oil, I was struck by a secret thrill, an enchantment known only to those who are able to, as we say, "come alive to history." *This is the floor upon which they suffered*, I'd muse, absently toying with an Eagle Stik—*This is the roof under which they perished*.

Although he knew nothing of that cryptic past, I believe Kenneth shared in a mutual pleasure: he would beg to come along, knowing I'd allow him to buy some little item—a Glu-Pop or a box of rubber bands—and that as we approached the checkout counter with our plastic basket of goodies, the owner's luggish nephew Charlie would dip his paw into the jar of pickled eggs, fish out one of those spicy, glistening treats, place it in a snack boat with a grunt of satisfaction, and offer it to Kenneth—*gratis*. My son never ate them, but oh how he loved to get them.

I puttered around our rented cottage, sweeping up, shutting off the water heater, mentally tweaking the acknowledgments page of my monograph. (A certain scrupulousness overtakes a man when preparing to collect a security deposit, or to submit the fruits of his labor to peer review.) I poured out the dregs of the milk, deflated and bagged the Poke-Bote. I was struck by a pang of nostalgia for a Munktohnville that even at that moment seemed far away, as if I were already gone. Latching my briefcase, thinking of my little carrel in the library, dust motes dancing in a beam of afternoon sunlight, I was embarrassed to find my eyes moistening with tears.

On the front porch, having locked the door, I remembered Lynne's sharp cry, paddling in the Poke-Bote in the brook behind our cottage, and the nervous smile on Kenneth's face as grinning Charlie delved for the lucky egg.

Yes, it had been a deeply invigorating summer and autumn. But the holidays were upon us; my true home beckoned. Juicy bird, gravy boat, plump pillow, warm wife. Creaking down the porch steps with bags in hand, I vowed not to look back. Time marches on: I had a four o'clock train to catch.

AS IF TO AFFIRM MY CHEERFUL RESIGNATION, the train arrived on the dot. Soon I was settled into my window seat—I had both seats to myself—with my briefcase snug at my feet. With a gentle *oomph*, the train chuffed into motion; frozen bluish fields slipped effortlessly past. It was dusk, and bits of sunset flashed through chinks in the wall of pine forest, like rose jewels glittering on dark velvet.

Soon the conductor appeared and requested my ticket. He was a pale and rather short elderly man, wearing a woolen uniform coat that was too baggy and long for him. He hovered over me eagerly—he seemed animated with a nervous, almost childish energy. Purplish blood vessels webbed across his bulbous nose and loose cheeks.

"Your ticket?"

He spoke in a disarmingly effeminate tone. I handed him the ticket. He glanced at it, said "Oh," and frowned. Then he peered more closely at the ticket, and scratched at it with his longish thumbnail. "Oh," he repeated with a nervous half chuckle—then punched the ticket, tore it, and handed me the stub. I slipped the stub in my jacket pocket and the conductor moved on.

I decided it would be relaxing to glance through the items in my "keepers" file: rare newspaper clippings I had managed to acquire in the course of my research. I unlatched my briefcase and fondled the clippings: the paper was almost translucent with age, soft and fragile, like dried skin. I sniffed it: rich and pulpy, with a faint acidic tang, the ferment of tangible history. *But even more tragick are the changes in moral character which often followe the disease. . . .*

These lines of text, I thought, are from a time not so unlike our own. You can hold them in your hand: you can touch them and read them. Outside it was almost fully dark, and in the window I saw a ghostly reflection of the clipping. Perhaps the window of some private carriage trundling urgently through the night had held the reflection of those very words, when they were real.

Someone coughed in the seat behind me. As I mused over the clippings, the coughing continued softly but insistently. Eventually, I was forced to acknowledge that the distraction was interfering with my quiet pleasure, and I replaced the materials in my briefcase.

I glanced to my left: in the seat across the aisle, a sullen-faced woman slouched against her window. She was enveloped in a shapeless yellow sweatshirt. Her eyes were shut, and her mouth hung open in a kind of grimace. Her legs dangled from the seat.

The coughing behind me continued. The coughs themselves were so weak and halfhearted that I began to think the cougher wasn't trying hard enough, or was somehow perpetuating the tickle by virtue of the feathery coughs themselves. I imagined it must be some frail or aged person who couldn't (or perversely wouldn't) muster the strength to break through the mucous blockage and bring the fit to a conclusion.

I decided to go find the café car. I was in need of a snack, and perhaps by the time I returned, the coughing (or the whole person) might have managed to go away.

But when I stood up and began to move down the aisle, I saw that sitting in the seat behind me was not the pathetic valetudinarian I had pictured, but a squat, robust man with cropped black hair and a thick mustache. He gave me a challenging glance.

Approaching the café car I heard a loud voice and caught a whiff of microwaved food. A few passengers stood waiting in line for service. The man directly in front of me was tall and fit, with a crisp green polo shirt tucked into stone-colored pants, and a blow-dried sweep of chestnut hair. I noticed that that his left arm—oddly well tanned for the season—ended not in a hand but in a kind of smoothly fused nub. He tapped a loafered foot with impatience. I wondered what he would order.

"Goddamn unrecognizable," boomed the voice I'd heard from the entryway. Beyond the small group of customers, a corpulent man leaned against the service counter. The elderly conductor who'd punched my ticket stood next to him, head bowed.

"The God's honest truth, I had thought it was a woman," said the fat man. His voice was loud and gregarious, with a folksy twang. He was bald, with a large moist forehead, and wore a waistcoat with his shirtsleeves rolled up. "Although

I think it can have an effect on the—well, on the physical side." The man seemed to be lecturing the elderly conductor, who, still looking downward, nodded soberly.

"Am I right?" he implored the conductor. Resting his elbow on the counter, he propped his mug in a meaty palm. "Eh?"

"Oh, oh yes," said the elderly man. "I'm sure it could."

"I know I'm right!" cried the fat man.

The conductor made a weak gesture of agreement.

The café attendant, a grave-faced man in kitchen livery, moved deftly about his confined space, preparing items and swiftly assembling them in neatly divided cardboard trays.

"But by then," declared the fat man with a heaving sigh, "little can be done." Retrieving a nasal spray from an inner pocket of his waistcoat, he plugged one nostril and then the other, shutting his eyes and squeezing the bulb with a deep sniff and a groan.

"Yes, I suppose that's true," murmured the elderly man, gazing at the fat man's procedure.

The well-dressed man whose hand was a nub was next in line for service. I watched him as he directed the server from one item to another—he seemed to want a series of complicated mixed drinks.

"You want ginger ale?" asked the server.

"No, I told you: the club soda."

The server seemed confused—he manipulated a number of miniature bottles of liquor and filled plastic cups with ice. "Lime?" he asked.

The nub man sighed and rolled his eyes: they landed on me with a glare.

I looked away. But as soon as I did, I felt the nub man's glare intensify, as if I had caused him offense. In the corner of my eye I saw him hold aloft the interrupted arm, as if to chastise me for some perceived squeamishness or pity.

"Low sodium, please. Low sodium," he barked as the server added the final items to his tray.

He paid the server, grunted his thanks, and laid a dollar bill on the tip plate. He held the tray poised between hand and nub, eyeing me sternly as he exited the café car.

I ordered my food: a chicken sandwich with cheese, and a lemonade. When the microwave stopped with a ding, the server peeled away the limp, steaming plastic from the sandwich. He accepted my money with a self-effacing nod and returned my change. I was discouraged to see that the tip of his index finger was enclosed in a grimy-looking bandage, but grateful that he skillfully avoiding touching that fingertip to my hand.

The fat man was tearing open a package of peanuts.

"Let me tell you something," he said to the conductor. He dumped the peanuts into his palm and slapped it to his mouth. Munching, he signaled a pause—.

As I steadied myself back down the aisle I tried to stare straight ahead, so as to avoid the gaze of the nub man, in case he happened to be sitting in one of the seats I passed.

Still, I couldn't help but sneak a peek at the seats. The passengers lolled in contortions of repose, in the dark or in pools of reading light. Some were collapsed across two seats, their feet or heads protruding into the aisle. Others sat upright, eyes shut and heads cocked back, Adam's apples sticking out like choked-on bones. Others hunched awkwardly over their fold-out trays, thrusting their heads into the seat backs in front of them. I hurried through this battlefield of exhaustion, trailing fumes of chicken as I went.

I couldn't find my seat right away. The café car was at the midpoint of the train. . . . Could I have walked back in the wrong direction? In my mind I began to retrace my steps, but I had lost my orientation. It seemed I could go in either direction, but instead I stood still in the dark aisle, holding my tray. A strange wave of fatigue passed through me. I shut my eyes, and saw a scene from the cottage: my papers stacked neatly on the good oak desk whose drawers could be locked with an antique key. Had I forgotten something? A dead bolt, the propane gas? I remembered my wife's face, paralyzed in bliss or terror as her Poke-Bote slipped over a little waterfall and down into the frothing spray—and felt the train plunging blindly, evenly across the darkened landscape.

But when I opened my eyes I saw a long pale face peering up at me in the dimness. I was standing beside my own seat. There was a strange young man sitting in it.

In retrospect, as stated previously, it seems that I missed some crucial juncture. And yet, what could have been done? When, on the edge of sleep—as now, with the snowflakes falling—some shadow of a voice whispers in one's inner ear that a grave catastrophe is imminent (a fire, a robbery, a secret evacuation), does that prevent one from slipping yet further into dreams—curious but harmless dreams, to which that vague warning turns out to have been merely the cryptic prelude, the quiet clarion?

THE BLOOD RUSHED TO MY FACE AND I SWOONED, for I could not see my briefcase, which held all of the documents crucial to my work. The man wore a loose green jogging suit trimmed with white stripes, and held a small red paperback book.

Beneath the reading lamp he seemed powdery, like a translucent moth. He wore round spectacles and his eyelashes looked white. Above a high smooth forehead his hairline receded drastically, but the pale hair was longish in back, clustering in curls around his ears and neck. Lips pursed, he gazed up at me with expectation.

Standing in the aisle, laden with cooling food, I broke my speechlessness: "Are you sitting there?"

The strange man's eyes came unfocused from mine. He rose gravely from the seat and gestured for me to sit back down in my place next to the window.

"Silly of me," he murmured. "I bet you think I must have been hit in the head by a train and then forgotten to take my medication!" He burst into a peal of sniffling laughter, clutching with three fingers at his sunken chin. "That's an old joke," he said.

I hesitated, then stepped forward, muttering an apology in my confusion.

"Hot snacks!" noted the man, oozing past me (almost through me) and reseating himself immediately to my left.

I gathered together my things, concealing my aggravation, and hunched against the window. I released the folddown tray, anxious to enjoy my meal. I felt uncomfortable that he'd been left alone with my briefcase. As soon as I finished eating I would inconspicuously check over it to make sure everything was in order.

The chicken sandwich was bland but warm. I ate quickly and mechanically, regretting the man's presence, and wiped my mouth with a napkin. Outside the window a cold moon fled through the dull purplish sky, keeping pace with the train over empty black-and-white towns.

"Clume," spoke the man sitting next to me. I turned: he extended his hand. "I'm Clume."

I wiped off my fingers, ruefully accepting his moist, limp grip, and told him my name.

"You know," he said, "that was pretty unfair. That scene back there in the café car."

"Scene?"

"You know, with the—." Clume balled his fist and retracted it into the sleeve of his warm-up jacket.

My face went hot with embarrassment. "You're referring to . . ."

Clume nodded knowingly. "It was like he imposed his own self-consciousness on you. Not your fault about the— you know . . . very bad taste. Speaking of which—." He gestured at my partially eaten sandwich. I searched my memory but was almost sure I hadn't seen this person— "Clume"—in the café car with me. There had been the nub man, the conductor and his corpulent friend, and the few other passengers in line.

"I just wanted to express my sympathies," said Clume. Then, in an arch tone: "I tend to notice the little things." He winked.

Clume's skin gave off a medicinal odor, as if he'd been rubbing himself with lotions or salves. He rummaged in a cloth tote bag near his feet, producing a plastic deli container. He popped it open, revealing an oversized golden-brown baked dumpling, like a calzone or knish. It smelled delicious.

"You sure didn't buy that on this train," I remarked.

Clume looked puzzled. "I didn't?"

"Back there," I said, gesturing toward the café car. "I never saw anything like that on the menu."

"Must have been sold out," said Clume. "Here—take this little piece."

I declined, but Clume insisted. He tore off a corner of the baked dumpling and dropped it on my tray. I now had no choice. It did look awfully good. But when I bit into the morsel I had to restrain myself from gagging. It was revolting—sort of like fish, but creamy and sweet, with an eggplantish texture.

Clume grinned at me as I forced a swallow; his round lenses caught the glare from the overhead light.

Steeling myself, I grunted and nodded in thanks.

Clume licked his lips. Looking at him in profile, you could see he had too much neck fold for a man of such slim build. The image reminded me of a sitting portrait of one of those angry and anemic English preachers from the enthusiastic era. I pictured him spitting forth godly language, condemning sinners to hell.

He pinced bits of crumb off his clothing, dropped them in the plastic container, and clasped it shut.

"I was noticing," he said, "your clipping."

At first I thought he was making some reference to my personal appearance. Then, with horror, I followed his eyes down to where my shoe tips nestled against the soft leather edge of my briefcase.

There on the floor—stray, single; a honey-colored

rectangle against the black foot pad—was one of my rare clippings.

I leaned closer. For a moment I felt as though I'd lost some part of my body: a tooth, a toe, or a finger. How had it gotten outside the sealed briefcase? What was it doing cast on the floor like a disused ticket or candy wrapper? A neat little hole was punctured in my warm humming world and a black breeze of panic seeped through. I thought I must have somehow gotten myself into a nightmare. Just then I felt terribly weary. My ears rang, and the reading light oppressed my eyes like a migraine.

"It's not yours?" said Clume. I smelled the lotion and could hear his faintly whistling, almost inquisitive nasal exhalations. He smacked his lips.

"Oh my God," I sighed. My voice buzzed in my throat, and the corner of my eyelid twitched.

"Here, let me—." Clume extended his fingers to retrieve the clipping.

"No!" I said, lunging forward to snatch it up, so that my head nearly knocked into his.

I held the clipping up close. My vision seemed to blur.

WARPED MINDES AND BROKEN BODIES:
THE HEARTACHE OF OURE SEPTEMBER.

"Are you a scientist?" asked Clume.

"What?" I said. "No, I'm . . . I am a scholar."

"Really? Well, you're looking at a fellow who knows his way around a library."

"I'm very tired," I said.

It was true. I felt overwhelmed with exhaustion. The

gently jostling train lulled me. I folded the paper and stuck it in my pocket, then jabbed at the reading-light button until I was in darkness. Pulling my coat tightly around me, I slumped against the window. The glass was cold against my cheek.

"I like research *so* much," continued Clume. "In fact, I've been thinking about a project of my own. Although, that kind of work has its risks, you know."

"Please," I begged, shutting my eyes.

For a moment Clume was silent. "Are you sure?" he whispered. "You know, with the digestion . . . so soon after you've eaten? Well, I suppose it's none of my beeswax."

My eyes fluttered open. Was Clume still talking? Through the icy glass, I saw something in the distance. I must have been too weary to register what it was—though in retrospect I should have paid closer attention. Whatever it might have been, it was the last thing I saw before slipping into a doze—it glowed there in the distance, hovering on the brink of my unconsciousness, like a dim signal sending forth some strange allegation.

ONCE OR TWICE, DURING THOSE WANING AUTUMN DAYS in Munktohnville, I'd stolen a nap in my library carrel. Perhaps I'd been reading accounts of the provincial postmasters who (not understanding the cause of the sleeping sickness) gingerly, using tongs, dipped the letters in vinegar before handling them; or of all those editions of the Munktohnville *Evening Gazette* that, before the day's alarming news of the plague's progress and the mysterious "walking cases" could be read, were disinfected with vinegar and dried before many a household fire.

My current dream must have drawn me back to those days, for I found myself seated over a thick volume the librarian had retrieved for me. Oddly, the tome was still in its packaging: a translucent, slightly tacky membrane, which must have escaped the attention of the librarian. I hated to mar this delicate skin, but I was eager to look at the words inside, words that would help me under-stand the terrible and baffling sickness. My monograph depended on it. I scratched with my nails, fearing that I might be wrecking something precious, or doing some-thing illegal. The membrane/wrapping came away unevenly, uncleanly, but I resolved to get the stuff off, rolling portions of the skin into pellets and flicking them under the table. I had just released the cover and was opening the book when I sensed a presence, spied a glit-tering eye—and there was Clume, snooping in the stacks; Clume, somehow disorganizing my work while I was distracted with the unpleasant packaging. (I wondered if the librarian was complicit—could they be collaborat-ing?) I heard him clear his throat; the odor of salves was unmistakable. I leapt from my seat, heart pounding, and caught Clume ducking into a restroom, avoiding eye con-tact yet obviously aware of me, feigning nonchalance yet hurrying in arrogant, effete little steps, a volume tucked in the crook of his arm. . . .

A clot of anxiety stopped up my chest, and I woke to a finger prodding me in the ribs.

It was Clume. I heard the whistling in his nostrils.

"I like the bones in your face," he said. "They settle nicely when you snooze. It reminds me of my cousin."

My head throbbed; my throat felt dry and constricted.

"Why isn't the train moving?" I asked.

Clume peered at me. "The train?"

In the wintry darkness outside the window, a cluster of lights, like flashlights or portable lamps, bobbed in the near distance.

"Did something happen out there?" I asked.

Clume leaned over to look out the window, his pale hair grazing my face.

"Hmm," he mused. "I don't know what that was. Some kind of accident?" He leaned back and settled his hands in his lap.

"What do you mean, 'was'?" I asked. "What accident?"

Clume seemed not to hear. He'd returned his attention to the paperback book.

"Don't you think we should ask the conductor?" I persisted.

Clume glanced at me. "I suppose, perhaps ... but wouldn't it be impossible for us to do anything? I mean, that accident—if there ever was one—had nothing to do with this train."

I looked out the window, but the bobbing lights had vanished. In fact, the train was moving again—so smoothly and evenly, it felt as though we weren't moving at all, but nevertheless I discerned the murky shapes of leafless trees and pointed rooftops passing slowly from left to right.

"Anyways," said Clume, snapping shut his book. "We were talking about your research. It sounds *so* interesting."

I continued to look out the window. I remembered the stray clipping—my nap had allowed no respite from this fact—and got a nauseous, sinking feeling. Was I becoming sloppy, my materials disarranged? The Krupp-Nudenheim wasn't going to sit around forever while I tinkered with my project. The Foundation would expect clarity and closure.

"In fact," Clume went on, "I've been thinking of doing an article myself. Or a book."

"What?" I said distractedly. "Which article?"

"It would be similar to your thesis. The expropriation. Involuntary committal. There were fakers, you know. It's compelling subject matter."

I found it difficult to listen to Clume's prattle, for that painful notion was nagging at me—had I indeed forgotten something back in Munktohnville? There was a kind of cubbyhole under the windowsill in my study in which I sometimes kept notes, but I remembered clearing it out, even cleaning it. The damp paper towel had picked up some insect husks and bits of mummified cocoon. Everything had seemed so secure, so wrapped up when I'd left: the book deal, the gravy boat, the four o'clock train. . . .

I had merely done what I'd planned to do all along: board the train and go home.

I MUST HAVE FALLEN ASLEEP AGAIN, because I felt a prodding in my ribs, and woke with a start, expecting it was Clume. But Clume was gone. The train was dark, except for the small bright lamp glowing over Clume's vacant seat. My mouth tasted rotten. The elderly conductor was standing in the aisle with a regretful expression.

"Um, ticket, please," he managed. He gazed down at me with his large, watery eyes.

"You already took my ticket," I said. "Much earlier. When I got on the train."

"Oh, gosh," said the conductor. He fidgeted nervously. "Yes, well, I know . . . but, you see, there have been some changes. May I see your ticket stub? The small stub?"

With a sigh, I fished the stub from my jacket pocket. The elderly man examined the stub, turning it over in his oddly tough-looking fingers, as if it were some interesting artifact. "Okay," he murmured. "Um, all right, well . . ."

"Is something wrong with this train?" I asked.

The conductor looked shocked. "Oh my!" He trembled. "Of course not. It's only the train has been delayed. So, you know, in the meantime, because of the delay, we won't be able to—"

"What delay?" I interrupted, unable to keep from raising my voice. "Does this have to do with an accident? There was a man, sitting in the seat next to me, I don't know whether you'd taken his ticket, but he must have . . . he boarded late, or . . ." I lost my train of thought.

The conductor patiently, almost pityingly, waited for my rambling speech to conclude. Then he said—now in a kind of rapid cheerful monotone, as if reciting some official statement—"Fortunately, because of your class of ticket, we are happy to provide you with a special accommodation for the length of tonight's trip."

"Accommodation?" I said.

"A Q compartment," he explained. "That's, well, a Quality Compartment."

"Compartment?"

"In, um, the sleeping car. Because of, you know, the delay."

"How long could the delay possibly be?" I demanded. "I did not purchase a ticket for an overnight trip."

"Oh, oh dear," stammered the elderly man. "We like to please all of our customers. I, um . . ." He bent down close to my face. There was a babyish smell on his breath, like apple juice or custard. "I think you'll find the accommodation quite pleasant."

"I am hardly concerned with that. As far as I know, this is not a sleeper train. What I wish to know, immediately, is when this train is expected to arrive."

"Oh, well," he continued, "a determination will be made, you know, in the morning. Or perhaps even sooner, sometime tonight. All passengers in the 'Q' receive a complimentary muffin, as well as a Preferred Traveler's Kit."

"Couldn't I be let off at one of the intermediary stops? Surely there's another train on this route."

The elderly man licked his lips and smiled at me sadly. "It's the express," he said. "I'm afraid there's only the one stop. At the end. And the train, you know, just doesn't go any faster."

THE "Q COMPARTMENT" WAS FURNISHED with a single fold-down berth. There was a brushed-steel washbasin, over which a square of mirror was affixed. The window's cream-colored vinyl curtains were drawn.

"It's a shared lavatory, I'm afraid," the conductor explained, hoisting my small suitcase with difficulty into the compartment. "But you'll find, um, the Preferred

Traveler's Kit, with an exfoliating cake and, you know, some other personal items."

After indicating the call button (a large blue knob) and urging me to summon him personally should I need anything, the conductor left me alone.

I stood there, eyes closed, feeling the jostling of the train. The whole business had left me physically and emotionally spent. I lowered myself onto the narrow berth and gazed grimly at the ceiling.

Someone knocked. I scrambled up and thought: *my briefcase!* and spun around, as if unable to locate it—but there it was, on the floor beneath the washstand. I seized the briefcase and popped it open, while the knocking at the door continued, and hastily rifled through my research. The mass of papers seemed perplexing and badly disordered. Bits of language from photocopied newsprint and my own vague scribblings leapt out at me: *Public papers were locked up in closed houses when the clerks left. . . . He promised to expose the doctor's reply to sun and air for some hours before handling it . . . the doctor seemed sure the disease could not be communicated in a letter.* The sentences confused me, and I panicked at my failure to recognize them. Which doctor was being referred to? A doctor from the Barn? Or was the doctor writing to a Barn administrator about some patient he had sent there? And what was contained in the papers? Information about the walking cases? I thought of the present-day Barn, with its brochures touting the caverns and the inner tubing, its shelves of Bisquick and fingernail polish; and poor Charlie, twiddling his fingers in the vinegary egg jar. . . .

"Knock-knock!" chirped a muffled voice, followed by

more raps on the door. I reached across the compartment, fumbled at the latch and flung the door open.

It was Clume. Who else? Alas, Clume had returned—and he held in his hand a single yellow cupcake in a fluted wrapper.

"I thought you might be hungry for a snack," he whispered conspiratorially. "The café car closed some time ago, and I thought . . ."

"No," I said. "I am not in the least bit hungry."

"Oh?" Clume replied. "Well, in my experience, I've found that nothing works up an appetite like some hearty research. Have you made any progress? I've been mulling over some ideas and I thought we could maybe compare notes. For instance—oh, I see you've got a Q!"

"Yes, that's right," I said. "Look, Mr. Clume. I appreciate your gesture, but I really, really must insist that—"

"Cut the shit," said Clume. He leaned in and whispered in my ear. His hair smelled like sebum. "I need to talk to you. Forget about the snack. This is serious. You'd better let me in and shut the door."

He glared at me through his spectacles. I noticed that his pupils were of slightly differing sizes.

"Okay," I relented, ushering him into the compartment and latching the door behind us.

Clume sat gingerly on the cot and sniffled. He peeled back the curtain and looked outside. I remained standing.

Clume took a deep breath. "I admit that I was wrong before." He nodded to himself. "I was mistaken."

"Mistaken about what?"

"When I told you that nothing was wrong with this train."

I tried to recall his earlier aggravating comments, but it all seemed so long ago. . . . Had I ever asked Clume if something was wrong with the train? Hadn't it been the conductor I'd asked?

"So what is it?" I said.

Clume sighed, as if he were trying to explain some simple but vital concept to a dull child. "Do you know what the 'Q compartment' really is?"

A flutter of fear rose in my chest. "Of course I know what it is. Naturally, it's this. If you're asking me why this train has been delayed to such a ludicrous extent that I've been obliged to—"

"That's not what I'm asking you," said Clume gravely. "I'm asking if you know what the 'Q compartment' is."

I stood glaring at him. His mouth twitched at the corners, as if he were concealing a smirk.

He said, "It's for *Quarantine.*"

"What's for quarantine?"

"The Q compartment," said Clume. "That's what I meant when I said I was mistaken when I said nothing was wrong with the train."

He crossed his legs, rustling the synthetic fabric of his jogging pants.

"Utter nonsense," I said.

Clume threw his hands up. "Okay," he said. "I'm just here to tell you some information. Apparently a rumor's been circulating. People on the train have been talking."

"What people?"

"I don't know," said Clume. "People."

He examined the tips of his fingers. I repressed a

powerful urge to strangle his fleshy neck. Then, collecting myself, I decided to humor him.

"Why," I asked, "would I be in quarantine? I am not ill. Are you in quarantine? Are you ill?"

"Ha!" he snorted.

"What's funny?"

"Let me ask *you* a question," he said. "Why are you still on this train? Didn't you have somewhere to be?"

I felt my head fill up with blood. I remembered the gravy boat. My family, and the plump pillow.

"The train," I said, "was delayed."

"By what?"

"By, I presume, an accident."

"I already told you," said Clume, "that accident has nothing to do with this train."

"Which accident?"

"The accident you just referred to several times." He squeezed and poked at the moist-looking cupcake.

"Look, Mr. Clume," I said. "If I'm in quarantine, then why am I free to roam this train as I please?"

"Are you?"

"How could I not be?" I laughed.

"Fine," said Clume. "Roam the train."

He tore off a bit of the cupcake and popped it in his mouth. He sat there chewing and looking at me.

"Get out," I said.

Clume raised his eyebrows. "Me?"

"You're like a bad dream," I said. "An infection. You're here and nowhere. I want you out."

"Who's nowhere?" said Clume.

"Out!"

He hopped up and oozed past me as I stood there shaking with frustration. I would have shoved him out the door had I not been so loath to touch his cringing form.

When he was gone I leaned against the door with my head in my hands, furious that I was now forced to contemplate the variety of absurd propositions uttered by the demented Clume. If only I could forget it all, go to sleep, and wake up to find that the train had gotten me home. As for Munktohnville and whatever holes still remained in the fragile texture of my research, whatever loose ends still lay about from the flurry of productivity in the final weeks of my sabbatical—whether or not I would have to go back and compile additional evidence, or reconsider certain of my earlier hypotheses—it would all have to wait until after the holiday, until after I'd had some rest.

While I stood there grappling with these thoughts, I began to hear muffled noises. I put my ear to the wall. At first I heard nothing. Then the noises resumed: a monotonous, repetitive moaning, then almost a lamentation or wailing. It would rise and subside, rise and subside. . . . Suddenly the voice burst out in a fit of what sounded like uncontrollable cursing. Then silence. The process repeated itself: moaning, wailing, fit of cursing, silence. I realized from the tone of the voice that it was the fat waistcoated man from the café car, whom I'd seen conversing with the elderly conductor. It was unmistakable. As I listened, I heard another voice, vibrous and murmuring, which belonged to the conductor himself. It was as if he were trying to calm or assuage the larger man, who was obviously in some type of distress.

I don't know what made me press the call button. It

was loosely attached, and I wondered if it was merely decorative. I didn't think it could really summon anyone. At first nothing happened. But then the noises fell silent. I waited. There was a vague shuffling—something bumped against the wall—and the sound of a latch. After a few seconds, there came a knock at my door. I hesitated to open it, suddenly abashed, as if I had intruded or interrupted something.

The conductor stood facing me. His thinnish gray hair was disheveled, his large eyes mournful and red. He grinned up at me weakly: "Is there, um, something we can do?"

"I'm sorry," I said sheepishly. "I hit the button by accident. But now, since you're here, I am wondering . . . because of the unusual delay . . ." I fumbled for a question, but I was confused. I tried to remember what Clume had said. "Could you tell me, is this a 'normal' sleeping compartment?" I had framed my question poorly.

"Oh, oh yes," he said, "it's the normal kind. It's quite normal. But, you know, with the upgrade."

"The 'Quality'?"

He seemed confused. "Yes, it has full quality."

"But it's not . . . *special* in any way."

The conductor fidgeted with his hands nervously in front of his uniform coat. "Oh, well, we consider all of our passengers special guests."

Whether or not it had something to do with the conductor's speech or mannerisms—he appeared to be alone in the passageway—I felt a strong impression that somehow Clume, wherever he might have been, was overhearing our conversation.

"Let me ask you this," I said. "I don't have to stay in this compartment for the duration of the night, do I? Naturally, the rest of the train is open to the passengers?"

"The rest of the train? Well, I suppose it is. Did you, um, need something? A pillow?"

I thought of the warm pillow I'd anticipated earlier in the day—a crisp, sunny morning that seemed so long ago. "No," I said. "But I might want to stretch my legs."

"Oh," said the conductor. "Stretch your legs—hmm."

After some pleasantries and confused assurances, the conductor left me alone.

I listened to hear whether he would reenter the compartment adjacent to mine. Beneath me and around me the train hummed, hurtling down its track.

The walls were completely silent.

PERHAPS IT WAS CLUME'S INANE SUGGESTIONS, or the elderly conductor's failure to address my concerns, or the fact that I may not have been able to clarify those concerns to myself. But at some point I decided to venture out.

Standing in the dimly lit passageway, I found no indication of the direction in which the regular section of the train might lie. I went left. When I came to the end of the car I pushed the rectangular button that opened the doors to the interstice between cars and continued through. This car was the same as the last—a narrow, carpeted passageway, also dimly lit, with three or four doors (presumably to sleeping compartments such as mine) on either side.

I passed through two or three more sleeping cars just like the previous ones—and while I was relieved to find that I was indeed perfectly free to "roam" the train as I pleased, yet I wondered whether all the other passengers with whom I'd been seated earlier were in fact occupying these compartments. I lingered outside the doors, listening for sounds of human activity—snoring, or conversation, or someone getting up to use the lavatory—but heard nothing. Perhaps this was simply on account of the very late hour.

When I passed through into the next car, I was struck with a sinking feeling. There, seated on a stool, was the elderly conductor.

As I came closer I saw that he appeared to be sleeping. Yet his body was slumped at an angle, as if he was very gradually falling off the stool. Carefully, I approached him. The conductor's cap sat askew on his head, his eyes were shut, and his large hands rested in his lap, where the woolen coat was bunched up. He was wheezing softly.

All of this made a grim impression. Had he been placed here as a kind of sentry? (And if so, by whom?)

I reached out and prodded him lightly on the shoulder. He didn't react. His face was slack, expressionless. Mottled. Somewhat corpselike. Almost peaceful.

Then his right eye opened, but only a bit, revealing part of the nacreous eye. Gradually it closed again.

What was I to make of this? I couldn't ascertain whether he'd seen me; perhaps it was merely some sleep tic, a myoclonic jerk in the midst of a dream.

I began to maneuver around the stool. Since the conductor was blocking the middle of the passage, I had to suck in my stomach in order to slip through the narrow space.

I'd nearly gotten past him when I felt a hand pawing

at my chest, and cried out as if in pain. The conductor was pulling weakly at my shirt.

"Nooo," he whined, grasping at my arms.

"Please, stop that!" I shouted in a whisper. "I am going past."

I was disgusted to find myself caught up in a physical struggle with the elderly man, as if he were trying to pin me against the wall or tickle me. His efforts continued, and I smelled the babyish custard smell as his breathing became labored.

"Um, the café car's at the other end," he protested. "Plus, it's closed now, or . . . or it may be open for night snacks . . ."

"I don't want any snack! Please, stop this behavior," I insisted.

"Oh dear, um, if you need something, you can press the call button," he said as he continued to grapple at me. "In your Preferred Traveler's Kit, you'll find—"

"Get. Off!" I grunted, shoving him away. I hurried to the end of the car, looking back over my shoulder.

"Oh, oh dear," he whimpered. "It's impossible . . . "

Moving quickly, since I couldn't see whether he was attempting to pursue me, I slapped my hand on the button, and the doors to the next car flew open with a shudder. The interstice rocked abruptly, and I gripped the doorway for balance. The doors remained open as I passed through into the next car, and glancing back I saw the hunched silhouette of the conductor resting against the wall at the far end of the passageway.

Finally, the doors shut behind me. I lurched down the length of the car, smacked the button for the doors, rushed through into the next car, and the next one, and the one after that. Every car I passed through was exactly the same as the one before: narrow passageway, dull carpeting, dim lights, closed doors on either side. On and on I hurried, ever more frantic, increasing my pace and determination, though I had no idea where I was going or what I hoped to reach. How many sleeping cars can there have been? And *where were all the passengers*? What sort of accommodation had been made for all those people I'd glimpsed in their seats, contorted and dozing in the pools of reading light, collapsed or rigid or hunched over their trays? Should I have banged with my fists on the doors to those compartments, shouting aloud that there had been an accident, an emergency, that everyone should wake up and come out of their rooms? But I did none of that, as if it was already far too late for a warning. And would I have been able to say what it was that I was warning them about?

It seems unlikely that a train should have been so long. Perhaps some illusion of perpetuity was created through the cunning use of a trick. But at last I came to the end of the very last car.

There was no door here, only a small window, partially frosted over. I went up close and peered through it.

All I saw were the wooden ties, ribboning out behind the train for a little ways before disappearing in the darkness and snow.

ADMISSION: I HAD BEEN FOOLED. Yes, I had roamed "freely," as it were, and had even gotten well beyond the point that the conductor had not wished for me to pass. Yet I now saw that all of this told me nothing with regard to the "Q compartment" and my ostensible access to the train as a whole. For couldn't it have been possible that the entire expanse of cars I'd just traversed had *all*, in fact, been "Q"? And that I alone had been set loose to wander in this godforsaken zone? That, indeed, the conductor had planted himself at his stool post as a kind of decoy (hence the feigned struggles), and the section of the train forbidden to me (the section where the other passengers had been relocated?) had been in the *opposite* direction—that is, toward the front rather than the rear of the train?

But these ruminations were useless. In a flash of horror, I realized that Clume's insinuations had contaminated my thinking, disabled my vigilance in precisely the manner he'd wished.

It was the briefcase.

I'd left it unattended—*again*. Good God. The Krupp-Nudenheim . . . the history, all those who had suffered . . . my months and months of effort . . .

Fine, his voice echoed in my memory, like a curse. *Roam the train.*

I spun around and set off at a full tilt. As I ran anguished through the empty cars I imagined the throttling I'd give the conductor, elderly or no, when I came upon him, conscious or not, perched on his stool. But no— there would be no time for a throttling, such measures would play further into Clume's hand. I had to get back to my compartment, to the briefcase.

I ran faster, and at one point stumbled over some soft object on the floor, though I had no time to stop and look. I kept expecting to find the conductor, and his absence only increased my panic and doubt (could I be going in the wrong direction *again?*) until at last I emerged through a set of doors and found not the conductor, but Clume.

I was back at my own compartment.

Clume leaned casually against my door.

He was nothing but a cipher, a rag doll, a chattering toy. It occurred to me that almost all of my troubles had been caused by the mistake of my having acknowledged him as an entity. I shoved him aside (he giggled; I smelled wine) and entered the compartment.

The briefcase was there—lying beneath the washbasin where I'd left it. As I knelt down to open it and check the safety of my materials, Clume spoke from behind me.

"I wouldn't do that if I were you."

He had come into the room.

"Of course," he said, "I'm not you. Ha!" (The sniffling laughter, the fondling of the sunken chin.) "My cousin used to say 'I am I and you are you' whenever we had a disagreement. She was such a card. Anyway," he continued as I fumbled at the latch, "like I said, that type of research frequently has its hazards: there's the fatigue, plus there's always the chance that the subject matter has already been 'handled,' so to speak, by others—"

"Shut up!" I commanded.

"And those libraries—*oof.* All that dust. One has to consider one's health."

Grabbing the briefcase by its handle, I stood up. The blood rushed from my head. My vision went gray with a snow of spots.

"I am getting off this train," I said.

"How?"

"I don't care. I'll notify the engineer of an emergency. I'll feign an illness. I'll jump out of a damned window if I have to."

Clume stepped closer. He'd been sipping something loathsome; the fetid wine smell was nauseating. "Well," he said, "I'll tell you a piece of information. I happen to know that shortly there is going to be a stop. An 'unofficial' stop. The only one before the terminus—which, as you might fathom, is still quite a ways off."

"Hmm, that's so interesting," I said. "Does it have to do with the 'quarantine'?"

Clume pretended offense at my condescending tone.

"Actually," he said, "it has to do with maintenance. No passengers allowed on or off. I think it's a place called Munktinburg, or Martonburg, or . . . "

The train began to slow. I could feel it—wheels and gears grinding and groaning deep in the floor.

As if sensing the same thing, Clume grinned.

"Get out of my way!" I cried. Briefcase in hand (forget the rest of my belongings) I pushed past Clume into the passageway. This time I knew what I wanted: I turned right, toward the front. The train shuddered and I lost my balance as I came to the first set of doors. Clume was close behind. As I hit the button, bells started ringing.

"We never finished discussing our research!" he called out.

The doors opened only a crack, but (holding the briefcase between my knees) I forced them several inches apart and squeezed through into the interstice.

"You know," Clume continued (he too was trying to squeeze through the doors), "I have to say that I think

I disagree—respectfully, of course—with some of your premises."

A loud siren began to whoop and wail over the noise of the bells and the sound of the train's brakes grinding.

"For instance, some of those 'walking cases.' Couldn't it have been that they only *thought* they were sick? . . ."

Thank God—here was an exit. The doors were shut, but there was a red lever marked EMERGENCY USE.

"Couldn't it be," he said, "that they got in the ambulance but somewhere along the way made a good-faith judgment that they were fine after all?"

I yanked on the lever and nothing happened. I stomped on it. Clume had nearly squeezed through the doors into the interstice and was reaching out his arm as if to grab me.

"It's a personal judgment call, wouldn't you say? *Be true to thine own self,* and so forth?"

"Aghh!" I grunted, heaving with all my strength on the emergency door's handles. The train had stopped, and the sirens had reached a deafening pitch, over which Clume shouted:

"Of course, it's easy to become confused . . ."

The doors sprang open—they were mounted on a sliding track—and a blast of cold wind rushed in. Getting on my knees, I began to lower myself off the side of the train.

"Deficiencies in moral character are sometimes known to result . . ."

My feet, kicking in space, at last found purchase on the ground, and I let myself down. A little squeal of pain escaped from my throat—I'd set my briefcase down while I was struggling with the doors; but the doors were still open, so I lunged up, reached inside and snatched it out. At the same time, Clume wedged his elbow in the doors, as though he were trying to follow me out of the train. I flung the briefcase behind me onto a bank of snow, and turned my attention to Clume's arm, trying to stuff it back inside.

"Ow!" he yelped, retracting the arm partway. I grabbed the exterior handles and tried to force the doors shut. But they kept jouncing off Clume's hand. And although I understood that rationally it didn't make sense for me to be slamming the doors over and over on Clume's hand, smashing it repeatedly, that was what seemed to be happening. In a kind of half dream I flung the doors together, so that they rebounded off the hand and came together once more, crushing the hand to a bloody pulp. ("Don't worry," he seemed to remark, quite matter-of-factly, in the midst of this punishment—"we've both handled the clipping.") My face was bitten by the freezing wind and my shoes scrabbled on the icy ground as I threw my weight into the slamming of the doors.

"*Uncanny behavior,*" muttered Clume, who finally pulled his pulverized hand back inside the train.

I staggered back and collapsed onto the snowbank. Out of breath and delirious, I watched as the train's machinery rocked slowly into gear, and it began to roll away.

And as I watched the cars glide past, I thought I saw people looking out at me from softly lighted windows: the elderly conductor and the grieving fat man in one window; in another, the sullen-faced woman with the yellow sweatshirt, and the grave-mannered café car attendant; in yet another, the carefully coifed head of the man with a nub for a hand.

There were many other faces in many other windows, all peering out at me—regretful, reproving, relieved—as they drifted past into the night. The one face I didn't see, thank heaven, was Clume's.

I AM NO LONGER CONVINCED THAT IT IS, IN FACT, the holiday season. Holiday is a time of cheerful and restful celebration with one's family—and this is decidedly not that. There is no turkey here, and no pillow. There is no gravy here, unless by gravy you mean howling wind. It has been a long, long night.

Where is here? I am not, as yet, in a position to investigate that. Shortly after the train left, I found that my motor coordination was poor. Bells rang in my ears unremittingly. There were certain ocular difficulties. . . . It would require too much energy to describe them. Or I could put it this way: I felt as though I'd been hit in the head by a train, so to speak, and forgotten to take my medicine. (Ha!—is that an old saying?)

I staggered over a hill and through a wood, not to grandmother's house, but to this structure in which I am currently—temporarily!—housed. I have no reason not to expect a prompt rescue and deliverance. Perhaps in the morning another train will pass through.

It now occurs to me that, in some sense (and despite the mess of papers scattered on the ground beside me), I believe I may have achieved the means to advance my research even further. True, I no longer have access to a library, and I may have to forgo, for some time, the beneficence of a Krupp-Nudenheim. But I have attained a power of mind that comes only when most of the senses have gone. I never expected the project to be easy. I like to think that today's scholar, plunging boldly into our collective dream of history, revivifying the dormant past, is the stolid pioneer of a new era: an era of reembodied knowledge.

There . . . I believe I have felt a sensation in my toe. Perhaps my limbs, after a brief winter's nap, are starting to reawaken to new life. Soon, indeed, the quickening will spread through me, as swiftly and surely as a fever, all the way up to my brain! Then—if I can only muster the verve to grab a pen—I will retrace my steps, stare down the evidence with a colder eye, and think my way to a new, uncharted place.

Here to Watch Over Me

THEIR SON ERIC'S FACE was not going to appear on a milk carton. He was too old for a missing child, nearly thirty, living an independent life, such as it was, up at the cabin. But for three straight Sundays, Harriet's calls to her son had gone to voice mail. The calls were not returned. Nor the e-mails.

On the third Sunday, Pat Guest woke up on the couch in the afternoon, the Ravens game over, a rerun of *Unsolved Mysteries* blaring, Harriet's face looming over him. The face implied a reproach. Pat was struck with a familiar sense of lapse, of unfocused guilt, as though he must have forgotten to do something, such as bring up the boxes of Christmas tree ornaments, ceramic figurines for the crèche, and the pentagonal wire frame he'd rigged up years ago, which he pulleyed up an elm tree and electrified with a string of extension cords, so that when plugged in—*voilà*, a blue star shone in the night above the Guest family home.

"I thought you said you would go today."

"Huh?" said groggy Pat. "Go where?"

She frowned down at him: "Go *where*?"

Pat scrunched his nose and stuck out his tongue. He instantly regretted it. Her mouth was quivering. "Something is very wrong," she said. Pat marveled at how suddenly she appeared to have aged. Pale downy hair, catching the after-noon light, outlined her jowl. Her face was still beautiful, despite the pouches, the lines of dissatisfaction engraved there; he felt a pang of tenderness knowing how bitterly she would feel the erosion of her beauty.

"Come on, sweetie," he said. "Bad news travels fast."

But he saw she meant business. Pat really didn't remember saying he would go to Hidden Valley today. But it was possible. And if he was just now getting the message, he knew, she likely had been trying to convey it to him for some time. For whatever reason, he just hadn't been able to hear her.

Three years before, Eric had given up his apartment in the city, where after college he had lived with roommates. When the roommates moved out, as Harriet feared they would, Eric had complained obsessively about noise from an upstairs neighbor. The woman, he said, had a dead leg—he'd said *dead leg* or *peg leg*—fitted at the foot with a Dutch clog. Eric had never seen her in person, but he pic-tured her hobbling back and forth across her hardwood floor as though two chores, one at each end of her apart-ment, alternately and perpetually consumed her attention.

Because of this Eric couldn't sleep. The cripple clomped into his dreams. It became, he said, the drumbeat of pur-gatory. He'd looked into solutions—such as adding a layer of sheetrock or something called "green glue"—but never pursued them. He alluded to problems—with his hands, with his brain. They bent their ears to this esoteric litany of complaint because it was, after all, the only information they received about their son and his life.

As his status grew more fragile (or refined), Eric spent

more and more time at the ski cabin up at Hidden Valley, in the Allegheny mountains. In the past several years, with Eric in the city and Annie out in Oregon, the cabin had been seldom used—until Eric started using it. After a while they realized he was living up there.

"He's given up," Pat had said.

"He just needs time," said Harriet. He probably took long walks in the woods, which cleared his head and helped him sleep. According to Harriet, he'd been exploring the area, working on a book.

What was there for a young man to explore, Pat asked, in a family ski resort? And did Harriet know what this book was about? (Eric said to tell his father that there was, believe it or not, "a world" beyond the resort. And no, Harriet relayed, no one knew what the book was about.)

To Pat, it sounded like his son had gone to Hidden Valley to retire. Nonetheless, Pat continued to pay the cabin's utilities, and mailed off a small check every month. He couldn't help thinking of it as a disability check. Sometimes Pat worried that his own foibles had contributed to the boy's morbid inwardness. Harriet's sister chalked it up to the difficult birth. Harriet herself, after the Cesarean, feared she wouldn't be able to love the baby enough, that the attachment wouldn't form the way it was supposed to. Pat had been scared out of his wits by the prospect of fatherhood, until little Eric was born—after that, he was scared only by the thought that some harm would come to the child, something against which he would fail to protect him.

The time had flown. This year Eric hadn't come home at Thanksgiving.

"Well, you know what," said Harriet. "You'd just better not go. Not by yourself."

How quick she was to play the brain card these days. After he'd smashed up the Chrysler in the spring, she'd insisted he go to the neurologist; dementia ran in his family. Pat waved it off. Harriet said he had a responsibility: not just to think what he wanted to think but to let an objective person, an outsider, see for himself. See what? said Pat; they couldn't prove anything until they autopsied your brain, and he wasn't yet ready for that. Their compromise was a visit to the family doctor Lorenzo, who couldn't say one way or the other, and focused his attentions on the heart, which he confirmed was as strong as that of an ox.

"I think I will have to go," Harriet said. "I'll cancel my Monday clients."

"Oh, shush," Pat snapped. "If you want me to go up to the cabin, I'll go up there right now."

"I've changed my mind," said Harriet. "It's getting dark. I don't want you on the roads."

That sealed it. He didn't even pack a bag. Pulling the car out of the driveway, he averted his gaze from the front door, where he knew she would be standing, glaring at him, mouthing words.

IT WAS SUNDAY. HE DIDN'T HAVE TO TEACH until Tuesday afternoon. Since retirement, Guest had taught adjunct, a couple of lower-level materials science courses. His students were incapable but he liked them. Some were sullen—not insolently so, just blankly impervious. It must have been this sullen minority whose poor evaluations had begun to turn up in the batch. They complained Professor Guest couldn't hear their questions and was easily distracted, going off on tangents and relating anecdotes whose connections to the lesson they were unable to grasp. These hurt his feelings, but he tried to disregard them. (He told Harriet that if he was losing his hearing, all the more reason to conserve it by using it selectively.)

He would have to distribute those evaluation forms on Tuesday. And finish preparing the final, which was easy—he could do it at the cabin, after he'd talked to Eric about why, even if you were depressed, or just didn't feel like it, you had to answer phone calls from your mother.

He tweezed the phone from his pocket: if he called Eric now and got him, he could turn around and avoid the whole trip. But he thought of his wife's face hovering over him, and dropped the phone in a cup holder. She wanted him to go in person.

AS HE DROVE NORTH THE HIGHWAY DRIED and the digital thermometer fell. At Breezewood, "City of Motels," he got on the Pennsylvania Turnpike and was seized by a beautiful idea: warm chipped beef on toast. It was served, he remembered, at a buffet-style family restaurant, the Something Smorgasbord, on the way to the cabin. A treat, a surprise compensation: the secret purpose to the trip. He pictured himself reaching with the tongs into the heat lamp's warmth, fetching two slices of thick toasted bread, then ladling out that salty, creamy porridge of meat bits. He might flirt a little with the waitress when she came to refill his iced tea. He liked to chat up a friendly young woman who didn't care about his weight or his health, who wouldn't mind, in theory, if he sneaked a cigarette or even had a glass of beer, though he'd given up drinking when the children were small. He thought he remembered live entertainment: an elderly man in a powder blue suit playing "The Carioca" on an electric organ. Desserts were arranged on a separate table called the Groaning Board. He would be there in an hour.

A silhouette of mountain loomed over the turnpike; Guest glided into the fluorescent tunnel. Then a second mountain, a second tunnel. Sparse snowflakes, set aflame in the headlights, shot toward him and vanished. Heat from the vents was lulling him so he cracked the window. A blast of cold air refreshed him; he could see stars above the dark hills: he craved a cigarette.

Guest switched on the radio and scanned the dial. He loved how on clear nights out here you could pick up stations far away. The scanner hit one, and an old country voice spoke out of the night, clear against the faint crackle—Hank Williams bantering with what's his name. The Grand Ole Opry. There came to Guest, as if riding on those airwaves, the smells of a living room rug and a July thunderstorm, rain on the roof and the sounds of his momma moving around in the kitchen.

He almost missed the exit when it came. He drove through the town of Hemperling and got on the state road. After a while he saw the lighted sign of the restaurant up ahead on the left. That was it: *The Oakhurst Smorgasbord*. The parking lot was almost empty—bad sign. Despite this, he got out of the car, despair filling his stomach, the idea of warm chipped beef slipping away. The doors were locked. Guest put his hands to the glass and peered inside. He could see past the darkened gift shop, back to where the buffet islands stood lampless and cold. The mocking melody of "The Carioca" drifted back to him like tropical music issuing from the bottom of a well. He could see, all the way in the back, a marlin suspended in a sea green alcove. Recessed lighting shone on the fish's striped flank, blue and silver, its spiked bill, serrated sail. *I'll be damn.* He hadn't remembered the marlin at this restaurant. He thought of his daddy's boat, the *Annabelle;* his daddy used to fish for big game like that. His big brother, who'd stayed down south, still did.

How the marlin hovered there, massive, curvilinear, in the dim dining room! He thought of Eric—saw him— floating over a blue abyss. How vivid it suddenly was.

It was a decade or more since they'd taken the scuba-diving trip to the Florida Keys. Just father and son, as odd a couple as could be. In the hotel Eric complained of tiny specks of blood on his bedsheet; he didn't rise for breakfast and at dinner he consumed his fish in sullen silence. Oh, it had made Pat mad. But when father and son geared up in their strange costumes of rubber and aluminum and tumbled over the gunwale of the churning boat, it was a plunge into a different medium, bracing and humbling. The equipment that had felt so clownishly cumbersome on deck became almost weightless. With ponderous ease they let themselves down the anchor line, listening to their long breaths, exhaling bouquets of silver bubbles that glooped and fizzed, ascending lightward.

There was a coral archway; it stood on the edge of

an underwater cliff. Pat, who'd been following behind, watched his son, who was wound up so tight, who carried so much anger or fear all the time, swimming now strong-limbed and graceful, disburdened of gravity, obviously in awe. When Eric had passed through the archway, he turned, his equilibrium perfect, his green fins barely stirring, suspended above the perspectiveless deep, and looked back at his father, speechless.

HE CONTINUED UP THE ROAD PAST THE WREN CREST MOTEL, recognizing the journey's landmarks, shadowy now, sketched out in the moonlight: a stone cottage with peculiar asymmetrical windows; a Boy Scout camp, its low log bunkers hidden in darkness. The road dipped into a hollow, swooped past the Church of the Brethren, and became a tree-lined corridor, which in summer was a dappled tunnel of sunlight and shade, the prettiest part of the trip; now in winter it was spooky, the moon sailing through bare tangled branches; and coming suddenly into view beyond the woods on the left were the white slopes of Hidden Valley, lit up for night skiing.

Guest heard a string melody, a horn intro . . . He turned up the radio: it wasn't the Beach Boys, wasn't the Four Seasons . . .

Da-da-da, to eter-nity . . .

The vocal harmonies gave him a chill, a throb that went straight through his loins to the depths of his very soul. The song *was* his youth, it was May-Lou McGonigal at junior prom—or close enough. He hummed along to its dreamy refrain, as though he had always known it.

Here—to watch over—me-eeeeee . . .

The DJ said, *That was "My Special Angel" by Hinkin County's very own Vogues.* Guest had never heard of it or them.

There was a little market up ahead—THE AMPLE HAMPER—and he pulled into its gravel lot. The cashier was an elderly man in a lumberjack shirt, with thick glasses and a shiny drooping nose. He was speaking to a young woman who was peering ambivalently into the deli case. The woman glanced up at Guest. She had big, heavy-lidded eyes, a round pale face with a poor complexion, and dark ear-length hair with red highlights. Her businesslike skirt suit was flattering on her figure, if a bit rumpled from wear. "You got a little flour, a little oil?" said the elderly man. "Fry 'em. I do." She turned back to the case, stroking her soft chin.

It was less a market than a pair of rooms where someone had arranged a number of items neatly but sparsely on the shelves. Much of the space was given to gallon bottles of soda, large bags of chips, and snack cakes. Specimens of bruised fruit languished in a bin; the dairy case had butter, baloney, and gouge-price salad greens. A circular rack displayed religious booklets. After he set his purchases on the counter he perused the deli case, which contained some cuts of limp meat, a tray of floating gherkins, and cellophaned packages of fish.

"What are those?" said Guest, pointing.

"Local kippers. Lake fish."

"Is that what you were recommending to the young lady?"

The elderly man studied him.

"She was buying some kind of meat?" said Guest.

"That lady is vegetarian," said the man. "What you see there is venison cutlets."

Guest nodded. "When did you all open up?"

"Been here twenty years," said the cashier.

He paid for his sandwich fixings, chips, and snack cakes. As he was backing out of the lot he saw the windows of the Ample Hamper go dark.

HE DROVE INTO THE HIDDEN VALLEY Four Seasons Mountain Resort past the waterwheel atop its cairn of decorative boulders. In summer it spilled forth a streamlet amid a profusion of zinnias and pansies, suggesting a trim, cheerful Swiss ambience. Now the wheel stood frozen. Straight ahead was the road down to the lodge. His car forked left, taking the dark residential road that crossed a fishing pond and snaked up the mountain to the condominium units. He took a curve too fast and braked for a deer; its eyes flashed silver; released from the spell it loped off into the trees. The cabin was nearly at the top of the mountain. As he pulled into a plowed parking space, he saw the windows were lighted.

Of course: Eric was in. Pat felt, along with relief, a surge of the old grim satisfaction at having confounded some adolescent mischief, foiled the sneak-out, broken up the party. "Bad news travels fast," he said aloud, as if Harriet could hear him.

But as he fumbled with his keys this feeling gave way

to another: the fear of embarrassment, of overstepping his bounds and walking in on something he wouldn't want to see. He paused on the plank steps; images popped up that his mind winced away from, flashes of ambiguous fleshiness.

He knocked firmly on the glass door, rattling the rosy-cheeked wooden skier dangling there like a talisman.

There was almost no wind. He could hear the *shusss* of snowmakers in the distance. He hesitated—but this was, after all, his house. He didn't have to unlock it: the soft turning of the unresisting knob was faintly sickening for a reason he couldn't place. With a little *screek* the door pushed inward, and Pat stepped into a warm haze of smells that made him think of many good times, the family all together in a cozy house on the mountaintop, with a roaring fire, the voices of children, nowhere else to be.

"HELLO," HE CALLED HEARTILY, MOVING TOWARD THE BATHROOM, sensing in the silence a presence, a hint that someone was in the cabin. He relieved himself, then thought to look behind the shower curtain. The right-hand door on the vanity cupboard was missing, as if removed from its hinges. The tap water wouldn't get warm. In the room with the kids' bunk beds Guest checked the fuse box and found the water heater was shut off. He flipped it back on: the switch cracked sharply in the quiet. The bunk beds looked absurdly miniature, beds meant for toddlers or midgets. The mattresses were stripped of sheets but blankets lay folded at the foot of each. Packing boxes were stacked haphazardly against the walls and piled in the closet. There was something exhausting and a little sad about all these belongings heaped here, in a room intended for leisure, for getaways.

"Eric," he called, emerging into the living room with its sea green carpet, rustic furniture, great triangular window. The room looked the same yet slightly altered, as though all of the furniture had been removed, then brought back and arranged by someone not confident of where everything went. This was the general impression—yet in detail all was familiar. Here, atop the stone mantelpiece, was the bowl of potpourri that still smelled spicy-sweet, the green-wimpled Santa on miniature skis, the twinned glass angels blowing fluted horns.

"Eric."

His son was avoiding him.

Then he remembered: he hadn't called ahead—had Harriet?—so Eric wouldn't have known he was coming. He was likely out skiing. Or down at the lodge.

The other bedroom on the main level was clearly where Eric slept. The bed was unmade and clothing was heaped in open suitcases, corroborating his sense that his son was here on an extended vacation. He lifted the flap of a packing box and felt an old twinge of forbiddenness at the invasion of Eric's privacy. It was only books: *Moon-Blindness and Other Stories*; *Principles of Hypnosis*; *Fibromyalgia: The Silent Mass Epidemic*. He'd have thought Eric would have moved into the master bedroom, but when Guest went upstairs, he found it undisturbed.

Coming back down, he saw the grocery bag he'd left on the floor. His hunger came surging back and he threw together a sandwich. While he was chewing, his phone rang. This touched him with dread—it was Harriet.

"Hi, sweetie . . . Mm-hmm. Yep. Well, I think he is . . . Huh? . . . No, in fact I have *not* seen the child as yet . . ."

Pat found himself explaining that Eric must be out skiing; yes (he lied), he had checked the ski rack and noted the absence of Eric's skis; he could not be out much longer because the chairlifts closed at nine-thirty, maybe ten.

"He will call you when he comes in . . . Yes . . . Yes, of course, I completely understand . . . I do too . . . yep . . . Okay."

Pat would not allow Harriet to panic, and so he didn't mind the equivocation as such. But he minded—and tried to ignore—the distastefulness of being obliged to cover for Eric, simply because of the young man's carelessness. Standing at the sliding glass doors which gave on to a little balcony, he watched the procession of skiers gliding past, the slower ones poling along, incognito in their garb, some still goggled under the night lights.

He prepared a second sandwich and scarfed it. Then he scavenged gear from drawers and closets—long johns, thermal shirts, neck warmer, gloves. His ski bib was too snug in the gut and crotch. Grunting, he squeezed into some boots that felt more or less right, and grabbed the skis he knew were his. The puffy jacket felt much too constricting when he zipped it up, but not till he was sliding down Lost Girl Trail, fiddling with his straps, did he realize the jacket was Annie's, or Harriet's.

THE CHAIRLIFT SEAT MET THE BACKS OF HIS KNEES with a love tap, then an impatient shove, and as his backside hit the bench—"Last run," the young lift attendant told him—he felt the old delight of being swept off his feet, airborne, self-contained on a wintry magic carpet. He clacked the edges of his skis together, relishing their stark music. The bench hung crooked from the lopsided weight of his lone body in the four-seater.

The whining cable bore him aloft and unobserved above the few remaining skiers. Guest loved a good chat on a chairlift, but riding solo was its own pleasure, a feeling of breezy omniscience. He listened to the oddly amplified scrape and scutter of skis carving turns on the steep crust of Cliffhanger, the humble mountain's only ◆◆ slope. Cresting the hill, he could see the pond called Tahoe Lake—black, ringed with pines—which the resort used as a reservoir for the snowmakers. The chair dispensed him and U-turned for its passengerless downward journey. From up here, Cliffhanger appeared steeper than he had remembered, the overhead lights weaker. The ungroomed terrain was a pitted patchwork of bump and shadow. He'd have to go cautiously, mindful of his knees.

He was struck to see a little one, alone at this hour, skiing down the left-hand margin of the slope, close to where the lighted portion ceded to darkness and tree trunks. The child snowplowed fearlessly into bumps nearly tall as he was, gliding up and over the moguls, dropping into their shadowed troughs. Up and over went this mufflered manikin, appearing and disappearing, never gathering too much speed, light as he was.

Guest tipped over the ledge of snow, dropping into gravity, following. He felt his muscles flex as he carved his turn, controlling his momentum in a complex negotiation between resistance and acquiescence. Astonishing that the body could learn to do this. He'd taught Eric not long after he'd taught himself, and little Annie more easily after that. Harriet, who never got the hang of it, kept to her "scenic tours" of Lost Girl Trail, and preferred hot cocoa at a sunny window.

"Watch it!" cried a deep-voiced figure in red, blindsiding him from the right and clipping his ski.

Guest pulled up short, heart racing, opening his mouth for a retort—then watched papa bear, who'd been following from uphill, catch up with his wayward cub.

"ERIC?" HE CALLED OUT, STOMPING HIS BOOTS on the doormat. The answering silence was vexing. Eric must be at the lodge, then—and Pat wasn't about to go chasing him around down there, exhausted as he suddenly felt. Collapsing on the couch in his ski clothes, he flipped through the cable channels, pausing drowsily on a religious station. It was one of those artless modern megachurches that look like small stadiums. The preacher had an odd accent. At first it sounded southern; then East Coast, almost Brooklyn. The preacher's looks seemed to match this: baggy dark suit, big block of a torso, the lugubrious face of an aging boxer, hair oiled back from a starkly receded hairline. *People are gonna say you* sound *different, you* look *different, you* think *different*, he was saying, the accent now sort of British, maybe Australian. The boxer-preacher stalked around the stage, speaking through a headset mike about *God as a river moving* through *you*, his big white hands held out at chest level, as if to say *this deep*.

Among the murmurous response of the audience a

man was laughing. In fact multiple men were laughing, but you couldn't see where it was coming from. The Aussie preached straight through it, about the river moving through you, changing you. Then, as if it could no longer be ignored, the camera panned to a young man near the front, in stitches, laughing convulsively. And another man off-camera—a black man, Guest thought—was whooping it up with even more hysterical zeal—*HA-ha-ha, HA-ha-ha*—as if on a loop. Was it some kind of laughing church? He couldn't tell whether the laughing was a deliberate part of the service—the river moving through you?—or whether, as now seemed the case, the Aussie was distracted by the whoops, prowling the room with increasing aggravation, dabbing with a handkerchief at his shiny brow. . . .

When he woke his phone was going off. The shrill jangle of the ringtone shook him like a wild accusation. By the time he understood where he was—saw the room's ghostly double on the darkness framed in the big triangular window—the phone had shut up.

He dragged himself upstairs. When he drew back the comforter, he noted skeptically, in the flickering portion of his conscious brain, specks of dried blood on the sheet.

He switched off the bedside lamp, thought *I've got to do something about that dang phone*—and was out.

HE WOKE MONDAY MORNING TO A SINKING FEELING. Fog pressed on the window; the world looked less solid. The unmade bed in Eric's downstairs room was still unmade, as though fixed in its posture of unmadeness. He poked around as if something might have shifted or altered since the night before. It had: he had missed the wallet on the bedside table, and now he opened it eagerly and apprehensively, as though it might yield a surprise.

The driver's license was the boy's, no doubt about that. So was the credit card whose balance Pat had been paying every month. He flipped through sundry business cards wedged into the pockets of the wallet. None of it meant anything to him.

The car, he thought, *how did I not think of the car?* Maybe Eric had gone somewhere in the car and forgotten to take his wallet. He pulled on some pants and went out in the fog. A family trio in snowsuits—a woman and two little girls—came clunking down the steps of an adjacent unit, bearing awkward armloads of skis and poles. It was milder; the snow would turn slushy by midday. Guest paced around the parking area until he spotted Eric's car, noting the Maryland plates.

So the wallet was here and the car was here—the key accoutrements of Eric. They must be good signs. But they didn't give him a good feeling.

Only one way in there and one way out, he heard a voice saying (the voice of John Wayne). The world of Hidden Valley had circumscribed boundaries, and within those boundaries, one way or another, was Eric.

Something strange may have happened, he thought, running his finger through the condensation on the car's rear window; and then again maybe nothing strange had happened. He tried to picture his son, at that moment, in someone else's condo—maybe with a group of friends, kids he'd met up here. Eric sleeping till noon in a strange bed. Eric eating breakfast, laughing with friends. He couldn't see it. Could he? Maybe he could see it.

The thought of Harriet's voice message oppressed him. He forced himself to listen to part of it, though he pulled the phone away from his ear when he heard her voice rising. When he brought the phone back to his ear, and the voice-mail menu gave him the appealing option to *send a reply message*, he took it:

"Nothing much happening up here, sweetie . . . I can't seem to find my phone charger and I don't have much battery left . . . uh . . . love you, sweetie."

Pat snapped the phone shut, ashamed and relieved. *Nothing much happening* . . . It was equivocal, perhaps cruelly so, but if he quit stonewalling and told her the truth—that after a whole night he had not yet laid eyes on their son—she would form the wrong impression, take the information out of context. Bad news traveled fast. *The truth*, at any rate, was provisional, was based on an absence of facts. When Eric appeared in the flesh— and he must do so sooner rather than later—the old *truth* would be obsolete.

He flipped channels, tried to work a little on his exam. He opened the sliding glass doors and watched the outlines of skiers gliding by in the mist, heard their disembodied calls and responses. He remembered how he'd once watched for the family cat, Garbanzo, to come home. What year had it been? By the third or fourth day of no cat, Annie'd been inconsolable, Eric silent. Pat had known cats to stray for even longer and return. He was drinking coffee at the bay window in the morning. It was one of those gusty fall days when you suddenly sense the end-of-year entropy spreading, in the branches thinning of their leaves, acorns bouncing off the skylight, the frenzy of bird and squirrel activity, hoarding of seeds and nuts, preparations for migration and burrow. The frenzy was centered on a lilac bush in the side yard. Little birds alighted on the branches; others just as suddenly took off; squirrels darted and paused along the grass. One moment the picture was crowded with quick life, the next emptied; then it reversed. It had occurred to Pat that if you counted the number of birds and squirrels at points along a time interval, the numbers would likely regress to a mean. The activity only appeared chaotic to our slow brains; in fact it was elegantly ordered, even harmonic, within its closed system. After half an hour of staring at birds and squirrels, he realized he had wandered into Garbanzo's dream.

Dusk came, dark. Once, then twice, the little phone, now set to vibrate, groaned its quiet convulsions. Outside the night lights came on.

He showered and dressed. He found a blunted Sharpie and a blank note card in the kitchen drawer and wrote, *Your father is here!—down at the lodge, please call when you read this.* He felt a little queasy taping it to the front door, which he left unlocked, as he'd found it.

THE TYROLEAN MOTIF OF STONE and varnished timber was unchanged since the 1920s. But the original lodge had been augmented haphazardly over the last half century—a new hotel, carpeted convention halls, duck-pin bowling, terraces, craft shops, swimming—resulting in a strange rambling structure whose wings were connected by stairwells and corridors, in which guests might easily get lost. It was a lodge with too many hiding places.

He emerged into the bright, warm lobby, surprised by its quiet. On weekend and holiday evenings it would be filled with a festive hubbub, the cries of children set free after mealtime, the merry clomping of ski boots. The air smelled of wood smoke, cigarettes, and french fries. Muted waves of groans, then cheers, issued from an adjacent pub room where the Steelers game was on. A fire blazed in the great stone hearth; the wall above was decorated with crossed pairs of primitive skis, snow-shoes strung with hide. Mounted heads of deer and bear watched over the lobby's few other stragglers: a roving trio of furtive-eyed boys in baseball caps and sweat-pants; a flushed, frazzled mom dragging a little one (still mummified in snow gear) across the flagstones.

A little diner was off to one side of the lobby. Walking past, he saw the back of a young man standing at the coun-ter. Gratitude ignited in his heart, flooding his chest like hot blood. He recognized the wavy brown hair curling at the ears. Those brown curls besieged him—they were like a slap to the face. He strode toward the boy, arms tensed as if for a fight, calling out "Eric" in a rasp that caught in his throat. But even as he placed his hand on the back of the young man's shoulder, he saw he had made a mistake.

"Oh," said Guest as the young man turned around. "My apologies," he added, backing away. The tall young man smiled tranquilly down at him. Guest noted his flat red face and small blurry eyes, the chapping around his lips and nostrils, his broad chest, snowboarding pants: an athletic boy; not handsome; not Eric. "My apologies," said

Guest, "I thought you were my son." The young man's face blushed redder. He mumbled something, then turning received his styrofoam take-out container from the girl behind the counter, and was gone.

Guest glanced around. A pair of older men in work jackets sipped coffee on stools, chatting with a fry cook. He noticed a woman seated alone in a booth, staring at him. She was pretty, with frosted hair, a tanned face, a self-deprecating smile. She was younger than he was; she winked. It was the wink that tugged him toward her booth. He saw she meant to speak to him; he had to come close to hear her.

"Oh good," she said, "good—you're okay. I saw that . . ." She waved her coral nails in the direction of the cashier. "Was there a mix-up with your order? You looked . . . angry."

"Angry?"

"Or maybe just mixed-up." She winked again.

"I guess you could say I'm a little mixed-up."

The woman's eyes widened; she let out a yelp of laughter. "You are, aren't you? You're a funny puppy. Let me guess—you're here for the conference. Dental insurance or something. Or, no—the polka thing?" She gestured at the opposite seat.

Guest shook his head, sliding uncertainly into the booth, noting the sparkle in the woman's coral lipstick, the untanned creases in her neck, her ample bosom beneath a hockey sweatshirt.

"Do you need something to eat?" she asked. "How about one of these?"

She jiggled her glass of white wine; a little sloshed over

the side and she frowned, patting the area with a napkin. He remembered how he had been prepared to order one drink at the Oakhurst Smorgasbord. The waiter appeared, an elfin, bushy-browed boy with a clip-on bow tie.

"A glass of white wine for the gentleman," said the woman. "We'll need another minute on the food. Do you like fajitas?" she asked when the boy had gone. "My friend Little Bit always gets the steak with Madrid sauce."

"Sounds perfect," said Guest, hearing *steak*.

She asked him his name.

"You're Pat?" she squealed. "Get out. My ex was Pat. You're not a stinker, are you? Joking! Oh, you're cute. Seriously, I feel like I've met you before. Have we? I know *everybody* up here."

This last remark caught his attention; he was opening his mouth when she said, "Thank you, Seamus," accepting from the waiter a wineglass and relaying Guest's order. Winking, she passed the glass to Guest.

"I'm Deb," said the woman. They cheersed and sipped. It was a little like nectar and a little like poison. But the tickle of fear under his ribs would grow fainter. He was an old man now; one glass of wine would not turn him into a drunk. Tonight he deserved it—and needed it.

"I was supposed to meet Little Bit before the show," said Deb. "She's been having a crisis. But I couldn't find her."

The elfin waiter returned and set before him a platter heaped with beef strips covered in a bright yellow sauce resembling Cheez-Whiz. Guest dug in: the beef strips were black and strangely tender. The dish was outlandishly salty. The woman continued to rattle on about her friend.

"It's just one thing after another with Little Bit. She had

to wear a leg brace after she got shingles. Then they said it wasn't shingles, it was something else. Then she was practically paralyzed. She's brilliant, don't get me wrong, but life just seems to crap on that girl at every turn."

Guest nodded, chewing. It sounded like Deb was bragging on her friend, or took some perverse pride in knowing such an exotically misfortunate person; and there was also a suggestion of *There but for the grace of God* that struck him as objectionable.

"She was an orphan. Found out all kinds of horrible stuff. It's a sick world, you know? Full of sick, sick people. Poor thing. I can't *think* what she'll do."

Deb was looking at something behind Guest. He glanced back; he didn't know what he was looking for. When he turned again she was sliding out from the booth.

"Would you excuse me for a sec? I just . . ."

He watched her denim-covered bottom as she sauntered away in the direction, he supposed, of the restrooms.

He waited and waited; she didn't return. Po-faced Seamus reappeared and asked him if he would like something else. "Just the check," said Guest. He polished off the remainder of Deb's white wine. When the check came, he saw that only one wine had been charged.

THE APPEARANCE AND SUDDEN DEPARTURE of the strange woman had baffled him; stuffed and sweating lightly, he wandered in the lodge a little stunned, feeling the wine's warm touch on his cheek, and the dread simmering underneath the wine.

He went down a passageway meant to look like a

village lane; behind darkened display glass a Santa figurine held aloft in its mitts a pot of hairstyling product. The air smelled of birthday cake and potpourri. Tacked to the door of the Leather Shoppe was a picture postcard of a man in a denim shirt cradling in his arms a cross between a fish and a groundhog. There was a handwritten inscription. Guest retrieved a broken pair of reading glasses from his jacket pocket.

> *Ole Man Winter proudly holds a record fur-bearing trout taken during the cold winter of 1992–1993. The trout was fooled by an all-leather "stream warrior" created and tied by us.*

"I'll be goddamned," said Guest, marveling. "Oh, excuse me," he said, backing into a group of men and women in polka costume, some younger, some elderly; they maneuvered complexly around him and continued toward the lobby, leaving him with the feeling he'd been twirled.

He went the way the polka folks had come. The hall became carpeted, low-ceilinged, the sconces casting yellow light on the pinewood doors of the guest rooms. Reaching a staircase he went up, hesitated, went down. He followed the sounds of muffled tuba and accordion, the sense of a great murmuring, until he came to a set of double doors, which opened, revealing not the polka hall but an indoor miniature golf course, wholly deserted. He could make out in the dimness a windmill, a giant shoe, a clown's face unfurling from its grinning gob a tongue of Astroturf. The oompah oompahed faintly from somewhere else in the building.

Guest set out to retrace his steps. He got a warm whiff of chlorine and found himself in the glassed-in swimming pool room. A man bulbous and slick as a manatee propelled himself along under the surface of the luminous water. One end of the pool room connected to a video arcade; when Guest opened the door he was jangled by bells and cascading bleeps, abrupt buzzers and revving engines, gun reports and taunting enemy laughter.

It's ridiculous, he thought, marching through the noise; ridiculous that Eric would be hanging around a place like this, that he would find some sort of interest or fulfillment here. Someone shouted "Shit!" as an air-hockey puck came flying off the table. (It was the teen-aged boys from the lobby.) A paranoid thought flickered to life in his brain: that Eric *was* here, ghosting the periphery—a mercurial arranger, somehow stringing him along by an invisible thread. And yet this paranoid idea gave him hope.

Escaping through a side door, he found himself in another hallway. As the chimes and bells of the arcade receded behind him, he began to hear music. It was familiar music, and he followed. The tender string melody and stately horns lured him on past a bank of coin-operated lockers and a fortune-telling machine (a green-turbaned head and pink mannequin hands, poised in a lighted glass box). By the time he arrived at the doors of the Tyrol Room, he'd recognized the song: he'd heard it on the radio driving up. But the voice he heard singing now was female.

The lounge was cavernous and smoky, unevenly lit. It was too loud but he didn't mind: the voice, sweet, ingenuous, washed over him like an enchantment:

> *You are my special angel*
> *Through eter-nityyyy*

He saw the stage on the right; footlights shone on the red cloth backdrop, tinsel glittered, and three older men in black velvet jackets stood behind a pale young lady in a blue low-cut dress. A pink neon sign behind the drummer read: THE VOGUES.

Those slow, dark eyes, the hair with a coppery sheen: it was the girl he'd seen in the market, the smartly dressed girl who was a vegetarian. The gray-haired men hummed and crooned in harmony. The song filled Guest's lonely heart like a drug.

> *I'll have my special angel*
> *Here . . . to watch over . . . me-eee*

The crowd on the dance floor looked boozy and well-fed; several wore name tags. He noted a young black man with large plastic glasses and a referee's jersey, slow-dancing with a woman in a muumuu. To the left, a somewhat rougher-edged crowd was arrayed around the bar.

> *Here . . . to watch over . . . me-eee*

He spotted Deb at one of the little lounge tables. She noticed him and waved him over. She was sitting with a man with thinning yellow hair and flowing slacks, crossed at the knee, who appraised Guest with polite interest.

"Pat, this is Ricardo; Ricardo, my friend Pat."

"A breath of fresh air!" said Ricardo, raising his glass. Guest nodded.

"Well, as you can see we found Little Bit," said Deb, glancing toward the stage.

"We thought she'd gone home," said Ricardo.

"That's Little Bit?" said Guest.

Deb shrugged. "The one and only."

"The girl—I mean young lady—up there on the stage?"

Ricardo said something he didn't catch.

"Say again?" said Guest, turning his ear.

"I love your white curls!"

Guest disregarded the comment. "I'm looking for a young man named Eric."

Ricardo raised an eyebrow.

"Do either of you know of someone named Eric?"

Ricardo and Deb exchanged a glance.

"Tall young man, brown hair," said Guest.

Deb shook her head—then caught Guest's eye and winked. He understood then it was only a facial tic.

"I need to speak to him," said Guest. "To Eric. My son."

Ricardo looked confused. He said he didn't know; he thought Eric was Trey's friend.

"Do you know where he is? Tonight?"

One of the elderly Vogues had assumed the lead, and belted forth in a rich tenor:

> *You-uuu are my reason to li-iiive*
> *All I own I would gi-iiive*
> *Just to have you ado-ooore me . . .*

Deb squealed with pleasure and tugged Ricardo onto the dance floor.

Guest took a big swallow of his drink. It seemed to him that Ricardo had all but confirmed that he knew of Eric. He felt suddenly, elatedly convinced that he was going to lay eyes on his son, come hell or high water, before the night was through. He watched the strange duo slow-dancing dreamily. Their eyes were closed as the lights came up and the Vogues bid the crowd good night.

Guest's phone vibrated in his pocket. He caught sight of the girl, Little Bit, at the foot of the stage. He made his way toward her through the humid bodies milling on the dance floor. She seemed to recognize him; he took her hands and over the din of voices spoke in her ear: "You were wonderful . . . just . . . wonderful." She blushed like a daughter. He could smell her shampoo.

"Where were you?" cried Deb, approaching with a greenish drink and Ricardo in tow. She pressed the girl's arm: "*Hel-lo*, did you not get my messages?"

The girl looked abashed. "I was here . . . "

"It's Trey's birthday. Everyone's going back to Swiss Mountain."

"Not me," said Ricardo. "Uh-uh. Been down that road."

Deb gaped at her friend, blinking her small eyes.

"No, ma'am, this boy's gotta work."

"It's Trey's birthday. We'll go for a minute. Big deal. I'll drive. Little Bit's coming," she said, tugging the girl's bare arm. The girl looked over her shoulder at the band members, who were packing up their instruments.

Deb was hastening Little Bit out of the bar among the

merry, dizzy throng. Guest followed. The crowd flowed up the steps, gripping the log railings, dispersing down corridors, rummaging in pockets for room keys. Guest looked back downstairs and saw Ricardo staring at the fortune-teller machine with a thoughtful twist to his mouth.

OUTSIDE THE LOBBY THE CHILLY REVELERS were clambering onto a shuttle bus. Guest lost sight of the two women. Then he saw them making their way across the parking lot—Little Bit with a fur coat around her shoulders—and hurried to catch up.

"Do you even feel safe?" Deb was saying.

"I don't know," said Little Bit.

"I can't be looking after you all the time."

There was something not right in the way Deb was dragging this young woman, who she'd said was ill, to a late-night party. But he felt that he needed to talk to Little Bit; he needed even more urgently to get to the party.

"I can drive us there," he said.

"You don't know the way to Swiss Mountain," said Deb. "I always drive." She struggled to get her key in the door of a white Plymouth. "Frozen," she muttered. She meant the lock or herself—she wore no coat over the hockey sweatshirt. "Come with us and I'll give you a lift back."

Little Bit, slipping into the backseat, mouthed something to Guest. He thought it was *Please come.*

He got in beside her, the backseat smelling of cold vinyl and perfume, his hand brushing the fur. Deb, firing up the engine, eyed them in the mirror and snorted.

The Plymouth took a hairpin turn onto the access road. A guardrail ran along the edge of a cliff. Headlights glared in the rear window; taillights glowed up ahead. Guest saw the hotel tower at the east end of the lodge, a few windows still lighted. Years ago, before they bought the cabin, he and Harriet and the kids had stayed in an adjoining pair of those rooms; that was when he'd taught them how to ski. The lodge receded behind them, the white slopes above still icy-bright in the distance.

"How could you stand to be up there with Haniver around?" Deb was saying.

"I needed to sing," said Little Bit.

A cluster of Bavarian-style houses went past, their windows dark. Then a gut-lifting swoop down a dip in the road, an ascent toward the resort exit. Guest glanced with regret at the residential road, the way back to his cabin, as they passed it. *I don't know where we're going*, he whispered to Little Bit. "To Trey's," she murmured. "It's easy to get lost." They passed the frozen waterwheel, turned onto the state highway, the old car grumbling, and roared off into the night.

THE PARTY WAS IN A SPLIT-LEVEL CONDO UNIT in a cul-de-sac in the woods. Guest found himself in the kitchen, backed against a countertop that was crammed with bottles and snacks. He clung to a bag of chili-cheese Fritos and a plastic cup of beer. Little Bit stayed beside him. She'd kept her fur coat on.

"Everybody drink, get fucked-up," said Trey, the birthday boy in the referee's jersey, as if laying down some ground rules for the party. "Have a good time, and remember, I've got a forty-five upstairs and my uncle can get me out of anything!"

"It's true," said a buxom young woman with an Irish accent (there seemed to be a contingent of them here)—"his father's top judge in Pittsburgh."

"Judge McCowan," added Trey. "Look him up. He adopted me when I was a troubled kid."

"He's a millionaire," said the Irish woman.

They hadn't been ten minutes at the party and already Trey had implicitly threatened his company with murder. Guest watched the young man's eyes; when Trey caught him looking, Guest broke off his gaze. Trey seemed too preoccupied (at least for the moment) to give a second thought to his age or his party-crasher status. He was getting some curious stares from the Irish gals, but no questions—perhaps on account of Little Bit. The party-goers seemed an odd mix of younger employees of the resort, snowboarders, locals from Hemperling and who knew where else. Through a kind of service window in the kitchen wall, he could see the dining area with a large glass chandelier suspended over a small table. There Deb was laughing with a member of the Vogues.

"I'm adopted too, you know," said Little Bit to Guest. "But my father's not a judge. Or a millionaire."

He nodded. "I think Deb told me that earlier."

"That my father's not a millionaire?"

"That you were adopted," he said.

"I'll bet she told you all kinds of things."

Thinking of Trey and his gun, Guest asked Little Bit about the man Deb had alluded to earlier, someone who (if he'd heard correctly) was frightening her. "Excuse me if that's too personal. I didn't understand what she was talking about."

Little Bit laughed. "Who does?"

He thought she didn't want to answer his question, but after a moment she said: "My brother." Her weary smile seemed to absolve Guest of prying. "She was talking about my brother. He's a killer. He just got out of prison. Sometimes he used to fill in with the band. He plays clarinet."

"Your brother was in prison for murder?"

"Rape," said Little Bit. Her eyes had a gentle expression—but beneath that was something opaque and inaccessible.

"I'm confused."

"His name is Bobby Joe Haniver. He is my brother. His folks adopted me when I was a newborn."

Little Bit's story was hard to understand. Haniver, the biological child, was ten years her elder. He'd been convicted of abducting and raping a boy in Maryland. That was the sentence just completed. But Little Bit believed Haniver had been doing it since he was sixteen, and was responsible for many more rapes—plus the murders of two boys. One of the boys, she said, had gone missing in Hidden Valley. This was years ago. It was all over the news at the time. She'd been talking to the families of the victims, who were trying to convince the DA to reopen these cold cases and charge Haniver with the murders before he got out of prison. But the effort was unsuccessful, or proceeded too slowly. Her adoptive parents had turned against her. She was a traitor, banned from the house.

As Little Bit spoke into his lowered ear, Guest had the

sense of a sleepy child recounting a nightmare to her parent; but although she was speaking and he listening, he felt as if *he* were the child with the nightmare, and she the assuaging parent. And behind her story the song from the bar—*forever angel, my ever angel*—kept drifting through his mind. He told his brain to fix and store the names of the people and places she mentioned: he would look it all up eventually.

"But how do you know this? How do you know he did those crimes?"

"He's my brother. I found out things in our home. And I've spoken with the families—I know what they know."

"But if all this is known, why would they let him out of prison?"

The girl shrugged. "Maryland does their thing and Pennsylvania does their thing. There are so many questions only he has the answers to. And some folks up here believe his side of the story. Like my parents."

Pat's mind cast vaguely back over many conversations with Harriet. Had they ever thought there was a chance Eric had been abused in some way? Maybe, but not really. Definitely not. A parent knew these things. You wanted an explanation for every behavior, but you learned sometimes there wasn't one. Children daydreamed; withdrew; protected secrets. It was only in middle age that Guest had thought about how much he might not know about his own life. The deeps, the dark spaces: they only grew wider, less fathomable, with the years.

The sweet stink of pot smoke wafted through the little window into the kitchen. Guest had put his hand on the back of her coat. He wanted to hug her—but he didn't know if he believed her. It was crazy. The drinks were a mistake. He didn't know what he should think. He reminded himself that he didn't know this girl. Maybe *she* was crazy.

He asked her what Haniver looked like. She described his bearish figure, his broad hips and soft voice.

"And where is he now?" Guest asked. "Do I need to be concerned for your safety? Where is Haniver right now?"

Little Bit's face darkened. He felt he'd crossed a line.

"I'm sorry," he said. "It's just that I'm trying to find someone. I'm trying to—" Little Bit was watching him intently; and he felt suddenly that she had read his mind, that she could complete his sentence for him.

"I'm looking for Eric," he said.

And as if confirming his thought, she said: "I think Eric is here."

"Here at the ski resort?"

"Here at the party," said Little Bit. "But aren't you . . ."

"I'm his father." Then he asked her: "Have you met Eric?"

She replied bashfully, almost blushing: "Of course."

"Where is he?"

She whispered: "You need to talk to Trey—it's his place."

Draining the beer from his cup, he followed the girl out of the kitchen.

In the shag-carpeted hall, he turned right, toward the dining area, but Little Bit headed the other way, down the steps to the lower level. He paused, watching her go down.

When he emerged alone into the dining area, several people turned to look at him. He saw Trey in the corner, talking with two of the Irish girls—they looked like sisters. He made his way to Trey's corner as the conversation hushed. Plumes of mellow smoke curled in the lights of the chandelier.

"Is Eric here?" said Guest. It was the most awkward introduction of his life. "I have to see him now."

Trey was polite, amused. "You *have* to see him—Eric?"

Guest nodded.

Trey looked stunned. "You *have* to see him. Shit, I don't even know who you are." He glanced around at his friends. "What would you pay?"

"Pay?" said Guest.

"To see Eric." When Trey said the name *Eric* it sounded like he had a stone in his mouth, or a piece of hard candy. Up close, his eyes were wonky somehow behind the thick glasses—a lazy eye, Guest thought, or a dead eye.

"I don't want to cause anyone any trouble."

Trey laughed. There were a few titters from around the room. "No, you certainly don't," Trey said.

Guest's heart was in his throat. He reached for his wallet and pulled out the largest bill he could see. His hand was shaking as he held out the bill toward Trey.

Trey glanced at the bill with surprise, then distaste, then what might have been pity.

"Oh, come on, man, I don't want your money!" He laughed.

The room erupted in laughter. "His father's a millionaire," said one of the Irish girls, smiling kindly at Guest.

"Eric!" shouted Trey. "Where's Eric?"

"He's asleep," someone shouted.

"Asleep," Trey repeated. "Well fuck, wake him up, he needs to see this!"

Guest pocketed the bill, his heart full to bursting. Why, he wondered, would Eric be sleeping in this place? He didn't care—whatever was going on, it didn't matter, it could all be sorted out. Suddenly Pat understood his true mission to Hidden Valley: it was to take his son home. It was to take him away from Trey and Swiss Mountain. It was to pack up those boxes and take him home. That was all that mattered. That was exactly what was going to happen.

"Is Eric up yet?" called Trey. "He's up? What's he doing?"

"Eric's the best, bro," said someone else.

"Kid is crazy."

"Kid's a genius."

They should never have gone along with this arrangement in the first place, never let Eric move up here alone, allowed the troubled young man this much solitude, this much awful freedom and boredom. He was still their child; they had a responsibility.

"Er-ic, Er-ic," they chanted, clapping: the Irish girls and Trey and even the Vogues crooner. They were all looking down the short carpeted hallway to where a tall, thin, delicate figure was emerging from a bedroom door.

I'll be goddamned, Pat thought, as a wingstroke of hope and fear swept him. A book indeed. What a book Eric must have been writing about this place, these people. How would he ever explain it all to Harriet?

"Oh shit, he's up!" bellowed Trey, his weird eye awobble. "Now it *really* kicks off!"

As the sylphlike person emerged into the lighted area, Pat saw the high white forehead, the close-set almond eyes blinking at the hoopla, the eyebrows that looked penciled on. This "Eric" could have been a boy or a girl. Fine, wispy hair stuck out from under a blue baseball cap; over the sheepish grin was a hint of mustache.

None of it was right. Pat couldn't see through or around these features to his son, to the real Eric. He thought of the first time his momma had looked up at him without recognition. He'd thought, *It's me, here—can't you see me?* Could this be what it felt like? Could it already have begun to happen to him?

It could—it could have begun. But this wasn't Eric. He seemed to watch the death of his idea, the idea that this was his son; yet it lingered from moment to moment as he bade his eyes reassemble the boy's features into those of the person he loved.

The boy looked like he had just woken up. He wore a white collar like a priest's, fitted around his bare slender throat. It was a cloth bandage, fastened with medical tape. In the center of the bandage, where the Adam's apple would be, was a kind of gasket.

The group received Eric unto them with boisterous acclaim. An Irish girl raised a glass pipe to Eric's lips; he closed his eyes and sucked, his hands raised stiffly before him. When he opened his eyes, pursed his lips, and blew forth a cloud of smoke, the party erupted in cheers.

Is he your father? someone said.

Eric turned and his strange eyes met Guest's: in them was something like love.

A SCRIM OF ICE WAS ACCUMULATING ON THE WINDSHIELDS of the cars out front. Guest padded back and forth looking for his car. The thought crossed his mind that one of those people could have stolen it. He was struck with a memory of the rage he'd felt one morning when he came out the front door and realized Eric—then a new driver at sixteen, and moreover grounded—had made off with his car. He'd felt not so much disobeyed as suckered, made a fool of.

Guest barked out a laugh, remembering that his car was parked down at the lodge.

He went back inside and searched upstairs and down for Little Bit, and then, when he couldn't find her, for Deb. Someone said that maybe she'd gone back to Pittsburgh.

The party was in full swing—no one saw him slip out a second time into the light prickling of sleet.

How far could it be? The night lights on the ski slopes were nowhere visible through the woods. The route to Swiss Mountain had been tortuous but mainly upward. If he just kept walking downhill, as he did now, cautiously for the ice, he would get there. But there was the cold, filling his lungs, worming into his ears. He didn't have gloves or a scarf. The road up here was empty and dark. He thought of his briefcase on the chair back at the cabin, with the exam he hadn't finished preparing. The unmade bed, the boxes of stuff, the wallet.

He remembered his son's driver's license. And he remembered the feel of the doorknob in his hand the previous night when he'd arrived at the cabin: how it resisted too little, being unlocked: how yieldingly the door had pushed inward.

He stopped in the road. Eric wasn't going to be there. The note he'd taped to the front door—*down at the lodge*—it hadn't been seen by Eric. It hadn't been seen by anyone. He stood watching his breath, listening to the ceaseless whisper of sleet in the branches of the trees, on the fallen snow, and terrible thoughts, the worst thoughts, winged toward him.

He saw scuba divers, police divers up in the pond they called Tahoe Lake. Alien figures, men in black. He saw their heads, neoprene-hooded, slick as seals. The water droplets flicked off their fins as they dived, their flashlights probing the icy murk. He saw police lights flashing, heard a dog barking on the pebbly shore, and the distant barking of other dogs back in the woods.

"Oh fuck, oh fuck, oh fuck me," said Pat Guest.

His legs marched stiffly, dumbly down the shoulder of the road.

He stopped again and thought: *I need to find the courage to think clearly about what is happening right now.*

He took a deep harsh breath and held it. He was forty feet under the sea, at bottom, looking up at Eric, stuck way up near the surface, clinging to the anchor line, the blue current jostling his body. Eric gave the hand sign for *problem*. He pointed to his ear.

Don't force it, Pat tried to say. *Just equalize. Take it gently—gently: it will happen.*

His son clung to the line, fins kicking, shafts of sunlight playing around him, shaking his head no—he wanted to abort mission.

Don't force it, Pat called in his mind. *Come down slowly, hand over hand. Equalize. Come down and join us. The whole good part is down here. You'll miss everything.*

But already their tanks were losing air; they were losing time. The guide with the other divers had gone on ahead. They were blue shadows in that strange perspectiveless landscape, growing fainter without seeming to move any farther away.

His shoes crunched on the frozen crust. He slipped, caught himself, nearly fell again. The tears burned on his numbed cheeks. He licked the salty wetness off his lip, shaking his head.

"I have got us into a mess," he said aloud. "I have gotten us into a terrible, terrible mess." What kind of a daddy lets one of his own fall behind, fall down the well, fall prey to the wolves or the hungry ghosts. "Not my daddy," he muttered.

But a voice, as if interceding, answered calmly: *Matter is neither created nor destroyed. Therefore nothing is lost forever.*

The phone came alive in his pocket. His numb fingers fumbled it out, a buzzing thing like a wasp—it got away, dropped on the gravel with a crack. He fished it up, answered.

His words came slurred and cumbersome.

"I don't know, sweetie. I'm sorry . . . Huh? . . . I don't know. I just don't know . . . Huh? . . . Tell me again. Again."

But Harriet was speaking, rapidly now, in a voice that sounded so like his momma's voice; and as he tried to hear what she was saying—to really hear this time—he saw headlights coming toward him round the bend, a vehicle making its way slowly up the mountain road.

Gumbo Limbo

THE VERY EXISTENCE OF THE TOWN of Gumbo Limbo, based on a murky distinction between land and fog and the gray-green waves, had always seemed doubtful at best, and in fact Gumbo Limbo may not be there anymore. But in the time I am thinking of—when a frail guest arrived on the shore, and lies spread like smut in a rotten hull, and rains of an impossible duration nearly smudged the village away—a boy did live in Gumbo Limbo. His name was Liam Murgen, born Van den Heuvel. He was the one who befriended the guest. This was quite some time ago, and both of them have long since left.

The boy lived there because when he was very little his parents died in the scenic railway fire in Canada, so he was sent to live with an uncle far down south in Gumbo Limbo. It turned out the uncle was dead, but the boy was taken in by the local apothecary Murgen, who'd been a friend of this uncle. The boy had little else than a box of clothing and toys mislabeled "Julius." He had an idea that his parents were resting in a fancy sanitarium in Massachusetts or Maine, and would return when the fire was over. In his mind's eye he saw a man and woman reclined on a balcony under a canvas awning striped yellow and lime; a nurse or butler pressed cool cloths to their foreheads and served them chilled milk in tumblers on a periwinkle tray.

But the boy no longer much imagined these scenes. He'd assumed his guardian's name, and was not unhappy living with the elderly man in the apartment over Murgen's Apothek on Creel Street. He watched the people of Gumbo Limbo in their long, inevitable parade through the pharmacy. He saw how, while one customer burdened with the most flagrant of maladies might futilely struggle to conceal it, another, with no evident disease of any type, would flaunt his imagined ill with vulgar show. He saw the discretion and care with which Murgen dispensed remedies for these afflictions, whether or not they were visible to the eye, whether they abided in the mind or the flesh. So the customers came with crepitus and albugo, quinsy and railway spine, split nails and sclerotic teeth, light sleep and dyspepsia. They came with rodent ulcer, stammer, and lily rash; Saint Clair's disease, limping, and glomus. Murgen pressed granules of medicine into hard little tablets, mixed acetous tonics and dissolving powders, compounded pots of waxy or oily unguents. He fermented widow's wood, crafted a debriding agent from the beards of blue mussels, and desiccated the milk from a rare deep-sea orchis. Sometimes these medicaments salved the afflictions and most of the time they did not. Murgen gave free treatments to those who could not afford them, like Mr. Hannity from the swamp, who came with an egg of a tumor on his face and went away weeping with gratitude and no hope, no hope. Murgen tried not to lie, and to those supplicants who wanted to be deceived he mostly kept silent. He knew their secret deformities and the fear those deformities wrought in them. He knew why they employed him: to kill off the half-dreamt, half-real monstrous versions of themselves they so hated and cherished.

Murgen cherished Liam, and worried for him. He believed the boy was losing his eyes. A customer standing near the medicine counter might have seen, through the wooden grille separating the front store from the back office, how Murgen would sit the boy across from the eye chart and, with practiced fingers trembling from palsy and concern, retrieve from the optical rack lens after thick glass lens, fitting them in the viewfinder and quizzing the child:

"Number one, or number two? Is this one a little clearer, a little sharper?"

The boy didn't know; he couldn't tell.

Then: "There. Something."

Liam thought he'd discerned something clear and sharp refracted convex in one of the big glass jars.

"No. It was nothing. Sorry."

Murgen sighed. "That's okay."

But it wasn't okay. The eyes were sick. Murgen feared to try his tonics on the child because he couldn't quite believe in them. He'd have gladly wrought an optical potion employing the blackest of diabolical arts if he thought its chemical burn might rend the veil on the boy's vision. But there wasn't any magic in Murgen's craft.

"Still," muttered Murgen. "Sometimes I think that boy sees everything."

IT WAS TRUE LIAM'S DREAMS WERE STILL OPTICALLY CLEAR. And that was why, on the gray and mild winter morning when the boy discovered the strange visitor, he woke early and hurried down to the seashore with the peculiar sensation that he'd had the exact same dream as somebody else—he didn't know who—and furthermore would see reproduced there in exact clarity the very thing he'd almost grasped in the dream. At the dunes he broke into an urgent lollop, but when he got there it was all gray on gray, beach and sky dissolving in a colorless mist: not the lapidary dreamscape, but the murky pannic haze of the boy's waking eye. And yet something out there held its form between the solute phases of saltswell and sand-flat: a darkly saturate spot. A thing washed up. The boy approached: it was a creature, that was true. But even up close it was hard to tell what the creature looked like. Was that a fin or lobe—some kind of sac? A slippery part, some scales—a portion of claw? Maybe the adumbration of a face. But it was tricky, similar to the way the mouth on a stingray's underside resembles a miniature little smiley face; but when you flip it over, it turns out the real face is on the other side: the eyes two wide-set dull expression-less beads. You'd rather have the more perfect little face on the underside. How much certainty ought one invest in a face, for fear it could be the false one? In the spirit of friendship, at least, one grants the benefit of the doubt to each and every possibility of a face.

"Hi," said the creature.

"Hi," said the boy. "What are you doing here?"

The boy bent his ear close, for the creature seemed to speak in the quiet susurrus of the surf itself.

"There is nowhere else," it said. "No farther to go. The sea keeps putting me up here, always at night. Always at night."

The creature sounded melancholy to Liam.

"Are you cold?" the boy asked.

"I start to forget what it's like to be in the water," it said. "And the air is cold. But I also forget that it comes again, the tide, and takes me back in. Then I remember water, and I'm not cold. But the next night it sends me up again, to the edge, where I'm cold."

"What do you do when it rains?" asked the boy, for even now a light prickling of rain fell on them.

"When it rains on the sea? You can hear it but can't feel it. It's just more water. Hardly that. More like the shadow of a cloud. But up here on the shore, I can feel it."

"Do you like it?"

"No," said the creature.

The boy nodded. Then he said good-bye and ran back home, because he knew Yak was approaching in his rolling chair, coming along the road behind the dunes, and Murgen had told Liam to steer clear of Yak, who was a crazy person, though wealthy, a shrimp speculator and owner of lime mines upcountry.

THAT NIGHT LIAM DREAMT OF A CREATURE. He saw it lying on the sand in the dark. He woke at dawn and went back to the seashore, and again the visitor was there.

When Liam touched the creature it was cold; it quivered and sighed. It was rough like a cat's tongue.

"Are you sick?" the boy asked.

"It's different in the sea," replied the creature. "Things have wisps and tatters, trail parts of themselves. Parts drift, tangle and separate. You're always inside everything, and everything is around you, and you move in it and it moves you around. But on the beach here it is different. On the beach, yes, here I might be sick."

"Are you sad?"

"Pick up that whelk shell," said the creature. "Put it to your ear. Listen."

Liam did so.

"That's what I feel like," said the creature.

Boy and creature spoke awhile, and though the creature had an elliptical way of expressing itself, they thanked each other for their friendship, because in the course of their talks they'd become friends. But kneeling in the sand the boy found a loose scale, a translucent tooth, a husk of something that snapped like a seedpod. He rolled the fragile bits in his fingers; he feared they were part of the creature, who was coming undone from the strain of being washed up night after night. It needed to be in the water all of the time and for some reason it couldn't be. The sea wouldn't let it.

The boy didn't want his friend to disintegrate. He decided, with some reluctance, to confide the matter to Murgen.

The next day he led the old man to the spot.

"There it is," said Liam, pointing.

Murgen craned his head (his hips were stiff) and peered. He seemed uncertain; there was a smell; he couldn't make much of what he saw there. He'd heard of the gourami, a fish capable of breathing the air. He'd heard of things caught in the nets by fisherman in Ireland or China.

"We should put it out of its misery, I think."

"No!" cried the boy, crouching protectively over the creature. Wordlessly the boy queried his friend. The creature indicated the waves—and just then there washed up a tiny snail shell. Liam picked it up and saw how the inside glistened royal purple.

"Look," he said, showing Murgen. "It's a gift. Like him. The sea keeps giving him back to us."

The elderly man fondled the rare shell and handed it back to the boy, who put it away in his pocket.

"I remember an old story," Murgen explained to the boy, "about a siren who slipped through the dike in Holland. She came to live among the people. Nobody could make out her speech, but they taught her to weave. It was argued that she was not a fish because she knew how to weave, but was not a woman because she was able to live in water."

Murgen's mind was drifting. The boy made no reply.

Murgen nodded. He agreed to the boy's wishes. The old man helped the boy put the creature in a big pickle jar of clean water. First they dropped a little cake of sodium in the water and Murgen stirred with a wooden stick until the cake dissolved. They took the jar to the back room of the Apothek where it was safe. Liam asked the creature if it felt okay there and the creature said that it did, but could they put the jar up on the high shelf, because it felt safer and more comfortable up there, and so they did.

Now in the mornings when the boy came downstairs he went to the back room of the shop and climbed up the stepladder to see how his friend was doing.

And were it not for Murgen's assistant—a youth by the name of Tim Rutter—the trouble in Gumbo Limbo might never have gotten started, and they all might have continued on okay.

RUTTER WAS A LANKY, FERAL-EYED PERSON with oily skin and a cruel streak that must have come from somewhere. He'd become attached to Murgen's shop some years back. He was not a good assistant, and customers patronized the Apothek despite his presence. Rutter had a repertoire of malfeasance not so much methodical as it was impulsive, arbitrary, and weird. Not only did he overcharge the customers and keep the money but he hocked phlegm in the philters and touched himself behind the counter when a pretty girl was in the shop, or sometimes a boy, or sometimes no one at all. He seemed too cunning to be truly touched, as the physiognomy of his head and face might have evidenced, though some found the feral aspect perversely attractive or even irresistible. He suffered from an irregular form of Saint Vitus' dance, whereby not a fit but a sudden glazed expression stole over him, a mask that suggested to those looking at him an odd mixture of contentment and consternation that seemed not to belong to his person. The frequency of the spells varied, but they tended to last several minutes. Privately Rutter referred to his condition as "the morbus," because that is what his aunt, a Mrs. Croat, told him it was called. This aunt characterized her nephew's rapt visage as peaceful, on account of Jesus was stroking his cheek in those times. She tried to take advantage of the spells to whisper in her paralyzed nephew's ear of the need of controlling his weakness.

Many people in Gumbo Limbo suspected that Tim Rutter had caused a dreamy, wild-haired girl named Oona LeMur to become pregnant after she welcomed his attentions, having mistaken the boy's hypnoid countenance for a complicated ardor. Oona lost her baby, though nobody knew for sure if the child had miscarried or if Rutter had employed some artifice he'd found in the pharmacy. Afterward Oona developed what they called the "woman's epilepsy"; she wandered the quayside at night, pushing an empty stroller, and after a while they put her away in a home.

Then there was the matter of Liam. Tim Rutter had always despised the boy even more than he despised his employer, Mr. Murgen. But after the business with Oona LeMur, his malice intensified—despite (or even because of) the fact that the old man, who was absentminded and didn't care for gossip, knew nothing of his assistant's connection to the girl's aborted pregnancy. Not only that, but Rutter's hatred became even more maniacally focused on the little boy. Perhaps Rutter had a notion that the boy had seen something, or knew something that most others did not.

"I dislike that crazy little blind boy," said Tim Rutter to Bobby LeMur, Oona's older brother, who, oddly, Tim still counted among his reliable acquaintances.

"What's wrong with the boy?" asked Bobby.

"He pees his trousers," said Rutter. "He's ugly. I don't even think he is a real boy. I heard he has got water on the brain. Murgen is a fool for keeping him."

Rutter said that he couldn't even be sure Liam was a true boy and not a strange, sexless, large-headed imp of some kind. Rutter also knew about the special jar that was kept on a high shelf in the back of the shop. He knew of it and despised what was inside of it.

"I can hear him creeping back up in there," said Rutter. "Saying baby talk to it. He is a spoiled child. I don't think he is blind at all. I think he fakes it for attention."

Liam knew that Tim Rutter knew about the jar. The boy couldn't see the strange smile on Rutter's face as the older boy watched him through the wooden grille, but he sensed it plainly enough.

Liam asked Murgen could they hide the jar someplace else.

"But why?" said the old man, laughing. "Who is going to mess with it?"

The boy suggested, without naming him, that Murgen's assistant might mess with the jar.

Murgen laughed again. "Timothy? What would he want with a thing like that?"

But the boy wasn't convinced. He carefully removed the label from a bottle of quinine and reglued it on the creature's jar, hoping it might serve as a disguise. The boy asked the creature if it minded the label and the creature said it did not.

THE VERY NEXT MORNING, AN UNIDENTIFIABLE BOAT was spotted in profile on the horizon. By noon the boat had doubled in size and rotated slightly toward land. In the afternoon a fierce little squall passed over Gumbo Limbo, obscuring the boat from view. Purple clouds heaped up over the village, rain spat and lashed, wind drove sea nuts and the grit of oyster shell against the windowpanes. The listless surf beat itself into an angry froth and threw all manner of slimed and twisted wrack upon the sand.

When the squall had passed, the strange boat was gone. But in Gumbo Limbo there was a weird hollow noise, a kind of dysphoric reverberation that seemed to come from everywhere at once and no place in particular. It made people feel like their heads were filled with rubber. A man returning from the cinema house said he'd been issued a blank ticket, and so had refused the admission. He said he had gone to the cinema every week for the past eleven years. He believed the unnatural ticket meant that he'd been sold a viewing of a nightmare not his own. When released from his hand the ticket blew away down Mutus Street in a vortex of queerly charged wind.

The windless rains followed. It rained three days and didn't stop. Gumbo Limbo receded behind a curtain of rain. The line between sea and sky dissolved, the line between sky and land. The lanes were canals of mud. Brine shrimp proliferated in the puddles. Instances of the sea louse and sea weevil were noted. A week went by; ten days. The rain was quiet, vertical, whispering, incessant. Mushrooms with unusual ocher labia sprouted in the cellars; rare black molds got a death grip in the walls. Mucus ran freely. Slimy heaps of refuse rotted in the breezeways. Some folks went a little deaf. The giant pods of some strange profligate plant crunched softly underfoot; the agglutinated seed husks clotted the wheels of local vehiculation. Two weeks into the slow deluge a kind of dentiform barnacle, lilac in color, had attached itself by way of a gummy tendon to every latch, newel, baluster, and gutter pipe; by the seventeenth day the peak of each chitinous bud had split and extruded a tiny fiddlehead nub, which within hours had unfurled, with obscene grace, into a false wind foot or storm tentacle. Citizens who sought the Apothek were obliged to ford a canal of mustard-colored slurry. They complained of head noise, skin blight, and geographical tongue; crepitus, night terror, and partial paralysis of the eye. Murgen shook his head and prepared tonics and poultices. Three whole weeks the rain went on. Instances of the marsh weevil were noted. In the unremitting gloom moods festered. Voices grew hoarse and decayed into angry whispers. Cases were mentioned of instantaneous death caused by lagoon-borne spores lodging in the lungs. It seemed that in some people the excess moisture had caused a perilous loosening in the delicate structures of the mind. Citizens complained of cryptopodia, cephalopathy, late rickets, anoesia. Snails and slugs reared their soft blind antennae from bed knobs and cupboard handles. In the cupboards themselves the water beetle clicked through the long minutes of the night.

The rumors Tim Rutter had begun to sow germinated in the fertile rot of Gumbo Limbo. Slouched on the porch railing of Mrs. Croat's home, he muttered to his companions about a special jar on a high shelf in the back room of the Apothek. A jar in which old Murgen kept a thing that, while strictly speaking unspeakable, it would not be past his powers to describe, should he choose to do so. As Rutter spoke he shifted and smirked; yet the listening boys felt that Tim's account, while definitely odd, conformed with what they felt they might already in some sense have known.

For indeed the attentive customer could have attained a partial glimpse, through the wooden grille, of a museum of the sort many apothecaries keep: specimens of local natural history as well as rare examples of corporeal perversion (omphalopagus, crinoia, *cutaneum cornu*), preserved in mineral spirits for the edification of specialists. But to those laypeople inclined to be appalled by jars of such prodigious content, their mode of display (obscured but not concealed by the wooden grille) might seem to reflect a subtle audacity on the part of the custodian—an implicit peep show, an inadvertent medical pornography. The pickled specimens could, in this way, be viewed as artifacts of life partially developed and misformed, stuck in time, suspended in globes of fluid, marinating in their own juices, unable to properly decay, disappear, pass on to the next world. Or else such examples of death enjarred might appear to conflict or, worse, conflate with the palliative, life-preserving purpose of the vessels of medicine alongside which they were shelved, making of the whole enterprise a relativistic and charlatanous fraud. The keeping of this sort of private museum may be one reason there has always been something suspicious about apothecaries, even kind and old ones like Murgen.

Whether or not the youths arrayed on the Croat porch believed the insinuations of Rutter is neither here nor there. They listened and would later repeat what they had heard.

Tim Rutter spat over the railing; the ejected matter plopped like a livid frog in a seething brownish pond.

He asked, "What kind of abortions he got in those jars anyway?"

The question discomfited the fellows; and they went home wondering about it.

LIAM CLIMBED THE STEPLADDER, FULL OF MISGIVING. He'd had a bad dream, and no breakfast yet to dispel the gray net the dream had cast over his mind. He'd dreamt his friend the creature had rebuked him—had called him a name like "goony" or "fat ass," or leveled some cutting accusation, such as the boy had failed to protect it or take proper care of it—then left the jar and gone back into the sea to become an argonaut, a night voyager that lives in a spiral shell, a narrow twisting house of diminishing chambers.

In his dream Liam heard a muffled scream and ran down to the beach, where a greybeard was hauling in his net—he dragged his catch through the surf and dumped it out on the sand. A little girl came running up to look. She jumped back and shrieked with terror or delight, while the old Triton worked at untangling his nets. . . .

When he woke, the boy tried to feel better about knowing it was only a dream, but the hurt feeling lingered until, having mounted the stepladder, he found his friend laughing quietly in the jar.

"Do you want to know a funny song?" it said.

"Sure."

"It's called 'Turkey Foot,'" said the creature, who taught the boy the song. It was a very comical song and tears filled the boy's eyes and rolled down his face because his friend's joke had caused him to laugh so hard.

OONA LEMUR DREAMT THE MOON RELEASED her baby back into the sea. Its sea mother called the child back to herself.

It was going to be named "Nelly" or perhaps "Merceau."

It had happened like this: The moon tugged and tugged until the bulb broke; it slithered out, oyster and seed pearl, over the cup's lip, down the whelk's tube, the finite whorl, hidden eye and sealed chamber, round and round to the vanishing point, till moonlight on cuttlewhite bone lit tiny stapes, no more than a whisper, seapolished glinting and gone.

"I named it Merceau," she said when she woke. "It is out there on the wide world now. It has gone to an olden home."

"OLD MURGEN, HE MADE A SIN," said a man called Crippen, who was known to be congenitally morose.

"A bad sin," he said. "I believe it cannot be put right."

The talk that led the man to his conclusion came from many quarters. But the most influential testimony had come from Mrs. Croat herself. Croat was a woman who even before the long rain had suffered in the nerves, and whom Murgen had treated, at her own insistence, with salves of black mercurial lard, green belladonna, and even a silken hood thought to restore sense to the lunatic mind. Mrs. Croat maintained that Murgen had captured a she-beast with no hind limbs and malformed breasts and hands that were flippers or flattened lobes.

"Like a mermaid," she said. "Or some type of female siren."

The apothecary, she said, was keeping the mermaid hostage in a bottle. The rain would not stop on account of her fury. The unwholesome liquid had pickled and shrunk her. Yet even as she physically weakened (her skin or scales had yellowed and begun to slough off) her mental powers only intensified. Mute, she convulsed in her jar.

"Truly the rain will not stop," declared the elderly woman, "until the mermaid is freed back into the sea where he got her."

It is always a difficult matter when someone else's nightmare gets caught in the tangled net of your dreams. A man named Onder said the creature had the head of a horse and the tail of a fish, but no one believed him. A man named Frye held that the creature was a tardigrade, otherwise known as the water bear, but no one believed him either. Nonetheless, everybody soon knew there was a mermaid ashore—or something close enough to a mermaid—and that Gumbo Limbo would drown like Atlantis, under a waste of waters a mile deep, unless the apothecary could be made to release her.

"If she is taken wrongfully from the sea," said Mrs. Croat, "truly the sea will come to her. Wherever she is taken, there too will the sea follow."

The man who said he'd been sold the blank ticket began to advertise a ten-cent fee for people to come inside his home and view something he called a "sea movie," a hastily crafted zoetrope or flip book, which may or may not have purported to show a picture of the mermaid.

It is a difficult thing when not only two but many people feel they have shared the same dream. When they feel they're still in it together. When suddenly everybody is.

"Murgen made a sin," declared Crippen. "A strange and awful sin."

Murgen himself, catching wind of the notion that a mermaid had been seen in the village, formed a hypothesis that a case of the sirenomelia or "mermaid syndrome" had at last befallen some unfortunate family. He said to the boy Liam that never in his long experience had he seen such a case, though he'd read of it once in a medical book, and the description of that particular birth deformity was so terrible it made him weep.

MRS. CROAT'S PORCH ROOF SAGGED under the weeks of water, seemed ready to break off like a slab of soft clay. Tim Rutter's urine arced over the rotten railing into the soup of the submerged garden. He said, "I saw Murgen's little retarded boy teasing the cripple fish-lady in that bottle."

Then he fell silent. Bobby LeMur watched Tim Rutter, who was dribbling pee on his foot. He stood there holding his member and gazing into some unfathomable distance; the queer glazed expression had stolen over his face.

Bobby LeMur frowned. He had never cared much for this Rutter fellow.

MURGEN DIDN'T SLEEP, DIDN'T DREAM; he lay on his cot and listened. A murmured demand rose in Gumbo Limbo. There was a freshly rotten stench, of something damp and spoiled, and many people gathered by the water. The sanitary wagon with its pale canvas hood drew up.

Mrs. Croat, standing atop an upturned shrimp

bucket, flapped her short fat arms like a penguin and expounded on her theory.

"She is alive!" cried the aunt, alluding to the mermaid. "It's her baby—her baby has been abandoned in the sea. The mermaid must be freed unto the sea so she can nurse her child there."

Croat painted for the crowd a picture of a baby floating in a cold limbo under the swells, a hungry baby crying out for its mama in the darkness far below the rainpocked ceiling of the sea.

This news of a baby fanned the outrage of the stench. A chlorotic woman named Lucy Graves suggested the mermaid's baby was dead. But such a thing was too awful to contemplate, for by that logic the rain might never stop, even should the furious and damaged mermaid be released.

From his window Murgen listened to the silence that followed the pronouncement of Lucy Graves; he listened while the wind drew veils of rain across the darkened plain of the sea; and he listened while, on the forty-seventh day of rain in Gumbo Limbo, the citizens coagulated in groups which, by the time they'd begun to clog the narrow lane before the Apothek, had formed into a veritable mob.

At the head of the mob was Tim Rutter. His face was red and strained and his sweaty arms gestured wild and inarticulate. An exhilaration swept through him like he'd never known except when he was fornicating with Oona LeMur. He shouted at the crowd, embellishing and reifying the dicta of his aunt: that Murgen the apothecary had a mermaid or other variety of fabled she-beast held hostage in the shop; that the mermaid was shrunken and deformed in Murgen's bottle; that she raged impotently in a slightly viscous lime green solution; that, in addition, old Murgen had unnatural designs on the female creature; that for all anyone knew he might have already begun to pursue those designs; that the rain was a curse put by the mermaid to punish Gumbo Limbo for the apothecary's secret crimes against her; that truly the rain would never end until somebody set her free.

As the words escaped his mouth, Rutter felt he believed them; as he convinced himself, so he hardened the resolve of the mob. They scooped up clots of mud and oyster shell and flung them at the shop. Two men climbed a drainpipe on the side of the building to try to get a look through the transoms at the famous hostage.

Murgen knew of the secret monstrosities wrought by nature in the bodies of God's creatures. And he knew it was their fear that made them truly monstrous. He suspected their rage had something to do with the boy's special jar, but he wasn't sure what. He looked for Liam in his room above the shop but the boy was not there. A clam shell thick and heavy as a horseshoe hit the window and cracked it. Rain blew in. The old man went to the window; he held his hands before his face and wept and begged the people to stop. He raised his voice to ask why were they angry with him, with the Apothek, but the sound was swallowed in the din of the crowd. Blinking into the wind he tried to survey the crush of faces in the lane. He saw his assistant was among them.

"Is that you, Timothy?" called the old man, hoping for acknowledgment and help.

But the dead-eyed youth was buffeted and sustained

in the surging press of people; his mouth hung open in a loose smile of childish incomprehension.

AGAIN AND AGAIN THE MOB SURGED against the Apothek. They had nearly smashed out every last shard of the display windows and were beginning to climb inside when a man appeared in their midst, a medical physician named Grover Stiles. Stiles was a large man and he pushed to the front and told everybody there to shut up and listen. He said Gumbo Limbo was sick—sick with rain. He told the people they had water on the brain and implored them to be still and regain possession of their persons. He told them they saw mermaids everywhere they looked. He said that he was going to walk into the Apothek and have a discussion with the apothecary Mr. Murgen.

"I intend to enter that store," he said, "through the doorway, not the window, and take an accounting of what all is in there and what is not."

So in the few moments of chastened bafflement the physician had bought with his speech, he entered and went upstairs to where Murgen sat on the glass-strewn floor with his back to the open window.

"I gave Leroy a syrup," he muttered, "a syrup for the cancer. But the cancer come back."

Stiles nodded. The apothecary's reason was impaired.

"It is not about a cancer or a syrup," he explained to the elderly man. "It is about this rain. And something those people think you got hidden down there in a bottle."

"That's all made-up lies," said Murgen.

"It may be," said Grover Stiles.

Murgen agreed to let Stiles search his shop in hope that the mob might desist. The physician went downstairs and announced that a deal had been brokered: He, Dr. Stiles, would search the premises. If any mermaid were discovered, she would be returned to the sea forthwith.

There rose a skeptical noise. The mob invested scarcely more trust in the doctor than in the apothecary, since in those days, as in ours, it was much the same business. A man named Horace Sympus stepped forward and demanded the liquid of the jar in question be tested for iodine to determine if the beast had lactated. Grover Stiles denied this request but said he would permit Sympus to join him in searching the Apothek. Sympus agreed, on the condition that he could, in turn, appoint two additional searchers, forming a citizens' committee of three plus the doctor. Stiles agreed. Sympus looked around and couldn't see anybody he knew, so he indicated at random a small round-shouldered man and a stern, sour-faced woman, whose names turned out to be Clive Dungeon and Elpiffany St. Clair. The four then entered the shop.

Murgen stood behind the counter, steadying himself. He tried to recall who these people were. He believed he'd treated the St. Clair woman for the limbic fever; to Sympus, who'd come confiding the shameful anomaly of his infant son Lyle, Murgen had been able to offer only condolence and discretion. Dungeon he'd neither seen before nor heard of. Murgen feared them: whereas before they'd come for help, they now came to ransack his shop because the wicked youth's mad aunt had told them lies about a decayed girl in a bucket.

They searched the Apothek from top to bottom and

front to back, and in the back room they found the wreck-
age of Murgen's stores. Somebody had smashed a cobble-
stone through the deadlight. Glass and spattered liquid
lay everywhere; volatile powders clouded the air, and the
room was filled with the bitter smell of potent chemicals.

There lay a piece of darkish matter on the floor that
must have come from one of the busted bottles. Clive
Dungeon prodded it with the toe of his boot, but Murgen
stopped him:

"That's nothing to do with it. That is only my concern."

Then they saw the big-headed child huddled in the
corner, his skinny arms hugging what looked like a two-
gallon jar. The boy wept over the jar and his knees shook.

The doctor approached the child and asked him what
he had there.

Liam, gazing up, could not make out the face that was
speaking to him. He said it was a creature, a creature who
had been ill and was his friend.

"I am going to need to take a peek at your friend there,
said the doctor."

The boy shook his head. His eyes were rheumy and
unfocused and he blubbered softly.

Murgen wanted to say something, but the words
caught up in his throat.

The three members of the citizens' inspection committee closed in. The doctor knelt and gently moved the boy's
arm off the jar. The boy cried out sharply. Then he began
murmuring to the jar.

"Where are we going to go?" Liam asked the creature.

His friend didn't know. It was comfortable in its liquid, unmoved by the great calamity.

"Do we have to let you go?"

Liam could imagine what would happen: The old man would put a hand on his shoulder—*We got to let it go, son*—and together they would carry the jar down to the seashore. In his mind's eye the boy saw how the villagers followed at a cautious remove like a throng of sodden mourners. He saw how the long rain had smoothed the features from their faces. Then the boy and the old man knelt on the sand; the ground-glass stopper was pulled, an odor wafted up; the jar was tipped; with a gulp the thing slid forth, landing with a meaty splat on the sand where the foam purled over it; and tipped all the way over, the jar's dregs piddled out like a faint green afterbirth. *I forget that it comes again, and takes me back in,* his friend had said. *Then I remember water.* The friend receded into the neutral gray distance where sea and sky dissolved; and Liam saw the rotten ropes of the fisherman's net, hemp gnawed by sea lice, the scream of the little girl, the awful discovery. *There's nowhere else, no farther to go. Isn't this the end of the sea?*

"I just need to be able to see what's in there," said the doctor.

Grover Stiles peered into the liquid and frowned. He retrieved his spectacles from his coat pocket and had another look.

Then he glanced up at Murgen. Sympus looked to Dungeon, and Dungeon to Elpiffany St. Clair, across whose sour face a strange placidness had settled. St. Clair looked to Sympus and Sympus to Grover Stiles, who nodded and cracked his knuckles and stood and replaced the spectacles in his coat.

THE CROWD PACKED IN THE LANE received the news with despair. The rain fell on their hats and shoulders; heads bent, they stood in puddles in blank amazement. They were bereft. Anyone who had harbored in his mind a special picture of the secret captive in the Apothek felt robbed of the chance to see that picture brought out alive in a jar of fluid. None of it was real but the rain.

GUMBO LIMBO WOKE TO THE SAME RAIN after a night of dreamless sleep. In the gray dawn light Tim Rutter stood in the empty, sludge-washed lane before Murgen's Apothek. He'd been up all night drinking a potent alcoholic clam broth. He was drunk and exhausted and vexed. He hollered in the lane and flung bits of refuse at the shop. A few people wakened by the noise, or who, like Murgen, had been unable to rest all the night, shuffled out to witness the commotion. Rutter cried forth deranged slanders against Murgen and the Apothek and the boy. He said the boy wasn't a boy at all, but a hermaphrodite with the God-granted bodily parts of both the male and female species. He said the old man and the child had deceived the search party and all of Gumbo Limbo, but he knew just where they had hidden the grisly specimen: he meant to smash out all the remaining windows and go in there himself, this very minute, and haul the thing out in the plain light of day.

The crazed youth was shouting such things when, as tended to happen, he was struck dumb. A paralytic innocence smoothed his contorted face. And all of a sudden that charmed face was transfigured by an unearthly light. The light seemed to emanate from everywhere and nowhere at once. The sun shone through: and it made Tim Rutter look a little green.

THE CLEAR WEATHER DIDN'T LAST FOR LONG. A mist rolled in, but a dry mist, softening and soothing away the vision that had fixed itself in such hard and burnished outline in the mind of Gumbo Limbo, a desiccant mist that seemed to dry up all the rotting remainders of nightmare and panic, the wet stench of the terrible festering wrack—a mist that swept down the coastal plain from higher, drier ground, and a wind blowing dust through the village and out into the sea.

It has never been known for certain whether Murgen and the boy remained in their home for a few days, quietly sorting through the broken things, or whether in fact they left Gumbo Limbo in the rainy predawn hours of the night following the mob and the search. Or whether they almost didn't make it out of town, the causeway being flooded, the marsh waters lipping the highway's edge, so that it might have appeared to a distant observer that their odd vehicle was skimming the surface of a vast gray lagoon.

And the boy, going blind from a secret cause that was a mystery to the old man, said:

"What do you see out there?"

"Nothing but water. Water and sky."

"All the same?"

"All the same. Lovely. And it looks like the rain has stopped."

The big glass jar sloshed on the seat, wedged between the boy's thighs, his hands on the lid.

The old man said:

"Maybe we'll just let it go somewhere out there."

LIKE THE RAIN PONDS AND STORM POOLS that took some time to drain, the rumors lingered. There had been a mermaid, but she'd grown so shriveled that no one could recognize her as such; or she'd shrunk to a size where the water in the jar suited her, and she stopped raging, and so the rain stopped. Or Murgen's boy did have a secret jar, but with nothing in it except a dead seahorse or maybe a horseshoe crab, which through blindness or insanity appeared to the child as something more—and the old man, not wanting to hurt the boy's feelings, had kept silent so as to protect his belief for a little bit longer. Or else a truly unmentionable thing had been quickly disposed of, out the back door in the night.

LIAM DREAMT HE'D WOKEN UP WITH A DISEASE, a seasickness that was an emptiness inside him, or a failing heart, seawater blood washing in and out of a grotto, a stony cave. He realized the creature was his heart and the creature was gone, back into the sea whence it had come.

"What do you think it means?" he asked.

"I don't know," said his friend.

Asking your own heart a question: how could it make a reply? It says only one thing ever, no matter the question you put to it. And even if you never ask one question your whole life, still it says that one thing, always and only that one thing:

I'm here. I'm going. I'm here. I'm going. I'm here.

The boy cradled the jar with a sad feeling of happiness in his heart: the feeling you get when you wake up from a bad dream to find out it's not true, it's still okay, and will be so for a long while yet, as far as you can see.

Love Trip

N THE SUMMER OF 1991, when I was sixteen, my mother gave me a brochure for the Cutty School. It showed smiling kids in ski sweaters, posed arm in arm in the San Gabriel Mountains. They looked preppy and sexually hale. In one picture, they did a trust-building exercise: a blindfolded girl, arms crossed over her breasts in a funereal pose, was about to fall backward off a picnic table.

It was an emotional-growth boarding school. My mother had learned about it from someone in the counseling community. She said she wanted us to look at the school, to think about it. "We're concerned that you're so unhappy."

I didn't think of myself as so unhappy. I'd gone through a histrionic phase around age ten, threatening to commit suicide. In middle school I'd had strange outbursts in class that I didn't remember afterward. From time to time they had threatened to send me to a private school. In other words, my childhood wasn't without its wounds, but whose is? I didn't see myself as more alienated or rageful than most teens. It seems strange that I should have been so out of touch with my feelings, given my family's history of dabbling in the human-potential movement.

We flew from D.C. to LAX. I fell asleep in the backseat of the rental car and woke to surreal visions: ranch homes with tinted windows cantilevered on the slopes of parched golden hills, phantom mountains outlined in the distance. The car struggled up switchbacks as if clawing its way out of the smoggy soup into blue skies and pine forests. We followed a dirt road into the compound.

A professional-looking woman in her sixties named Darlene Allgood took my parents for a separate orientation while Brandy and Cathy showed me the log bunkhouse. They said they were going to be my Big Brother and Big Sister. "This is your cot. This is where you have to put your toothbrush." There were no doors on the toilet stalls or partitions in the showers. They sorted through my duffel bag, setting aside my Walkman, my rap tapes, my Bart Simpson T-shirt. I explained that I was visiting and would leave soon, that they had to put back all of my things. They gave me a stuffed animal and a welcome card full of signatures and hearts and smiley faces, like a get-well card from people who didn't know me.

When I asked Darlene where my parents were, she said, "They are where they need to be. Just like you are where you need to be." She spoke like a grade-school teacher, but her eyes, as I've since noticed in the faces of other North or South Dakotans, seemed to gaze from out from a deathly distance into something even remoter.

I pictured my parents in the rental car, winding down the mountain, and swore I would never forgive them.

MY PARENTS FELL IN LOVE 1969 AND WERE MARRIED the same week as Altamont. After the miscarriage of their first child, my mother went to stay with her friend Patti at a commune in

Antelope Valley. She saw how the women opened themselves up to one another, in pairs and in groups, nude or clothed, expressing feelings that in other settings might have seemed ugly or strange.

When my mother got pregnant with me, my father started going to Synanon meetings. It was a new kind of therapy meant to induce self-knowledge through an aggressive confrontation with one's peers. He was looking for structure, for something that would get him squared for fatherhood. This was years before Synanon put a rattlesnake in Paul Morantz's mailbox, and began assigning chemical castrations.

They lived in a two-bedroom house with a lemon tree in the yard. Not long after I was born in the Los Angeles winter, under the sign of Aquarius, my father had to go away to help his mother, who was ill. It was during this time alone with her new child, my mother later said, that everywhere she looked she saw the signs of danger and despair. A black man weeping or laughing on the corner. Children playing alone in little sunbaked yards. News reports of the boy in Costa Mesa who disappeared on his way to the bus stop. Pied pipers in that sunny land, strange melodies played on bone flutes. You could feel it in the atmosphere, like a queerly charged wind blowing in from the desert, snaking through the canyons, stirring the eucalyptus leaves. One night someone kept calling; when she picked up the phone, she heard only the sound of the wind. She put me in the car seat and drove out along the freeways, because she felt safer in the car and I always slept.

My parents quit their jobs and moved East to raise

our family. It was 1980, when the heads of Ronald Reagan and Nancy Reagan rose into the sky like psychedelic visions. My mother got involved in a new kind of counseling. One spring we went on a retreat for families. In a vast carpeted room with windows looking out on the woods, a facilitator named Gene had us whack one another with foam bats. He led us in a hugging exercise. It was supposed to be about regression, about reestablishing attachment. The more I squirmed, struggled, and fought, the more squishily forgiving and ensnaring the group hug became, like a tar baby. A snuggling blanket, tented around us, made the cluster of bodies all the more sweaty and intimately odorous. I slapped at Gene's chest, grappled for his ear, felt the scratch of whiskers on my arm. *Let it out*, he soothed: Gene was laughing, his eyes closed. I pummeled something soft and heard him cry *Oof! Not in the balls! Not in the balls!*

If you gave up struggling, all it was was a hug. It was the resistance, the fight, that made it seem scary or unpleasant. That was supposed be the lesson: Give up the fight, enjoy the love. Love would prove itself stronger. Back at home, when we did the hugging exercise, I felt suffocated and powerless. It was almost preferable when, on occasion, my father would pull out his belt, ask me to take down my pants, stand me with my shins against the bed, and whip me in the way of old.

Years later, when I asked my little brother Peter about that family retreat, he said he remembered it as one of the most enjoyable trips we ever took.

THE EVENING I GOT TO THE CUTTY SCHOOL, I was in my first Circle of Disclosure. They called it a "rap": twelve kids in plastic chairs in a circle, with pillows for hugging or pounding, and tissues scattered around. That was how, less than a day after leaving home, I found myself struggling on the floor with a teacher named Rudy, a type of wirier, more implacable Gene, a Gene who wouldn't let me out of the hug so easy.

With my face smushed into a patch of snot-damp carpet, and his knee pressed into my back, he whispered in my ear that he loved me, that he didn't believe a word I said, that I was *in my lie* or *in my I*, that unless I gave up the ego trip and *got into my feelings* I was bound to end up shooting smack, or sucking cock for money, or dying in a gutter of AIDS. It was like I had fallen through a time warp, to relearn some lesson I had failed to get right the first time.

MORNINGS WE CHOPPED WOOD, DUG PITS, and built retaining walls. Or we filled in those pits or dismantled those walls. The classes described in the school's brochure were just fiction. No one at the Cutty School was qualified to teach an academic class. One of my jobs was digging a trench to run PVC pipe out to the Wilderness Hut. I liked working out in the cool air of the woods. It was the only chance for my mind to go quiet. The body ache at the end of the day felt good. I was getting muscular, and the sun browned my arms and chest.

Klaus Wouters, the handyman and music teacher, would appear as if from out of the woods, like a figure in a folktale. He was a stout, bowlegged man with a mustache and wavy dark hair slicked back over his thinning patch. He might have been in his forties. He would sit on a log and watch me dig. He might have been supervising my work as a member of staff. I was never sure if he was obligated to be there, or just wanted to. He lingered like an ambivalent hotel clerk, or a checked-out guest who isn't quite ready to leave.

I knew Klaus from the Smush Pit. This was a circular recessed area in the fireplace room, with two steps down, an orange-carpeted amphitheater filled with pillows and cushions, where the obligatory snuggling ritual called "smushing" took place. You would see Klaus on a stool by the fishbowl window, against a backdrop of darkening trees, bent over his guitar. He held the neck in his good hand, working the frets with blunt, strong fingers, while he strummed with his disabled hand, using the long, thickened nails of his thumb and forefinger. He played "Moon Shadow" or "Michael Row Your Boat Ashore," while down in the pit we petted and hugged, whispering the secrets of our lives.

Klaus gave me unhelpful pointers on digging the trench. He nibbled his mustache, hands folded on his paunch. Maybe he was watching how I would respond to his presence. He asked if I had thought of going to college.

"I'd planned on it," I said, "but every day I spend here I get stupider."

He asked if I had read a book called *Inversions*. When I said no, he asked whether I had studied the ex-patients' movement.

I said I had never heard of it.

It was, he said, a radical political movement. He said that he and the members of this movement were survivors of psychiatric violence. While I heaved shovelfuls of dirt and rocks, Klaus described these broken creatures wending their way from all corners of the nation and converging on the golden hills of San Francisco. There, in a storefront on Noe Street, they hugged and laughed and cried. Young and old, he said, they were people who had suffered alone with bad memories and bad secrets.

"They say you've got the family you're born into and the family you choose. Those people," said Klaus, "were the family I chose."

"There was a boy with blond hair," he said. "About your age. Maybe a few years older. He and you have a similar type of face. The same bone structure." This boy had been a history major at Stanford, and had gone without complaint to hundreds of electroshock treatments. Afterward he went to a Bible-reading class in the mornings, and spent the rest of the day in his room, relearning words by copying them onto recipe cards.

Klaus never looked straight at me, but kept his heavy-lidded eyes trained on my knees or up in the branches. He said the leader of the group had been a silver-haired, red-nosed lion named Papp, who would declare in his Tennessee drawl: *There is no cure because there is no disease.*

"The first time Papp laid hands on me," Klaus said, "I broke down and wept. Because the hands felt so warm."

Papp said the nuclear family itself was a form of disease. He said madness was growth, and growth meant change; since the social order hated change, they policed it like crime. The doctors were the henchmen of the State, breaking people who refused to believe in their illness. They took scalpels and cut into minds, severing the links between parts of the human being. Or else, through drugs, they took the bricks and mortar of the old asylums and rebuilt them inside the person.

Papp's partner, who was called RaeAnn Pape, said mental health was a bourgeois idea. They wanted you to cling to the good thoughts or happy thoughts, crouching behind a bulwark of fear, shutting your eyes against what was Outside, and the Others who dwelt there. *Let them come, let them come!* RaeAnn would cry, *let them come and knock down these walls.* Klaus, eyes shut, head thrown back, impersonated the righteous cries of Pape in the quiet of the forest.

I set down my shovel and stood in the trench, my sweaty hair cooling in the mountain air. When Klaus became animated by his ideas and memories, his lips glistened with spittle and his hands jerked about. I thought that Klaus, in some ideal world, would have liked to address the whole student body, expounding on his ideas in a speech.

I asked Klaus why he didn't go back to San Francisco, but he seemed not to hear me.

The things Klaus told me in the woods sounded crazy. But crazy in a different way than the Cutty School. He never said a word against the school. But I knew, or thought I knew, that he wasn't on board with what Rudy Hamer and the staff were doing. I felt that, for different reasons, both Klaus and I had wound up at the school by mistake. That was why I came to trust him, why he made me feel that I wasn't so abjectly alone.

I told him how, in the raps, you were supposed to *find out your lie*, but I didn't know what mine was supposed to be. Cathy and Brandy, and everyone else, including the staff, had been abused, or abusers, or addicted, or suicidal, or had run away on the streets. Everyone came here with a story, and everyone knew the smell of ugly truth when at last it got pried out.

Klaus didn't coach me on what to say in the raps; I'm not sure that he would have known how. But he kept my secret, which was that I had no terrible secret. The most dangerous thing you could say at the Cutty School was that you didn't understand why you were there.

YOU COULD BE WOKEN UP AT ANY TIME OF NIGHT for a dorm inspection or an emergency meeting, or just by a student, male or female, or sometimes a staff member, needing to get in your bed and smush for a while.

One night I woke up in this way, a warm body pressing against me. It was Cathy, my Big Sister, spooning with her back to my chest, her rear snuggling into my crotch. She smelled good and was beautiful in a rustic, German kind of way, with her cheekbones and fine blond hair, her thick lips and widely spaced eyes. She began to relate a story I'd heard fragments of, or variations on, several times before. She included the part about her older brother's friends. *Do you know what it's like*, she asked in her smoky, sleepy voice, *to have two cocks inside you at the same time?* She giggled.

In the rap next day, she accused me of getting the feel-goods off of her. The betrayal confused and stung me, though in theory I couldn't blame her. The preemptive attack was a survival strategy; the only way to keep that burning beam of attention off your face was to seize it and turn it on someone else.

Rudy had a high, sunburnt brow with a fluffy strip of receding hair. His face lit up at the mention of feelgoods. He asked me to describe exactly what was happening when the offense occurred—how our bodies were positioned, what Cathy was telling me.

"There is a part you're leaving out," he said when I'd finished. "Something you must think we are not fit to hear."

"Did you tell him it was private?" Darlene said to Cathy. "Did you ask him to keep secrets for you?" Darlene perched erect on her seat, hands on her thighs, her face composed in an expression of concern.

Cathy sniffled, her eyes fixed on the carpet.

"Okay, okay," I said, adding the details of Cathy's story about the brother's friends, the two cocks.

Darlene gaped at me in seeming disbelief, then turned back to Cathy. "Did you ask him to violate your trust in this way?"

Cathy looked at me as though she didn't know me—and shook her head, teary-eyed, her fine hair wagging limply.

"He violated her trust," Rudy clarified. "He turned her story into a secret, something shameful. That's about him, not her."

A chorus of assenting murmurs rose through the room. Rudy did a neck stretch, cranking his head to each side. "I'm interested in his focus on these cocks. Maybe he needs to prove he is a big boy. Is there some concern here about his penis? Is he interested in penis?"

Darlene nodded soberly, her fingers touching the silk print scarf at her throat.

"What happened to you?" Rudy said, regarding me with interest and disgust.

"What happened to his Little Child," Darlene echoed.

I could feel the other kids tensing on the edges of their seats. Nothing I could offer would have diffused what was coming, so I turned to Darlene and said, "Maybe nothing happened to my *Little Child*. How would you know anyway?"

Darlene's mouth opened in mock surprise. "How would we know? Because of your parents," she said.

Her answer surprised me into silence. As if on cue, kids leaped across the circle to scream in my face, *Run your anger, man; Take care of your feelings!* One at a time they took turns, my face getting flecked with spittle—*You're out of your feelings!*—while Rudy sat rigid in his tracksuit, eyes closed, as if suppressing fury or relaxed in deep meditation, or as if it were all unfolding in the theater of his mind; while in the background, as I remember it, a song played over and over, as if on a record player that someone kept resetting.

ONCE I TOLD KLAUS THAT I INTENDED TO GET OUT. The compound was remote, but not as remote as it seemed. Little Eagle-neck Village was down the road. On foot, you could make it there in a few hours. There were stories of kids from earlier years who had "split." One boy showed up at the ranger's station demanding asylum, swearing up and down the school was a cult, that they wouldn't let him make a phone call and were trying to turn him against his family. The sheriff's deputy listened to the young man's story, nodding in sympathy, then helped the boy into the patrol car and gave him a lift back to the school.

I remember Klaus saying that I might not be as trapped as I thought I was. Later, he told me what sounded like a secret, about some people on the mountain, or near the mountain, who knew what went on up there, who could help.

But that might have been in my head. Klaus might have been talking about inner freedom, a way of "splitting" inside of yourself.

When the first snows blanketed the woods, Klaus stopped coming to the log.

My parents came to visit before the holidays. I had fantasized about this moment—how when they arrived I would call out Rudy and Darlene in front of everyone, eloquently detailing their crimes, exposing the school, its sickness, its cruelties and perversions. I went through these scripts in my head, lying in my bunk at night.

But when my family showed up, my little brother Peter was with them. I put on a grown-up face and acted like it was all no big deal.

I hugged Klaus when we said good-bye. He felt sturdy but hollow, like a barrel or drum. His good arm was around my neck; his other arm, small and rigid with its clawlike hand, was squished against my stomach. I knew my family could see me crying, snotting on Klaus's hair.

We flew home for Christmas and I asked not to go back. In the end, my parents agreed.

I HAD IMAGINED RETURNING TO MY HIGH SCHOOL like one of those freed hostages, humbled by suffering, the object of awe and respect. But I found myself on the other side of a pane of glass from my old friends. I'd imagined regaling them with stories of the freaks I had known in California—I would use that word, *freaks*—and had pictured how they would laugh with me. But it was impossible to joke about, much less explain, what the Cutty School was, what that episode in my life had been about.

Rumors circulated: What had I *done* to get sent away (or what had been done to me)? When a kid named Fleischer asked if it was true I'd been brainwashed in a cult, I punched him in the nose. My punch was reflexive, and shocked me, and it stunned me when Fleischer popped me back. The blood clogging up my nose felt like snot. It was the only fight I'd ever been in.

I had nightmares, waking up convinced that I had done something to cause my little brother harm, leaving him paralyzed or deaf. In other dreams I struggled to bury physical evidence of a crime people thought I was guilty of.

I went through that spring, and then senior year, quiet and detached, applying myself to my classes.

I never tried to contact any of the kids I had known at the Cutty School. I had told them shameful and embarrassing things, stuff I would have liked to erase from universal memory. I looked forward to a time when I would forget their faces and names. Even Klaus, I would have been happy to forget.

IN 1993, I RETURNED TO THE SCENE OF THE CRIME, or not far from it. Glenwood College was, as the brochure said, nestled at the foothills of the San Gabriel Mountains. I liked being thousands of miles away from home, where almost nobody knew who I was. Walking across the quad, you had a clear view to the mountains. In September, those peaks were hazy outlines that would disappear behind the veil of yellowish smog. But by December, the rains washed out the dirty sky and the mountains reappeared, looming above the campus, bluish and white-capped with snow. Back in those mountains was the Cutty School. Knowing that, being so close by, gave me a kind of sick thrill. It was why I wanted to go to Glenwood College. Looking back, it seems perverse, but understandable. It's how people are when they have unfinished business. You get stuck.

My dorm room, a single, was a comfortable cell. I hung out with Joe from my Rodney King seminar. He lived in the basement, in a back wing, where the hallways were narrower, mazelike, and poorly lit. An empty display case was set into the wall, and the wood paneling was carved with old graffiti. One said JIM JONES WAS HERE, and one said simply, KENT STATE.

A rotating cast of characters would drop in on Joe, including a pair of hippie girls who lived on the hall, agoraphobic, codependent roommates: Melissa Baum, with her flaming red hair and Cheshire cat's grin; Charity, pretty and exhausted, with her big apologetic eyes. They ate only ramen and Campbell's chicken and stars. Charity had that lost, ageless quality of the psychedelic waifs of the nineties. Once I saw her above-ground in the daytime, standing under an oak tree in a baby-doll dress, and she looked like a ghost.

TIME FELT SUSPENDED IN THAT BASEMENT HALLWAY. Smoke plumed and subsided, wreathed itself round. To speak, to try to be understood, was like launching little frail boats across that drift of smoke, not knowing where they'd end up. When Joe's sister visited from San Francisco, where she was in med school, she claimed that every student on the hall, including Joe, was at risk for preschizophrenia—a condition, she said, where the personality fails to cohere.

"Do you think I'm crazy?" I asked Baum. She grinned inscrutably and said everyone was crazy. *We're all mad here.*

On Halloween night, a Sacramental Farce and Fire Opera was staged in the rock quarry east of campus. Giant puppets lumbered through the smoke from the whirling Mexican *castillos*, while the disembodied voice of a poetry professor chanted verse through amplified speakers.

That night I wound up so high, I thought I was having a stroke. I had to lie on the floor in the dark while the high ran its course. Baum discovered me and put on a tape. Each instrument seemed to emerge from a separate region of space: a soft jangle guitar, a noodly electric guitar, the skittering drums, and the liquid, spooky voice of the singer, like a silver-throated wraith, who sang about spending some time on a mountain, spending some time on a hill. The music was a lucid dream, like the palliative for an illness, but it was also part of the illness. Baum smoothed my hair with her smoky hands while I tried to let go of my spiraling thoughts and submit to the song and the touch.

In the middle of the night I walked home over lawns wet from the sprinklers, across a courtyard where a stone fountain splashed and birds sang in the dark. The bathroom lights were fluorescent and jittery. I wondered who was this person, long-haired and red-eyed, staring back.

When I woke, it was sunny, as it was every day. I could hear a hedge trimmer from my window. Wherever you went on that garden campus, you could always hear some type of machine—mowers, trimmers, blowers, saws—buzzing in the middle distance.

AN ENVELOPE CAME FROM MY MOTHER. It contained a plane ticket and a letter about life at home, including her concern for Peter, who was now in middle school. It also contained an envelope from Klaus Wouters, which had been mailed to my parents' house. The return address was General Delivery in Little Eagleneck Village. I opened it right away, marveling at the spiny crawl of his handwriting. He wanted to know how I was. He said nothing about life at the Cutty School except to mention that a boy named John had gone missing several months before and still hadn't been located.

I remembered the boy Klaus mentioned. His name was John Cressey. He'd seemed younger, but was older than the rest of us. An accident as a baby had left him with a shortened leg and a paralyzed vocal chord. John's hair had been long in back and shaved close at the sides, with his bangs cropped high on his forehead in a precise bowl. He was fascinated with frogs and toads, which he pronounced *tades*.

One time I had been in the Smush Pit with Big Sister Cathy and Big Brother Brandy. In the standard smush positioning, I sat between Cathy's legs, leaning back onto her sweatered breasts, and Brandy sat between my legs. John Cressey was lingering nearby, and Cathy called him over to smush with us. He came bashfully and sat between Brandy's legs. The four of us reposed on the carpeted floor, linked butt-to-lap, as though seated on a toboggan, about to go whooshing down a snowy hill. Brandy hugged John Cressey in his strong, tanned, knife-scarred arms, eliciting from the damaged boy a gurgle of pleasure.

I remembered Klaus on his guitar stool, picking out his tune, watching us. Once I asked Klaus why they made us smush.

He said he it wasn't a bad thing. He wondered aloud where we got the idea of good touch versus bad touch, and answered himself: society. It was society's hang-up, not ours. Society taught us to fear our bodies and the bodies of other people, whereas in truth we were all connected.

But I never once saw Klaus in the Smush Pit after dinner, though staff were allowed, even encouraged, to join in.

I wondered what he wanted from me. Maybe writing notes to old students and sending them out into the world was just a thing he did.

I'D BEEN LETTING MESSAGES FROM MY PARENTS pile up on my answering machine. When I finally spoke to my mother, I felt her sense of how far away I was. The distance felt crushing, but I resolved not to succumb to that gravitational pull.

I made up a story about how I was going to spend Christmas with a friend whose family lived in Pasadena. This make-believe friend was female, and I let my mother infer that she was a girlfriend. My plane ticket could be refunded.

Joe said I was an idiot, that they'd kick me out of the dorms. Baum agreed to leave me the keys to her Saturn.

Joe was wrong. After everybody cleared out, I was able to stay on quietly in my room. The custodial crew gave me interested looks, but after a few days of cleaning, the dorm was silent. My key card continued to work.

When the winds blew up from the pig farms in Chino, the air had a tang of manure. It blended with the odor of rotting eucalyptus nuts, with all that strange Pacific vegetation getting its first winter soak.

I walked around campus, along its empty colonnades and porticos. The mountains looked naked and wet, almost black. I spent a morning at the pool, reading in the chilly light, watching the wind pinch and drag the surface of the water like a milk-skin. I smoked a cigarette and wrote a perfunctory letter to Klaus.

The next day, I posted the letter, then went to the library, where I looked through old editions of the *Courier* and the *Los Angeles Times*. A grotesque image kept bothering me: John Cressey fumbling his way down the mountainside, confused and alone, tripping in the crumbly rock; the boy gasping in his odd piping voice, scraping his hands on the pine trunks when he clung to them. But I couldn't find any mention of Cressey in the papers, or notices of a boy who'd gone missing in the San Gabriel Mountains.

The reply letter from Klaus came right away. He included a phone number and asked that I call him.

I held off for a few days. I slept in a sleeping bag on my bed, with the window open, got up around noon, and took most of my meals at a taco stand on Central. I would park the Saturn and order chicken enchiladas from the window, then carry the styrofoam container to a picnic table at the edge of the parking lot. I would eat my lunch under a dusty-looking pepper tree, listening to the freeway traffic in the distance.

When I called Klaus, he sounded unsurprised to hear from me. At first he seemed to think I was speaking to him from the East Coast. I almost let him think this. But then I clarified that I was in Glenwood.

Klaus asked about my plans. Would I want to get together for Sunday dinner? He pointed out that he had access to one of the school's vans, but only for school business. Did I have a car?

After a pause, I admitted that I did.

THE ROAD WOUND THROUGH HILLS OF DRY GRASSES dotted with scrub brush and entered the national forest: bristly pines on a slope of crumbly ocher rock. Coming into Little Eagleneck Village I got a rush of dread. When I saw the Alpine-style building with the post office and ranger's station, I pictured Rudy Hamer emerging from the door. I had fantasized this in detail: I would see Rudy and honk, watching the flustered surprise in his face; I would roll down the window, give him the finger and a piece of my mind. Now I felt sure I wouldn't be able to do anything like that.

When the Eagleneck Inn, a log cabin–style restaurant, appeared on the left, I pulled off the road into the gravel lot and spotted Klaus on the porch. He had his back to me. He appeared to be reading a flyer tacked to the corkboard next to the entrance. He wore a fringed buff-colored jacket I'd never seen—like a cowboy or Native American jacket. I felt certain I'd made a mistake. I was going to drive away, when Klaus turned around, saw the Saturn, and recognized me.

He approached the passenger side, casting a few quick glances back at the restaurant and up the road, as though he were concerned someone might see him, then opened the door and got in.

"Let's not go here," he said, thumbing at the inn. Ensconced in the seat he seemed shorter and thicker than I remembered him. He wore baggy jeans and a mustard-colored shirt. His cheeks were pink, his hair combed back, clustering in curls at the nape of his neck. I could smell his suede jacket, and another scent that might have been a hair oil.

I asked him where he'd like to go. He said it didn't matter to him, he would eat most things. There was a hamburger restaurant down in the valley that he remembered having enjoyed, though he couldn't recall the name. Pop's, it could have been, or Happy's. He said you could get a good meal just about anywhere in Los Angeles.

I took a curve a too hard and told myself to slow down. A scenic overlook swung past, a glimpse of the endless city spread out in the valley below. Tremendous boulders were strewn along the edge of the road in the shadow of orange cliffs towering on the right.

I popped in a tape. The road descended into the foothills and came to the intersection of old Route 66. The Inland Empire stretched in both directions. "Swing a left here," said Klaus, meaning east toward the desert and beyond. We passed a car dealership decorated with garlands of red, green, and silver tinsel.

"You go to the college now," said Klaus, gesturing out the window. He said I must do a lot of reading. He asked if I knew of a book called *The Shroud of Reason*. By what author? I asked. He couldn't remember. It was a good book, he said. He asked me whether the football team had had a good season. I told him I had no idea. I had never seen the football arena. I wasn't sure whether Glenwood College had a football team. Klaus said he remembered attending a football game in Omaha, Nebraska. "Nineteen sixty-five, it must have been. Or '66."

I began to dread the empty silences lying ahead. Klaus kept glancing in the side-view mirror, and I got the strange idea that he was eyeing a gray minivan that had settled into the lane behind us.

We passed a sign for the city limits of Casterly, which rang a bell with Klaus. He said he remembered a restaurant shaped like a boat. "I always thought it would be interesting," he said, "to eat at a place like that." As the highway came into the center of town, I asked if he knew the name of the restaurant. Klaus shook his head: "You can't miss it. It's huge and painted blue."

"Turn left up here," he suggested. We drove through a subdivision of wooden bungalows, past plowed-up grove land and a fenced-off industrial zone, always with the mountains behind us, or off to the side, blocking out half the sky, blue and massive and veined with white powder. They were closer and taller here than in Glenwood, but with a flattened perspective, like paintings on a Hollywood set. We never saw anything like a boat-shaped restaurant. The choice came down to Casa Dinero and a Sizzler in a fake adobe building. Casa Dinero was closed.

We sat opposite each other in the booth. Klaus ordered a shrimp basket while I had a burger and fries. The food was delicious. Klaus dipped his shrimp first in the cocktail sauce, then the tartar sauce, holding his arms, elbows out, somewhat high above the table to keep his sleeves from getting soiled in the food. He crunched off each shrimp at the tail stub; his mustache bobbed up and down as he chewed, grunting faintly with contentment. When he'd finished he hailed the waitress and ordered a second basket and asked if I wanted another burger; the entire meal was on him, he said, down to the tip.

"What happened to John Cressey?" I asked.

Klaus glanced at me with his heavy-lidded eyes and continued to chew for a while. "They've got a shrink up there now," he said, as if that explained something about the unknown fate of Cressey. I knew Klaus hated shrinks and feared them. "I'd like to believe," he said, "that no harm has come to John. Maybe he knew some people who were able to get him out of there." I was struck by that last phrase.

Then he began to recount a story from the papers a few years back. A hiker had found some bones in a ravine out by Lake Elsinore. There was a jawbone with braces still attached. They thought it might have to do with a boy who'd gone missing in the seventies. But when they sent the bones in for testing, it turned out they were the bones of a girl. "Of course," added Klaus, "that wouldn't have anything to do with John."

He ordered a brownie sundae with vanilla ice cream. When he came back from the restroom I noticed he was wearing pointy black boots, that his feet were unusually small, and that he was grinning broadly.

Outside it was cooler in the late-afternoon shadows, and I zipped up my hoodie. Klaus seemed fortified by the meal and invigorated by the atmosphere.

"Casterly," he said. "I remember Casterly. You can feel how close the desert is."

He said we should keep heading east on Route 66; we should go see a little of the desert. I said I thought this basically was the desert.

"No, I mean the real desert." He wanted cactus plants and Joshua trees and lines of tall, thin palms stretching to the white horizon. "The kind of place where you have to knock out your boots for scorpions."

I said we didn't have a map, that maybe we could go another day. He said all we had to do was go east, keeping the mountains on our left. I had never been to the desert either, but, as I told Klaus, the sun was getting low and we would never make it there before dark on the old highway. He agreed that we should take the freeway.

"There is plenty of light left. We'll be there in no time."

Once we were on the freeway, I popped in one of Baum's Grateful Dead tapes, a live recording of a show from the seventies. "I remember this music," said Klaus. "I saw this band play in Omaha, Nebraska."

"The Dead? You saw the Grateful Dead play?"

Klaus shrugged. "You could get lost in that music." He was smoothing his shirt down over his belly. Within minutes he asked me to pull over.

"Klaus," I said, "what is it?"

"Pain. Bad pain." His face looked a little greenish.

"Where is the pain, Klaus?"

"Stomach cramp."

I took the next exit and pulled over onto the shoulder. When I turned off the car, he was groaning softly.

"Do you need an ambulance? Should I go get help?"

Klaus shook his head, opening the door. I got out and came around to his side, thinking he was going to vomit. But what he did was get into the backseat. He lay on top of the stray pieces of paper, clothing, cassettes, and CD cases scattered there. He had his knees bent, his small pointy boots up on the seat.

I watched him for a minute. "You're going to need a doctor, Klaus," I said.

I worried that he might be having an attack of diarrhea. There wasn't much around; down a service road, I could see a low white building that might have been a garage or small warehouse. Behind us the setting sun was globular and shimmery, submerging itself in a hot-pink bath. Scrub bushes along the side of the road cast spiny shadows on the dry, pebbly dirt. I figured if it were diarrhea, Klaus couldn't play it off; there's no way to dissemble in an emergency like that.

"Keep moving," he said. "Motion is the best thing for it."

When I started the engine, I said I was taking him home.

"The desert," Klaus said. "We're going to see the desert. It's okay. I know how this goes."

"We won't get there in time," I said. "We have to go back."

"There's plenty of light," he said.

It had an absurd ring of fatalism, like a final wish, and I suddenly had an apprehension that if Klaus died out here, nobody would come to claim the body. When I steered the car onto the eastbound ramp, I didn't know if what we were doing was right. I drove with the passenger seat empty, Klaus lying back there like a patient. The valley opened out before us. I could see the windmills ranked in the distance, their white sails turning against the darkening sky. I could even see the shadows cast by their towers. The rearview mirror blazed with a golden-pink light. I had turned off the music.

"I remember drives," Klaus said. He explained that he'd grown up in a prairie town, and when the summer heat became uncomfortable, his mother would take him and his sister, Gerthe, on long drives in the loess hills. "All three of us sat up front with room to spare. No one wore seat belts back then." One time, he said, they stopped at a tourist motel that had a swimming pool and a diesel-powered train you could ride along a track that circled the motel. The gift shop, he recalled, sold pelts of small animals, Indian arrowheads, and corked glass vials filled with a mustard-colored powder: the glacial silt that the winds had blown, over millions of years, into fantastical dunelike drifts all along the eastern side of the Missouri River valley. "That was the summer after I came back from the hospital."

And he added: "It's all just pictures, isn't it?"

Then he fell silent. We passed the exit for Banning. Dusk fell over the landscape. A cluster of phantom mountains rose up on the right, while the range we'd been tracking on our left sank and dissolved; then the mountains on the right also sank and dissolved. I thought Klaus might be asleep. But when he resumed speaking, I realized he was alert.

"I was five years old," he said, "and I thought I would never go home. I was in an iron lung, and they said they might never let me out. They put a little mirror on the front, so you could see behind you. You could see people coming in and out of the room. It was supposed to make it less claustrophobic."

His father, Klaus said, was a railway clerk and his mother stayed at home with Klaus and Gerthe. Their next-door neighbor was Mr. Early, a World War I veteran who wore circular wire-rimmed glasses and never went outside. From his bedroom window, Klaus could see across the yard to Mr. Early's window. One time he saw Mr. Early take off his glasses, and he could see how part of the man's face, including an eye and part of the cheek, came away with the glasses.

Klaus remembered how, when he was in the lung, he

hated that mirror, because it constantly drew his eyes to the doorway, in which, for some reason, he expected to see Mr. Early.

But the time after the hospital, he said, was the happiest he could remember. He was shy, with few friends except for a young music teacher at the junior high, Richard Mundt, whom the kids called Richie. Richie worked part-time as a salesman at the music shop downtown. He lived above the shop, and Klaus had fond memories of afternoons there. Richie gave him accordion lessons, showing him ways to compensate for the crippling in his arm and hand. It was Richie who sang him old shanties like "Maggie May" and "Hangin' Johnny"; it was Richie who taught him his first chords.

One summer a boy was found murdered at the edge of a cornfield. An atmosphere of grief and paranoia settled on the town like snow. The boy had been two years younger than Klaus, a tough character. Once, walking home from the bus stop, Klaus had passed a yard where the boy was playing. The boy stopped, staring hard at Klaus, and flashed him a gesture—wrist bent, hand clasped like a flipper—meant to make fun of Klaus's handicap. Klaus blushed and hurried home, mortified and ashamed, then angry. But after the murder, when the whole town slept in the heat of July with their windows locked, Klaus remembered the boy's face and crew cut, and the flipper gesture, and he felt ashamed of his anger.

When the new school year began, Richie Mundt was gone. Klaus didn't know where he'd gone, and didn't feel permitted to ask.

He said his memory of those years was run through

and through by the sounds of flood sirens and tornado sirens, and a song called "Young Lovers" spinning over and over on his sister Gerthe's turntable.

One summer Klaus saw Richie Mundt coming out of the movie theater. Richie was squinting in the glare off the sidewalk, and looked pained and bedazzled, as though he hadn't been in sunlight for weeks. "He didn't see me," said Klaus, "across the street, looking at him." Richie never came back to the school or the music shop. Klaus eventually learned that he was living with his parents in their bungalow.

I HAD TO PEE. I SAW TINY CLUSTERS OF LIGHTS in the distance and, seemingly closer at hand, on the left side of the freeway, a service island glowing in the surrounding dark. When I took the next exit, I found myself on a one-way road heading away from the island, but I continued on in the hope that, being so close to the freeway, we'd soon come to another gas station or a McDonald's.

The road stopped abruptly at a high chain-link fence. It suggested the perimeter of a small airport or a prison, but I couldn't see any structures, only a dark and evidently vast area of land. I turned left. The road passed through a small neighborhood or town in which nothing was open for business, and then it seemed we were really out in the country. Finally I pulled over and got out to pee in a ditch. Klaus said, "Let's not stop just yet. I need to keep driving for a bit." A bright moon hung in the sky, and in the course of that long pee, as my eyes adjusted to the landscape, I realized I could see twisted black shapes in the moonlight—oddly tufted trees out of *The Lorax*, which is to say trees like souls, ancient souls or punished souls out of Dante, frozen at intervals all the way to the edge of visibility, where I could make out the silhouettes of huge rock formations.

Back in the car, I said, "Klaus, you've got to see this. I think it's the desert, the real deal."

"I'm tired," said Klaus from the darkness of the backseat.

"You don't want to see the desert?"

"I'll see it in the morning."

"What do you mean, the morning?"

"We must have come halfway across the state of California. We must be about halfway to Phoenix."

It did feel incredibly late, but when I started the car and pulled back onto the road, the dashboard clock said it was not even ten.

"We won't be making it back tonight," said Klaus, "that's for sure."

"I don't think it'll be a problem. We just need to figure out where the freeway is."

"There's too many cops on the road at this kind of hour. You didn't see them. I did."

Something darted across the headlights, my foot hit the brake, and I swerved into the oncoming lane. I swerved back and knew I had missed the animal, a rabbit or hare, but suddenly I saw in the sweep of headlights a boy standing on the gravel shoulder. When I blinked we'd passed him. I slowed the car, convinced I had seen him in that flashbulb instant, shirtless and shoeless, with a blond crew cut and a scar across his chest. I stopped the car and

turned to look back. Klaus, too, was sitting up and looking out the rear window. I thought we were looking for
the same thing, a boy back there on the shoulder, and was
about to speak, when I realized he was looking at a pair
of headlights in the distance. It was hard to tell how far
behind us they were, but they seemed not to be coming
closer, as if they had also stopped.

"Who is that?" I said.

"Them?" Klaus said. "The Grey Family."

I didn't know what he meant, and for a moment I
thought I must be going insane—but then Klaus was
laughing, hacking and spluttering, and I realized he'd
only been kidding.

A business district emerged up ahead, with a Wendy's
and a couple of motels. I knew we couldn't be far from the
freeway and could ask directions. But Klaus said we should
stay in a motel. "I just need to call it a day." He would pay
for the room, he said—for two rooms, if need be.

I said, "Don't you have to get back to the school? Don't
you have to go to work tomorrow?"

"I might be done with that school," said Klaus after a
pause. He added, "They're going to the medical model."

The choice was between the Desert Palms Motel and
the Desert Oasis Motel. Those might not have been the
names, but they were something like that, and the one
I chose (the Desert Palms) had a blue neon sign with a
trim of yellow bulbs. I parked under the portico and saw
the gas needle was on empty. When I got out and Klaus
didn't follow, I went into the lobby without him. I already
had an idea of what was going to happen. The clerk, an
older woman with garish makeup, looked straight out of

central casting for a scary nurse in a comedy or horror. I paid for the room with cash. Filling out the registration card, I didn't know the license plate number, so I went back out to look. Klaus was sitting upright in the back-seat. When he saw me he waved through the window.

We drove around the side of the motel and parked in front of our room. There were only two or three other cars in the lot.

"At least we got some place to lay our heads," said Klaus when I unlocked the door. He spoke as if we were hoboes or bone-weary pilgrims. The room was a smoking room and smelled like one. There were two beds. I flipped on the light, then turned the knob on the AC unit to fan mode; the machine clattered to life and exhaled a sigh of musty air. Klaus sat on the bed closest to the window. He patted the comforter, plumped the pillows. He slid out the bedside drawer and removed the Gideon Bible, inspecting the front and back covers, as though he'd never seen one before. I lay on the other bed in my shoes, watching as Klaus removed his Native American jacket and hung it up, fastidiously, in the closet, which was a narrow recess in the wall. My dorm room, I thought, couldn't be more than a couple of hours back west. I could easily be there, in my sleeping bag, by midnight. I wasn't sleepy in the least. But Klaus, for his part, seemed happy to be here. I still didn't know where he lived—at the school, or maybe in an efficiency apartment in Little Eagleneck Village.

"No toothbrushes," he said, emerging from the bathroom. "They used to give you those little toothbrushes."

He wondered aloud if there was anyplace such items could be had.

I offered to go find us some toiletry products. "Ah, who cares," he said. Then he reversed himself and said it was a good idea. He pulled out a fat brown wallet. He peered inside, seeming to poke around in it. He produced a limp bill and handed it to me gravely. It was a ten. When I left the room, Klaus was removing his pants.

Outside in the night I saw a mini-mart a little ways down and decided to walk. I got the toothbrushes, a travel-size tube of toothpaste, and a small blue bottle of Scope. I also picked out some jerky, a bag of peanuts, and a small bottle of orange juice. Then I thought of Klaus and went back and got a second of each. Standing at the checkout counter, I noticed a pair of unusual men emerge from the back of the store and make their way slowly toward the exit. They wore dark suits and had long red-dish beards and skullcaps. The shorter man was blind, feeling at the floor with his white cane, while the taller man escorted him by the elbow. I wondered if there were colonies of Amish in the desert.

From across the road, the motel's coffee shop glowed like an aquarium. I sat on a bench near the lobby, eating the jerky and peanuts, then smoked a cigarette, watching an occasional car pass. When I got back to the room, I looked through the gap in the curtain. I could see Klaus in bed. Television light flickered over his face and his arms— he had the covers pulled up to his chest. I tried to open the door quietly. The room smelled steamy, and an MTV veejay was yammering. A bath towel hung on the back of the chair, and Klaus's clothes were stacked neatly on the

round table. I set my items on the bureau and stole a glance
back at Klaus, watching his eyelids. I couldn't tell whether
he was asleep or pretending. I took off my shoes, turned
back the covers, and lay down in my clothes. I watched
MTV for a while and must have drifted off, because I
found myself in a troubling phone conversation with the
front desk clerk, who was trying to explain that something was wrong with the bathroom, that I shouldn't go
in there. *My bathroom? What's wrong with it?* I demanded.
It's handicapped, said the clerk, and I didn't know whether
she meant the bathroom was reserved for the use of the
handicapped or the bathroom itself was handicapped.
Then I realized I was controlling both sides of this conversation, that I had been dreaming but now wasn't. The TV
was playing a Cranberries video. I glanced at Klaus: he
was flopped on his stomach, his head turned to the window. I got up and turned off the TV, then tried to go back
to sleep—but I knew this disjointed feeling, and I knew
I wouldn't be able to sleep. So I tiptoed out of the room,
trying not to make the latch click too harshly. Out in the
night it felt better. I took huge breaths of the desert air,
then lit a cigarette and wandered through the breezeway
into the pool area. The pool was illuminated and, when
I dipped my hand in, pleasantly warm. The moon had
disappeared; the black sky was filled with stars. Aside
from the pool and little accent lights in the cactus garden,
everything was dark. All at once I felt urgently horny—or
maybe it was just giddiness—but I stubbed out my cigarette, stripped naked, and slipped into the water. I let my
air out gradually, sinking till I was crouched on the bottom. Then I pushed off and burst up through the surface,

shaking my hair and squeezing the chlorine water from my eyes. I frog-kicked up and down the length of the pool, stopping to hold my head back and gape at the unthinkable, fragile mass of stars. Is it sad that this was one of the most genuinely erotic experiences of my life?—not just up to that point but ever? No one in the world knew where I was at that moment, except for Klaus. Who was Klaus? Who was I, for that matter? Just some sensory holes for the world to seep in, to leak through—a sieve. Yet I *was* here now, even if no one knew. Nothing could undermine that feeling, by which I mean it could never be erased, even were I to lose all memory of it. I saw how the last day of my life, the day I died, whether tomorrow or in a hundred years, would be a day made from the same substance as this day, that finally there was no difference.

I squeezed out my hair, dried off with my boxer shorts, then put on my jeans and shirt, my hoodie, socks, and shoes. I lay on a plastic chaise and smoked a cigarette. When I got back to the room door, I realized I didn't have my key.

Through the gap in the curtain I could hardly make out anything. I could have gone to the lobby and rung the night bell. But I imagined that parody nurse groaning on a cot, groping for a wig.

I rapped lightly on the window.

I waited, listening. I didn't want Klaus to wake up, but I rapped again anyway. Then I checked all my pockets and discovered the key in my hoodie.

When I let myself in, the TV was playing an Alanis Morissette video on low volume. "I wish I could get them to play that one over and over," Klaus said. He was stretched out in his underwear, the oblong sack of peanuts on his furry chest, squinching his toes in sync with the beat. "The music now is better than it used to be. In a way. The production values are better."

"Aren't you tired, Klaus?" I asked. "Don't you want to go back to sleep?" I got up and closed the curtain and went back to bed.

He shook some peanuts into his palm, cupped them to his mouth, chewed, and shrugged.

"We could go back," he said. "I know you're probably eager to get back to the college."

"You mean now?"

He shrugged again. He said that he felt refreshed. He'd just needed to clear his head. He clamped the bottle of juice in his armpit and cranked off the top with his good hand. He said he felt fine, that he could drive the car if I wanted.

"Do you have a license?"

"It's okay," he said. "I'm a pretty good driver."

"Klaus," I said. "What are you going to do? If you don't go back to the school?"

He was thinking, he said, of getting back into the Movement. There were some people he hadn't talked to in a long time, but he was thinking he could try to reconnect with them.

"People from San Francisco?"

He didn't reply. Then he said, "I heard there's a lot going on in Germany. After the Iron Curtain. A lot of people are going to need help."

He asked if I had ever been to Europe. I could come with him, he said. We would have to go soon. Everything was opening up. He had an idea of a Safe Home for young people, run by psychiatric survivors. He'd been thinking about a new kind of peer-to-peer therapy. It would involve music and the body, and very little talk. "Like a dance."

"Klaus," I said. "Do you remember when you played 'Puff, the Magic Dragon'?"

"Which time?"

"In the rap," I said. I was thinking of the time I got called out for getting the feelgoods off my Big Sister Cathy. That was the day I got punished for challenging Darlene, when Rudy pressed me about the two cocks, about my penis. I got blown away by the group that day—a real shit storm. They weren't going to stop until I gave up the goods: a bona fide trauma, the *lie behind the lie*. So I had gone on a rant about an older cousin, a Halloween party. I invented details about a Dracula cape and glitter on his skin and the plastic fangs he took out of his mouth. I used the name of a real cousin—Jamie—and said that for days and even weeks afterward, I kept discovering little bits of glitter in my bedding. I invented the part where Jamie coached me to say, and believe, that this hadn't happened.

I remembered how, as I told the story about Jamie, I had felt myself moving outside my body, outside the Circle of Disclosure, to the far side of the room. I watched myself break down and sob real tears of catharsis. The other kids backed off, having gotten the spectacle they'd been taught to require. Part of me was aware of how strange this was, being forced into a lie about being forced into a lie. I was thinking how ashamed I was to have given Jamie's name, how I would never again be able to look my cousin in the eye when I saw him at Christmas. At some point, at a signal from Rudy, "Puff, the Magic Dragon" kicked off. It was a song of reward for my Little Child, a song of forgiveness. Klaus played it on his guitar, sitting on a stool in the corner.

Klaus shook his head: "Not in the raps."

"Yes you did. You were there in the corner. I remember." I wanted Klaus to verify that he had been there, that I had told the story I remembered having told. I wanted him to confirm what had happened there, what it had been like.

He was smiling. "I remember that number. I sang it sometimes. But not in the raps."

A gray light was seeping into the room, from around the edges of the window curtain. I looked at Klaus's little feet, at his brawny white thighs and stout torso, at his arms, one strong and one stunted, at his lips and heavy-lidded eyes.

"But why," I said, "did you ever want to work at a place like that?"

He thought for a minute. "I guess I wanted to be on the side of the underdog, on the side of the person who is in trouble."

"But Klaus," I said, "the school *was* the trouble. It was a joke. A horrible charade. A nightmare. They taught me not to trust anybody. They taught me not to trust my own mind."

"They said you kids had been on a fear trip. Up on the mountain, we were running a love trip."

"But was it love, Klaus? Do you believe that? Was it love?"

AFTER MY FATHER DIED from an aggressive form of prostate cancer, I was living at home with my mother. We began enjoying each other's company in a new way. I felt closer to her—this new, grief-changed version of her—than I ever had before. It was during this period that she talked about Patti from the commune, my father's explorations at Synanon, and the traumas and consolations of my sudden presence in the world, in that little house with the lemon tree that she could still very clearly remember.

I don't know how much of the mellowing between us could be chalked up to the loss we'd endured together, and how much to the effects of the psychotropic medications we were both taking. I had started taking them after my year at Glenwood, when I transferred and moved back East. People said it changed your personality, blunting the emotions and memory.

Maybe it did, but I never sensed it. I just wanted to feel better, more alive. The psychiatrist said we didn't have to explore the origins of unhappiness or the roots of fear. The goal, he said, like the goal in all medicine, was to fix the problem, just like you would with an infection or a broken arm.

My mother had stopped doing talk therapy years before. She had become more involved in the church.

One evening in early June, when the house felt submerged in a sea of green, and my mother and I had finished a meal on the side porch, I asked her: "Why did you and Dad do it? What went through your heads?"

She gave me a wounded look—but then, when she

realized I was talking about the Cutty School, her expression grew thoughtful.

"You imagine all kinds of things," she finally said. "There is so much you don't know. In the early years, you know everything about your kid. But it changes; you know less and less. Something happens . . . you feel it slipping away. It's like mourning. Like the stages of grief."

She stared at her salad. "To tell you the truth, your father was more worried than I was."

I was afraid of what she might say next. But what she said was: "Sometimes you could be such a little shit."

We laughed. That made me feel better.

That summer, I helped her sort through my father's office. I turned up letters from friends I'd never known about, and drafts of carefully rhymed poems, one of which seemed to be about the fear of losing one's mind. It must have been the feeling of handling materials never meant for my eyes that led me to look for my old diaries and, when I couldn't find them, ask my mother if she knew where they'd been stored.

"You didn't keep diaries," she said. "You wrote stories and made little storybooks."

"There were also diaries," I said, "or journals. We had to do them for school."

"Hmm." She drifted into her closet and emerged with a cardboard shirt box containing a neat stack of marbled composition books. "Maybe you're talking about these."

My handwriting at age eight and nine was bubbly and dense. The younger me described playing arcade games at a seafood restaurant, and a spring-break trip to the Epcot Center in Florida. What I was really looking for, and afraid of finding, was something about my cousin Jamie—some evidence that the stories I had invented at the Cutty School could have had some basis in fact. That when I made up those lies I was drawing on a scrap of truth buried in my subconscious mind.

I had sometimes imagined my parents seeking out these journals, nosing around in them, making a discovery. Now I found myself in that parental role, snooping on my old self, reading between the lines for distress signals, traces of something bad.

But I found nothing of the kind. I did notice a narrow strip of paper where a page had been torn out—which could mean anything, and probably meant nothing at all.

Jamie, by that time, was married. They had a two-year-old boy and an six-month-old girl.

THE CUTTY SCHOOL CLOSED ITS DOORS FOR GOOD IN 2003. I was searching on the Internet and found a message board for former students, "A Gathering Place for Survivors."

> *I have close to no memories of the entire two years in the program. I happened to remember some details this morning, and that's what led me here.*

I was amazed, though not surprised, to see posts like these, in which former students, anonymous or identified only by handles, testified to something like a years- or even decades-long amnesia.

A few of the posters, to be sure, avowed that Cutty had given them the self-understanding they'd needed in order to live what they described as productive and happy lives. But the majority were angry, and focused their ire on particular members of staff. My heart sped up when I came to a series of posts, a debate in fact, about Klaus Wouters. Someone called blownaway wrote that it was easy for staff to be indoctrinated in the same way as students; there were people at the school, including Klaus, who had genuinely wanted to help kids who were in trouble. HatedCutty disagreed. He or she wrote: *but klaus was not a decent person. he was just as crazy as everyone else. he loved having favorites and secrets. he chose to go along with it. he chose to see what he wanted to see. I sort of hate him for that worse than I hate rudy even. but that's just me.* Someone called darkstarcrashes went so far as to say that Klaus had something to do with the disappearances of John Cressey and of another boy who'd gone missing after John.

Reading that part made me angry. I drafted a long, detailed reply, but in the end I deleted it. I wasn't sure what to think.

The following year, shortly after Labor Day, I flew to Los Angeles for a conference. My girlfriend Adrian, who'd never seen the West Coast, came along. I dozed on the plane, and woke high above a landscape carved into puzzle pieces of orange and pink, with poisonous-looking eddies of yellow and swirls of pale green. There was no sense of proportion or scale: I couldn't tell whether these were geologic formations, or something man-made, a chemical farm spreading out over dozens of miles.

The next morning it was bright and breezy in the Marina, but as we made our way inland on the 10 freeway, the landscape grew hazy. We stopped off in Glenwood, where I meant to show Adrian the place where I'd spent that strange year. But it was sweltering and smoggy, with newly arriving students swarming everywhere.

The shimmering campus, with its palm trees and eucalyptus, was like a mirage, and my dorm, where I'd lived alone in December of 1993, had been renovated almost beyond recognition. It looked white and naked, and the students and their families carried boxes in and out of big new glass doors.

We got sandwiches and iced coffees in town, then drove up into the mountains. Adrian was the only person in my adult life who knew about the Cutty School. She knew that I still played and replayed episodes from that time in my head, often just after waking. It was her idea to go there. She thought it would help me, as she put it, find closure.

The air cleared as the road ascended. I pointed out the Little Eagleneck Inn, not mentioning that was where I'd once picked up Klaus in a borrowed car. Driving into the compound I felt sick. I didn't want to get out of the car, but Adrian was curious to look around. The log buildings, and especially the dormitory cabins, had the look of structures newly evacuated. Their windows were dark in the sunshine. I expected, any second, to see Rudy Hamer come banging out of a screen door.

We hiked a trail up to the top of the ridge. I remembered walking up this same trail on the day I'd arrived in 1991, after my check-in, after Darlene Allgood told me that my parents had left. I had thought I was alone in the woods, but Big Brother Brandy had been following me up the trail. He caught up with me, tall and grinning and slightly stooped, saying it was time to come back, that I had to come back down now.

Adrian took this snapshot, in which you can see the dining hall, the wing containing the fireplace room and Smush Pit, and part of the admin building.

I asked her not to include me in the picture.

Driving down the mountain, I was thinking about Klaus, where he was now, and wondering how our road trip to the desert, which felt so much like a dream, could ever possibly have happened.

Some communications from Klaus reached me over the years, but they were never from the places I imagined him to be—San Francisco, dressed in his Indian jacket, or some halfway house in Slovakia or Finland.

Once an envelope came with no return address and only a newspaper clipping inside. The article was about a case Klaus had once mentioned to me, about a boy who'd gone missing in Southern California in 1975. A hiker had found some bones in a ravine near Lake Elsinore, and those bones were determined to be female. But a new analysis, with DNA testing, had found they were indeed the remains of a boy—of the boy, they believed, who'd gone missing in '75. This discovery, which reopened the long-cold case, had led to the filing of murder charges against a man named Raymond Lee Hipple.

The truly mind-bending part of case, as the article made clear, was that it was Hipple himself, posing as a hiker, who had alerted the police to the bones in the ravine that day. As Klaus himself had scrawled in blue ballpoint pen along the margin of newsprint: *Why do they always go back to the scene of the crime?*

I spent a long time thinking about what Klaus meant by sending this clipping—was it a provocation, or some kind of tacit admission? Was he trying to say that nobody goes missing permanently?

In the end I decided his motive was only nostalgic, an allusion to the time we'd spent together, when Klaus had shared something that, for whatever reasons, continued to haunt and trouble him.

Another time I received a postcard mailed from Brunson, Iowa. Klaus was in a nursing home there, recovering, he said, from shingles. He'd returned home to care for his aged mother and had fallen ill himself. The idea struck him—at the age of fifty-three, he noted—that he would never be able to begin his life, the life he wanted to live, while his mother was still alive.

I wondered how ill Klaus was, if it would be the last I heard from him.

But one more letter came. He'd sent it, like the others, to my mother's house; she forwarded the letter to the apartment where I'd been living alone since ending my relationship with Adrian.

It was written with a kind of manic energy, and was mainly about a young musician and artist named Tim Winterman. Winterman, wrote Klaus, was a human rights refugee. He had been under forced psychiatric drugging at his home in Michigan. With help from an underground network of activists, Winterman had escaped across state lines.

Klaus wrote at length about Winterman's music and his political ideas. *He believes we make choices. Each of us controls the choices that determine our fates. We are each responsible for creating our own realities.*

Klaus had offered him refuge in his mother's home in Iowa. "Political asylum," he called it. Even now, Klaus wrote, the young man was heading west by bus or boxcar. Any day he expected a knock on the door.

He'd been washing bed linens, stocking the cupboards with snacks he thought Winterman would like.

I imagined Klaus in his old bedroom, looking out the window, awaiting the young man's arrival.

Acknowledgements

I AM GRATEFUL to the journals and magazines in whose pages versions of the following stories were originally published: "A Drowning Accident" in One Story; "The Sleeping Sickness" (as "Train Delayed Due to Horrible, Horrible Accident") in TriQuarterly; "Gumbo Limbo" in Conjunctions; "Love Trip" (as "The Love Trip") in Vice; "Brace for Impact" in StoryQuarterly.

This book would not have been possible without support from the Iowa Writers' Workshop and the Robert Schulze Memorial Fellowship. Special thanks to my teachers: Charles Baxter, Ethan Canin, Sam Chang, Daniel Orozco, Marilynne Robinson.

And to Iowa friends: my perennial workshop coconspirators, Jake Hooker and Sarah Smith; Alexia Arthurs, for dialect and teas; Casey Walker, who told me everything I didn't know I didn't know about publishing a book, and a lot of other helpful stuff too.

Thanks to the Fine Arts Work Center in Provincetown, and to Salvatore Scibona. To my FAWC friends Sara Majka, for enchanted hotel dining rooms, and Margaret Reges, who keeps following me around the country in her car.

Thanks to the Wisconsin Institute of Creative Writing and the James C. McCreight Fellowship, which helped me finish this book, and to Ben Hoffman, whose editorial genius made a few of these stories much better.

Thanks to Ben Boyer, best road-tripper and first reader, and to Gabe Alkon.

"Gumbo Limbo" is based on folklorist John Bennett's "The Apothecary and the Mermaid."

To the Pennsylvania Turnpike, runway to the zone, and to Seven Springs H5, gateway to the zone.

To The President and The Ape.

BELLEVUE LITERARY PRESS is devoted to publishing
literary fiction and nonfiction at the intersection of
the arts and sciences because we believe that science and the
humanities are natural companions for understanding the
human experience. With each book we publish, our goal is to
foster a rich, interdisciplinary dialogue that will forge new
tools for thinking and engaging with the world.

To support our press and its mission, and for our full
catalogue of published titles, please visit us at blpress.org.

BELLEVUE LITERARY PRESS
New York